Serena looked a

'But why should you
all this just to attract

'I have been pursued by the fair sex, Serena,
since I was old enough to notice. But I am not
so green as to believe that they loved me for
myself. My family's fortune is famous. It's
only too obvious where my attractions lie.'

'We have agreed, have we not, that attraction
is not a question between us?' Serena said,
adding, 'In any case, I had no idea — still have
no idea — who you are, so how could your
riches appeal?'

Dear Reader

Wonderful summer reading for your holidays this month! Sylvia Andrew gives us a cracking plot in her latest Regency, SERENA, full of intrigue, and Valentina Luellen takes us to Scotland in 1740 where clan feuds were rife in HOSTAGE OF LOVE. Our American offerings both have fascinating people you'll love in THE RELUCTANT BRIDE by Barbara Bretton, and Louisa Rawlings appears again with WICKED STRANGER. Happy reading!

The Editor

Sylvia Andrew taught modern languages for years, ending up as Vice-Principal of a sixth form college. She lives in Somerset with two cats, a dog, and a husband who has a very necessary sense of humour, and a stern approach to punctuation. Sylvia has one daughter living in London, and they share a lively interest in the theatre. She describes herself as an 'unrepentant romantic'.

Recent titles by the same author:

A DARLING AMAZON
PERDITA

SERENA

Sylvia Andrew

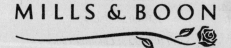

MILLS & BOON LIMITED
ETON HOUSE, 18–24 PARADISE ROAD
RICHMOND, SURREY, TW9 1SR

To my daughter Catherine

MILLS & BOON, the Rose Device and LEGACY OF LOVE are trademarks of the publisher.

First published in Great Britain 1994 by Mills & Boon Limited

© Sylvia Andrew 1994

Australian copyright 1994   Philippine copyright 1994 This edition 1994

ISBN 0 263 78629 3

Set in 10 on 12 pt Linotron Times 04-9407-82196

Printed in Great Britain by Centracet, Cambridge
Printed in Great Britain by BPC Paperbacks Ltd

CHAPTER ONE

THE late afternoon sunshine pierced the blinds over the veranda, dazzling in its intensity. Reluctantly Serena moved to close the slats. It was very hot, and the breath of wind coming off the sea had been welcome. She returned to her seat and waited for her visitor's reaction to her plan. 'Well, Lady P.?' she asked finally. Very few people on the island were permitted to use this mode of address for the governor's lady, but Serena, a Calvert of Anse Chatelet and one who had known Lady Pendomer for most of her life, was one of the privileged. However, Lady Pendomer, normally the most placidly optimistic of creatures, said firmly, 'You will never manage it, my dear! You can have no notion of the cost of a London Season — it was more than enough for us, I assure you, and, sad though I am to have to say this, your circumstances are not such that you could afford anything like the amount needed!'

Serena lifted her chin, and the look she gave her guest was slightly cool.

'You needn't give me one of your father's stares, either, Serena. I would be doing you a disservice if I did not speak plainly now, rather than later. The project is doomed from the start — you simply do not have the resources to carry it through properly. And unless you do the thing in style it is better not to do it at all.'

Serena said with a teasing smile, 'You are suggesting

that we lack the necessary style, Lady P.? I am surprised.'

'You lack the necessary funds, my dear! If you wish the ton to take note of you, you will need to hire a house with an impeccable address, and have an extensive and fashionable wardrobe — shoes, fans, shawls and all the other bits of nonsense. And then you will need servants, a carriage and horses. It's not as if you have any sort of base in England — you would be arriving with everything to find! When we launched Caroline we were at least able to stay at Rotherfield House with Henry's cousins. You have no one. No, no, it is quite beyond your means! Unless Lord Calvert left some secret Eldorado which I know nothing of?'

This time Serena's smile was bitter. 'No, there were no pleasant surprises in my father's will. The family fortunes are quite as you describe them. The estates bring in just about enough to keep us and to repay a little of the mortgage each year.'

'You are surely not contemplating raising more money on the plantation?'

'I doubt we could.'

'Well, then. . .?'

'I have managed to put a little aside. And I have some jewellery ——'

'No, Serena! You must not! If and when you ever agree to marry anyone, that jewellery will be your dowry! And if you do not marry it will be your only safeguard for the future. You must not spend it on Lucy!'

'I wouldn't have to sell all of it, Lady P. Possibly just the Cardoman necklace ——'

'The Cardoman necklace! Sell the Cardoman necklace?'

'Why not? It's not even particularly beautiful——'

'But it's a priceless heirloom! Serena, I really think you are not yourself. It may not be beautiful to modern eyes, I grant you—it is, after all is said and done, over a hundred and fifty years old—but how many families can boast of a necklace made for one of their ancestors by a king? There are those who say that King Charles would have married Arabella Cardoman if he could. No, no, you must not let it go out of the family. Besides, you would never find a purchaser.'

'Now there I fear you are mistaken. I have one already. And as for the family. . .have you forgotten that Lucy and I are the last Cardoman Calverts? The name will disappear when we marry—or die. And Lucy must be given a chance to. . .to escape, before it is too late. The loss of the necklace is a triviality compared with that.' Serena walked over to the edge of the veranda, released one of the blinds, and gazed out over the sea. The dying sun had laid a path of golden light across the waves, which rolled lazily into the cove below that gave the estate its name. 'You seem surprised that I have never married. Tell me, if your Caroline had been forced to stay on the island, or if she had not met Lord Dalcraig during her Season in London, would you wish to see her accepting an offer from one of St Just's "eligible bachelors"?' She turned back to look at her old friend and, without waiting for a reply, she continued, 'Of course you wouldn't. You were wise enough to see that both of your children left the island while they were still young. This climate seems to bring out the worst in the men who stay here. They are either weaklings, sapped of energy, lacking in any kind of enterprise, content to let others direct them. . .or they become self-indulgent, vicious——' She broke off suddenly, and turned away again. After a small pause she said, 'Lucy is a lovely, high-spirited girl. I will not see her married to someone who would break that spirit, nor yet to someone whom she would eventually despise.'

'You are very harsh in your judgement of island society, Serena.'

'Have I not good cause?'

There was another, longer silence. Finally Lady Pendomer sighed and said, 'I know the importance you place on seeing your niece safely established, and I cannot deny that the possibilities here on St Just are few. But the cost of such an enterprise as a Season in London for the two of you——'

'Oh, but I should not go!'

'Not go? Why not? Who would look after Lucy?'

'Lucy would take Sheba with her to England, and my Aunt Spurston would chaperon her. I could not leave the management of Anse Chatelet in the hands of anyone else for such a length of time. The situation is precarious enough.'

'But you must go!' said Lady Pendomer, quite forgetting that she had been protesting just one moment earlier that the whole scheme was impossible. 'If there is to be a trip to England at all then you must go too, Serena! You are so concerned for Lucy's future — surely you should be thinking of your own?'

'Oh, come, Lady P.! Who would look twice at me — a middle-aged spinster, with no dowry to speak of? No, we must concentrate on happiness for my niece.'

'Serena, I could become very angry with you if I did

not know how hard you have fought to keep Anse Chatelet in the family. You are twenty-six, not middle-aged. You may be somewhat thin, but that is because you do not look after yourself. You could be a very handsome girl if you bothered to dress properly. And, whatever fears I may have had for you when you were a child, they have now disappeared——'

'Fears? Surely you mean disapproval, Lady P.?'

'No, Serena, I was afraid for you. Wild, hot-headed, lacking any kind of discipline or self-control—faults I lay completely at your father's door, I may tell you.' Serena's chin lifted again and she stiffened. But Lady Pendomer swept on, 'And you were both so completely dazzled by Richard. . . Everyone was, if it comes to that. But even after the rest of us knew your brother for what he was, you and your father still idolised him. Your hero-worship I could understand—both your brothers were so much older than you—but your father. . .he should have known better——'

'He was cruelly punished for his blindness. We all were.'

'Yes, Serena.' Lady Pendomer bit her lip. 'Forgive me. I did not mean to remind you of the past.' She returned to her former theme. 'I should not be at all surprised if you were to find a match for yourself as well as for Lucy in London! You rate yourself far too low.'

'You are mistaken! It is rather that I rate myself too high!' Serena smiled at Lady Pendomer's exclamation of disbelief. 'Let me explain. My brothers almost ruined Anse Chatelet before they died, and you know as well as anyone how we have fought to save it ever since—I am still fighting. I never had the sort of girlhood I have tried to give Lucy——'

'You could have had one with your great-aunt in England, Serena. She invited you to live with her long ago.'

'I know, and I was grateful to her. But you must know how impossible it was. There was Lucy. . .and as my father grew older he depended on me to run the estate — there was no one else. And indeed, I think I have done as well as any man — better by far than my brothers would have done. I assure you, I wouldn't marry and give up control of Anse Chatelet, not after all these years, unless I found a husband I could trust to manage it better than I can myself. And if such a paragon existed — I say if — he would surely find a better match than a spinster of uncertain age with a run-down estate in the West Indies!'

'Yet you say you rate yourself too highly?'

'Yes. I rate myself too highly to accept less. In any case, what man could tolerate less than total control of his wife's estates? Would I respect him if he did?' She smiled at Lady Pendomer. 'No, I am doomed to die an old maid. And now let us talk of something else. Lucy may come in at any moment.'

But Lady Pendomer was not to be deflected. She said obstinately, 'Whatever rubbish you talk, Serena, I will tell you that I still consider you eminently suitable to be a dutiful and loving wife to any man fortunate enough to win you.'

'You make me sound such a dull creature!'

'Nonsense, my dear! In fact, I think you might well make a very good match. And I might just be persuaded to help in this ridiculous scheme of yours if you were to accompany Lucy to London. Surely Will Norret could run Anse Chatelet for one year? Pendomer will keep an eye on him. And there are other ways in which I could be of some assistance — your wardrobes, for example. I fancy Maria might be of some use. . .' Serena's eyes lit up at this. Lady Pendomer's maid had at one time worked for Madame Rosa, the noted London *modiste*. If she would make some dresses for Lucy there would be a great saving. But Lady Pendomer was continuing, 'And, most important of all, I shall be very surprised if you can persuade Lucy to go without you. Think it over, Serena. Your mad scheme will very likely fail in any case. But if you force Lucy to go alone — '

'Sheba would be with her!'

'A slave!'

'Sheba is a freedwoman, Lady P. We have no slaves on Anse Chatelet.'

'That might be so, Serena, but, slave or not, Sheba is as ignorant of England as Lucy herself. A former nurse is not quite the company Lucy needs! If, as I said, you force her to go without you, then you are being quite unnecessarily cruel to the child. And I will not help you in that.'

After Lady Pendomer's departure Serena was left in a most unusual state of indecision. For years she had practically run the estate, for her father, the nominal head of the family, had been a sick old man, and there had been no one else to shoulder the burden and make the decisions which affected all their lives. Now her father too had died, and Anse Chatelet was hers — hers, that was, except for the massive mortgage which had been raised years before to pay off the family's creditors. She lived in constant fear that she might one day, through mismanagement or some oversight, fail to pay

the instalments as they fell due. The agent in Barbados
had left her in no doubt that the creditor for whom he
was acting would foreclose. It would be folly to risk
such a disaster by leaving Anse Chatelet to the care of
someone else, even for one year.

On the other hand. . . Lucy was growing up fast. She
was now well past her seventeenth birthday, and if she
was to be prepared for presentation to London society
then a voyage to England could not be long delayed.
And go to London she must! It was unthinkable that her
beloved niece's beauty and vivacity should be wasted
here on St Just. If Caroline Pendomer, who was a girl of
very moderate charms, could capture a gentleman of
such breeding and fortune as Lord Dalcraig in her first
London Season, then Lucy's success would be certain,
and her future secure. And at least one of Serena's
private worries would be set at rest.

At this point Lucy came running on to the veranda.
'Sasha, Joshua and the others are having a crab race on
the beach — do come and watch it!' She grabbed Serena
by the hand and attempted to pull her back through the
house.

'Wait, Lucy! I have something important to discuss
with you. And how many times ——'

'Must I tell you to call me Aunt Serena?' finished
Lucy in chorus with her aunt, adopting a disapproving
frown. 'Lady Pendomer has been here.'

'If you know that, why weren't you here to speak to
her?'

'I didn't know — I just guessed it from your
expression — you've got your Aunt Serena face on. And
you're not often stuffy, Sasha. Do come down — Joshua
won't wait much longer!'

'Lucy, my love, you're no longer a child.' Serena hesitated, then went on, 'You know I've always tried to do what is best for you. . .'

'Goodness, Sasha, what a Friday face! What has Lady P. been saying?'

'Nothing that need concern you. But I think it's time we talked about your future. I have been thinking of a Season in London for you.'

Lucy's eyes grew large, and she sat down rather suddenly on the stool by Serena. 'We can't possibly afford it!'

'Yes we can, with a little planning and management. I shall sell the Cardoman necklace.'

'But, Sasha, that's a Calvert heirloom!'

Serena said innocently, 'Oh, forgive me, Lucy, I thought you didn't like the necklace? But, of course, if you wish to keep it, then there's no more to be said. . .'

'I think it is hideous! But it's been in the family for such a long time, Sasha ——'

'Too long! Your grandfather was considering whether to sell it when he died. It would fetch a pretty little sum — enough to pay most of our expenses, at least. What better use can there be for it?'

'It's yours, Sasha. You mustn't sell it for my benefit.'

'Why not, pray? Let us talk no more about it. We are the last of the Calverts, Lucy, and if you do not wish me to keep the necklace in trust for you, then it will be sold — in an excellent cause.' Serena smiled lovingly as her niece's anxious scruples gave way to excitement and she threw her arms round her aunt.

'Oh, thank you, thank you! I hadn't thought. . . I never imagined I would ever see England! Oh, Sasha! It would be beyond anything! I've always dreamed of

London, but I never thought I should go there! And to make my come out. . . I can't believe it! London! Oh, how soon are we going?'

'Wait a moment! I'm not sure that I can come with you.' Serena put her hand over her niece's mouth. 'No, listen to me, Lucy. Our resources are not great even if we sell the necklace, and it is important that they are wisely spent. You will need clothes, lessons in deportment, a suitable background, and lots more besides. If I came I should also need clothes and the rest. It's not as if you would be alone in England. Sheba will go with you, and I am sure Aunt Spurston could sponsor you in society better than I could. And you know the estate needs my attention here.'

'*I* need your attention, Sasha. How could I manage without you? Can't you forget Anse Chatelet, just for once?'

'Anse Chatelet is our only real asset, Lucy. It is a far greater part of the family heritage than the Cardoman necklace. I dare not forget it.' Serena watched as the bright hope on Lucy's face faded.

'Of course. It was stupid of me. But if we cannot go to England together, then I do not wish to go.' Lucy walked out on to the veranda and Serena's heart sank. This was worse than she had bargained for. She started to follow her niece but then changed her mind. She would avoid further confrontation for the moment. Lucy was impulsive, but essentially reasonable, and when she had had time to consider the advantages of a Season in London she would probably agree to the plan.

In the weeks that followed Serena was able to judge how wrong she had been. Lucy remained adamant in her refusal to go to London without her. Reason, persuasion, threats — all failed. Lucy merely said that she could enjoy nothing without the company of her aunt, and that they could perfectly well be two old maids together on St Just. When Serena turned to Lady Pendomer for support, her old friend merely replied, 'I have never been one for saying "I told you so", Serena, but did I not warn you that this would happen? And much as I disapprove of Lucy's refusal to obey you, I do in fact agree with the girl. I'm afraid you must reconsider your position. Either you both go to England — and I have already expressed my doubts on that head — or Lucy must make do with St Just!'

So Serena was already weakening when a letter arrived from England which took the decision out of her hands. Aunt Spurston offered to accommodate them in Surrey, and to help in preparing Lucy for presentation to society. However, for Aunt Spurston herself, a London season was out of the question, her doctor would not hear of it. Serena, as Lucy's guardian, must accompany her niece.

Serena was resigned, Lucy was overjoyed, and Lady Pendomer exerted herself on their behalf. She wrote to her friends in London, she spoke to her husband to engage his help in overseeing Will Norret's work on the plantations, and, best of all, she commissioned her maid to make some dresses for them. The necklace was sold and preparations were soon under way for a voyage to England.

Lucy's début was of enormous importance to herself and her aunt, but they would both have been very

surprised to hear that four thousand miles away someone else was looking forward to their departure from
Anse Chatelet and their arrival in London with an
eagerness that almost equalled their own. . .

CHAPTER TWO

To THE discerning eye the gentleman striding through Grosvenor Square in the direction of Upper Brook Street was unmistakably wealthy. His buckskin pantaloons and dark blue superfine coat were plain, but superbly cut, and his starched muslin cravat was secured with a very fine diamond pin. His cane was discreetly mounted in gold, and his boots were of the finest quality and polished to gleaming perfection. His dark hair was fashionably dishevelled under his beaver hat. This was no fop, however. There was a suggestion of power in the broad shoulders and lithe figure, and he had an air of one accustomed to command. Many would have called him handsome, but there was an indifference, a coldness even, in his ice-blue eyes, and a hardness about the well-shaped mouth which was not prepossessing.

The gentleman turned in to one of the houses at the nearer end of the street, where he was met by Wharton, his butler, and two footmen.

'Bring a bottle of Madeira to the library, Wharton. I am expecting Mr Bradpole,' was all the master of the house said as one of the footmen reverently received hat and cane.

'Yes, my lord. Your lordship may wish to read this before Mr Bradpole arrives.'

Lord Wintersett, for that was the gentleman's name, took the card which the butler offered him and looked at it impassively. 'When did Mr Fothergill call, Wharton?'

'Shortly after your lordship went out.'

'If he calls again, tell him I'm not at home.'

As Lord Wintersett closed the library door behind him and Wharton disappeared to the wine-cellar, the two footmen retreated to the rear hall. Here they lost their professional stiffness and became more human. 'Cold fish ain't 'e?' said the younger one. 'Wonder if old Fothergill will call 'im out?'

'Not if he wants to live, he won't. And you mind your tongue, Percy. If Wharton hears you, you won't last long in his lordship's service, even though you are my own sister's boy.'

'I'm not sure I'd mind. A proper frosty-face 'is lordship is, no mistake. I don't know what all those gentry females see in 'im.'

'His wealth, that's what they see. And as for you — let me tell you, Percy, you don't know a good place when you see one, you don't. His lordship may be a touch cold in his manner, but he's fair. You could do a lot worse, a lot worse. Anyway, what makes you say that Fothergill would want to call his lordship out?'

'I thought you'd know. They're saying 'e seduced old Fothergill's daughter.' Percy looked in astonishment as William burst into chuckles.

'Not another one!'

'What do you mean?'

'I'll bet you a tanner it's a try-on. The Fothergills aren't the first aristocratic coves who've had an eye on the Wintersett gelt and attempted a bit o' genteel blackmail. But they'll be like all the rest. They won't get far with him.'

'You mean ——'

'I mean it's time we cut the gabble-mongering and did our jobs. Off you go, young Percy, I can hear a carriage. That'll be Bradpole.'

'Oo's that?'

'The lawyer, you nocky!' Once through the door to the entrance hall they resumed their air of stately indifference and went to stand by the door to the street.

After Mr Bradpole had been received with dignity he joined Lord Wintersett in the library. First they spent some time clearing up odd bits of family business, and then the lawyer was offered a glass of Madeira and a seat in a more comfortable chair by the fire. These he accepted with pleasure, saying as he sat down, 'I have something further of interest to your lordship.'

'What is that?'

'News from our agent in the West Indies.' Lord Wintersett frowned.

'And?'

'Lord Calvert is dead. He died at the end of May.'

There was a pause during which Lord Wintersett got up and poured some more Madeira. Finally he said, 'I'll drink to that. Damn him!'

'My lord!'

'Oh, we're all damned, Bradpole, but he, I fancy, more than most. Who inherits?'

'His daughter.'

'Sasha Calvert. Or has she married?'

'Not yet.'

'She's unlikely to do so in the future. Whatever her attractions were in the past, they must have faded by now — the tropics are notoriously hard on women, and she must be nearly forty. Over thirty, anyway. And her fortune is small enough. I'll drink to her damnation, too.'

'My lord, I must protest. You do not even know the lady.'

'But I know of her, Bradpole. Oh, I know of her.'

'Lord Wintersett,' said the lawyer gravely, 'have you never considered that Mrs Stannard, your sister-in-law, might have been influenced by her own very natural feelings in presenting the circumstances of your brother Anthony's unfortunate death. It all happened so long ago—some thirteen years, I believe. Would it not be better to. . .to forget the past? After all, Lord Calvert and his sons are now all dead.'

'But Sasha Calvert is still alive, Bradpole—and has inherited everything, you say?'

'There's also a granddaughter, Rodney Calvert's child—but she has no share in the estate, merely a small sum of money. I understand that Miss Calvert is her guardian.'

Lord Wintersett said swiftly, 'I have no quarrel with the granddaughter.' He sat down on the other side of the fireplace. 'So. . . Sasha Calvert is now mistress of Anse Chatelet—but for how long? Now that the father is dead, surely the estate cannot survive?'

'I understand from our agent in Barbados that Miss Calvert has been running the estate herself for some years now. Indeed, he is full of admiration for her courage and spirit—in the past year or two Anse Chatelet has made some recovery——'

'A lady of many talents, it seems. But I don't believe she can keep it up forever. And the estate will survive only as long as the mortgages are paid, Bradpole—paid on the day they fall due and not a second later. Do you understand me?' Lord Wintersett's lip curled. 'There is to be no extension of time, no soft-hearted response to appeals from a lady in distress.'

Mr Bradpole looked at his client in silence. Finally he said, 'Am I to understand that you wish to deprive Miss Calvert of Anse Chatelet if you can?'

'I not only wish to — I shall, Bradpole, I shall. One of these days she will make a mistake — and then I shall have her.'

'Before that time comes you will have thought better, I hope,' said Mr Bradpole soberly. 'I very much doubt that your lordship could take pleasure in such a victory.'

'Pleasure! No, there isn't much pleasure in the whole damn business. When the Calverts drove Tony to his death they ruined the lives of half of my family — you know that as well as I do myself.'

'And in return your lordship has done his best to ruin the Anse Chatelet estate ever since. Yes, I know the story.' The lawyer chose his words carefully when he next spoke. 'Lord Wintersett, do you think what you are doing will improve the state of your mother's mind? Or make Mrs Stannard happier? Or give your nephew the use of his legs?'

Lord Wintersett's voice was glacial as he replied, 'Bradpole, your family has served the Wintersetts for many years. You are one of the few people in this world in whom I have confidence. But I will not tolerate further doubts on this matter. Do I make myself plain? I intend to deprive Sasha Calvert of her home and her happiness.'

Mr Bradpole started to put his papers together in silence.

'God's teeth, Bradpole, why do you feel the need to defend the woman? She's a harlot, a Jezebel. My poor brother was so ashamed of falling victim to her that he——' Lord Wintersett swore and turned to the window. His back to the room, he said, 'On the whole I do not admire my fellow creatures, and with few exceptions remain indifferent to them. But Tony was. . .unique. A gentle scholar who loved the world— when he noticed it, that is. I would have sworn that his honour and integrity were beyond question. That's why he shot himself, of course,—having betrayed his marriage, and with such a woman, he could no longer bear to live.'

Mr Bradpole started to say something, then stopped as Lord Wintersett swung round.

'I wish to be kept informed of every circumstance on St Just, do you hear?'

'Of course, Lord Wintersett. I will see to it. Er. . . there is something else, in fact. I understand that Miss Calvert is thinking of bringing her niece to London—to present her during the next Season.'

'Sasha Calvert in London, eh?' A most unpleasant smile on his lips, Lord Wintersett added, 'Good! Not only will Anse Chatelet be left in less watchful hands, but Miss Calvert will be within my reach at last—and on my ground. Excellent! Let me know as soon as you hear of her arrival in London.'

Mr Bradpole's face was impassive as he left the room, but once outside the house his expression revealed his worry. He had long known Lord Wintersett's feelings on the subject of his brother's death, and, convinced as the lawyer was that the true facts had yet to be established, he had frequently attempted to argue his client into a more temperate frame of mind. In everything else Lord Wintersett was scrupulously fair, capable of objective judgement — almost inhumanly so. But in this one matter he was unapproachable. Mr Bradpole returned to his chambers filled with foreboding.

It was unfortunate that Mr Bradpole's departure coincided with Mr Fothergill's return, for that gentleman took advantage of this to force his way into Lord Wintersett's presence. William and Percy would have removed him, but with a resigned wave of the hand Lord Wintersett took him into the library and shut the door.

'I've come to demand satisfaction, Wintersett.'

'Pistols or swords, my dear fellow?'

Mr Fothergill stammered, 'No, no you misunderstand, by gad. I mean that I. . .we — my wife and I — expect you to make an offer for our little Amabel — after the situation you placed her in last night, that is. She was very upset.'

'You surprise me, Fothergill,' murmured Lord Wintersett. 'I quite thought that it was the lady who had placed herself in the "situation", as you call it.'

Mr Fothergill shifted uncomfortably under Lord Wintersett's cynical gaze, but the memory of his wife's words as he had set out, and even more the consciousness of what she would say if he returned without result, spurred him on. 'Amabel wouldn't compromise herself — for that is what being found in a private room with a man of your reputation must mean — without encouragement! My daughter knows what's expected of her!'

'Now there I am in complete agreement with you, Fothergill,' said Lord Wintersett with a sardonic smile.

'She does indeed — a very able pupil. Who coached her? Your wife?'

'What do you mean by that?'

'I mean that I am far from being the flat you think me. If I were green enough to be taken in by the kind of trick employed by your wife and daughter last night, I would have been married long since. Do you think they are the first to have tried? Believe me, the ladies find me almost irresistible.'

'You take pride in that, do you?'

'None at all. I find it excessively tedious — what tempts them is my wealth, not my person. I assure you, Fothergill, whatever your wife may have said, your daughter's good name has not been damaged by me — I have learned to be far too wary a bird. At worst she might be accused of a slight indiscretion — which will be forgiven because of her youth and high spirits. But her chances of making a respectable match will be much reduced if society hears how you have pursued me this morning. Bad losers are never admired.'

'But the private room! My wife said. . .and your reputation — — '

' — — is not for seducing young and innocent girls. You may be assured of that. Your daughter followed me into Lady Glastonbury's winter garden — which can hardly be described as a "private room" — without my knowledge, let alone my encouragement. I think she realises that now. Go back to your wife — tell her that I am neither worthy nor desirous of Miss Amabel's attentions. She is a pretty enough girl, and should look elsewhere.'

'But — — '

'My man will see you out. No, really, I have had

enough. And Fothergill——' He waited till Fothergill turned. 'I am indifferent to what society thinks of me. But I should warn you that you will only make yourself even more ridiculous if you persist in these accusations.'

After Fothergill had left Lord Wintersett found himself unable to settle. He was conscious of nothing so much as an overwhelming sense of boredom. The scene that had just been enacted was not the first such. London was full of pretty, empty-headed little dolls, whose chief, if not only, ambition was to marry a wealthy man. The thought of marriage to such a one appalled him. Yet he ought to find a wife before long. He could not in all conscience let the title and all the responsibilities of the estates fall to young Tony—delicate since his birth and now confined to a wheelchair. He frowned as he thought of his nephew. Perhaps he should take more of an interest in him. The boy was intelligent, but hopelessly spoiled. Alanna was far too indulgent. . .

His gloomy thoughts were interrupted by another unexpected, but far more welcome, visitor. A warm smile transformed Lord Wintersett's face as Lord Ambourne came into the room.

'Ned! What are you doing in town? Is Lady Ambourne with you, or can you dine with me tonight? I need you, dear fellow, how I need you! I was rapidly falling into a melancholy.'

'I can and shall dine with you. Perdita is down at Ambourne, supervising the packing. We are off to France in three days.'

'Well, then, where shall we go? Or would you prefer to dine here? Albert has a way with a capon which I think you would find acceptable. And I have a very fine white burgundy. . .'

After it had been decided that Lord Ambourne should dine in Upper Brook Street, and orders to that effect had been sent to the kitchen, the two men settled down with a bottle of wine in the most comfortable chairs by the fire.

'What's wrong, James? Or can I guess? Fothergill?'

'You heard? No, that's nothing. I'm used to it.'

'From what I hear, you were not very kind to the young lady.'

'I should think not, indeed. If I were, she'd have cast herself on my bosom and matters would have been much worse. The chit will recover.' His tone was indifferent.

Lord Ambourne's face was troubled. He hesitated, then took the bull by the horns. 'Probably. However, there have been others who have not found it easy to recover from the public set-downs you have given them. I dare swear they have deserved them. But do you have to be quite so brutal, James? Perdita and I do not enjoy hearing what society says of you.'

'I am indifferent to what society says of me. You should try not to care, too.' James glanced at Edward's set face. 'I mind what you and your family think of me, Ned. Am I such a monster?'

Edward sighed in exasperation. 'You've always been the same! The best friend a chap could have, but the coldest fellow in creation towards anyone else. Why don't you find a wife?'

James smiled derisively. 'You think that would cause me to love my fellow creatures more, Ned?'

'Perhaps not. But at least these poor girls would stay

away from you. Though I'd feel sorry for your wife. Unless. . .'

'Unless what?'

'Unless you found someone like Perdita.'

James laughed, a warm, human sound. 'Impossible! Perdita must be unique. If you can find me her double I'll marry her on the spot. Now, you've done your duty, let's change the subject. Tell me what you've been doing.'

Later that night, after Lord Ambourne had returned, with a certain deliberation of movement, to Rotherfield House, James thought over what his friend had said. Ned was right, he ought to get married. He promised himself that after he had settled the affair with the Calverts once and for all he would seek out some amenable débutante, the least stupid he could find, and beget some heirs. Meanwhile he would wait patiently for Sasha Calvert to walk into his parlour. . .

CHAPTER THREE

SERENA kept her expression of polite attention firmly in place as she wondered for the third time in as many minutes how much longer the visitors would stay. They were sitting in her great-aunt's drawing-room, a somewhat dismal apartment made gloomier by the heavy grey skies outside. She and Lucy had been staying with Lady Spurston ever since their arrival in England two weeks before, and it seemed to Serena that she had not seen the sun in all that time. In spite of the large fire the drawing-room was chilly, though Mrs Galveston and her daughter seemed not to notice. For the moment Serena was free to follow her own thoughts, for Mrs Galveston, an imposing dowager in plum silk and an amazing hat, had finished with her, and was now quizzing Lucy. Miss Eliza Galveston was timidly displaying her velvet reticule to Lady Spurston, her fingers twisting the strings nervously as she explained how she had painted it. Mrs Galveston was one of her great-aunt's closest friends, and a member of one of the first families in the county. Aunt Spurston had said it was important to please her for a number of reasons, the chief one being that she had an elder daughter, Maria, married to a peer of the realm, whose own daughter was about to make her début. . .

Though Serena herself had been amused rather than intimidated by the dowager's trenchant remarks, she was anxious about Lucy. But her niece had so far done well, answering Mrs Galveston's questions with charming deference and remembering not to put herself forward. This was not easy, for some of Mrs Galveston's remarks would have been considered impertinent even among 'colonials'. The constant guard on tongue and behaviour which her great-aunt deemed essential for Lucy and Serena were not apparently necessary for this dreadful old woman. The corners of Serena's mouth lifted in a hint of a smile as she listened. Lucy was not giving anything away, for all her pretty ways.

'Serena?' Lady Spurston's voice was reproachful. 'Miss Galveston was asking about the flora of Jamaica.'

'I must tell you, Miss Calvert, that I positively dote on Nature. I have quite a collection of pressed flowers at home, have I not, Mama? Perhaps you would like to see them?'

Before Serena could reply Mrs Galveston cut in tartly, 'Do not encourage her, Miss Calvert. She spends far too much time as it is with her collections. But there, what else is there for the poor fool to do — unless it's daubing paint on velvet!' She turned to Lady Spurston and pronounced her verdict. 'Miss Lucy has a pretty way with her, and once she acquires more polish might well take. But it won't do for Miss Calvert to be her niece's sole chaperon.'

'Why not?' asked Serena in astonishment. 'I'm Lucy's guardian.'

Mrs Galveston eyed her with scorn. 'Whatever they might do in the colonies, Miss Calvert, it is still necessary here for a chaperon to be married! You are not married, I take it?'

'No, but I have surely reached the age of discretion.'

'No spinster, of any age, not even Eliza here — and

she is well into the age of discretion, one might say almost beyond it!—can be a young girl's sole chaperon—not in the kind of circles I imagine you wish to move in. It is unfortunate that your great-aunt's indisposition makes it impossible for her to be with you in London, but without a chaperon to assist you you may as well abandon the whole scheme.'

Serena looked at her in some consternation. Was her beautiful plan for Lucy's future to fail after all? Mrs Galveston looked speculatively at Lucy, and then back at Serena.

'Perhaps Miss Lucy should meet my granddaughter and her mother, Lady Warnham. Maria's as much a fool as Eliza—I am singularly unfortunate in my daughters—but at least she married well. Isabella is the same age as your niece, and is making her come out at the same time. We might be able to arrange something. . . I will see.' She looked with disapproval at Serena's sober dress. 'It would not be impossible to find you a husband, too, Miss Calvert. . . Some respectable widower, perhaps. But you are sadly brown—I'll send some Gowland's lotion round. You won't find it here in the depths of Surrey, but I have a supply from London. Applied nightly it might repair some of the damage done by the tropical sun.' She cast another speaking glance at Serena's dress, but decided to say no more and got up to go. She took her leave of Serena and Lucy, then kissed Lady Spurston's cheek. At the door she stopped and said, 'See that Miss Calvert takes some of Dr Massinger's beef extract, Dorothy. She's far too thin. Come, Eliza!' She sailed out with supreme assurance.

After Mrs Galveston had gone Lucy said passionately, 'I would rather die than spend another second in that woman's company! Do not, I beg of you, Sasha, have any more to do with her!'

'That will do, miss!' said Lady Spurston sharply. 'It is kind of Mrs Galveston to take such an interest in you. She is extremely well connected, and you might consider yourself fortunate indeed if she decided to help with your début. You must curb that unruly tongue of yours, Lucy. Pert young ladies are not admired.'

'My dear aunt,' Serena said swiftly before Lucy could reply, 'After this afternoon I am sure you must agree that we may have every confidence in Lucy's ability to behave well, whatever the provocation.'

'Provocation? What provocation, pray?'

'Surely Mrs Galveston's questions passed the bounds of discretion?'

'Serena, you do yourself no credit in taking exception to Mrs Galveston's very natural interest. She must satisfy herself that you are both worthy, before assisting a young girl from the colonies with little dowry and only a maiden aunt to protect her.'

'We are nevertheless Calverts of Anse Chatelet, Aunt Spurston,' said Serena, always sensitive about her family's name. 'I should have thought our credentials were sound enough for anyone, however well-connected they may be.'

'Besides, Mrs Galveston is so unkind!' Lucy cried. 'Sasha doesn't need her Gowland lotion and. . .and. . . beef extract!'

'How many times must I tell you to call your Aunt Serena by her proper name, Lucy? Mrs Galveston may be somewhat blunt in her pronouncements, but she knows the world as you do not!' She looked at Lucy's

downcast expression and said more gently, 'I am sure
you are fond of your aunt and would not wish her to
have wasted her efforts in bringing you to England. So
you must exert yourself to conform—I cannot tell you
how important it is. And now I would like to have a
word in private with your aunt.'

Lucy glanced at Serena, saw her nod, and reluctantly
went out. Serena waited calmly for her aunt to speak.
Finally Lady Spurston began, 'Why are you here in
England, Serena?'

'You know why. I want Lucy to meet the kind of man
I would wish her to marry.'

'Have you any matrimonial ambitions for yourself?'

'Oh, no. Mrs Galveston may confine her good offices
to Lucy. They would in any case be futile—I cannot
imagine who would be interested in me. I have too small
a dowry to attract a man in search of a rich match, I
have neither youth nor looks to attract a romantic, and
I'm afraid I lack the docility required by a man simply
looking for a wife to run his household. No, my
ambition is purely to see Lucy settled, after which I
shall return to Anse Chatelet.'

'And die an old maid. Not a very attractive prospect.'

'I fear that is the only prospect left for me.'

Lady Spurston considered this for a moment. Then
she said briskly, 'I am not yet convinced of that, Serena,
but at the moment I wish to discuss your niece's future,
not your own. Lucy is very pretty, and her liveliness will
do her no harm in the eyes of the young men. She will
take, no doubt of that. But the world in general will
judge her as much by your demeanour as her own—you
are her guardian, after all. If you wish her to move in
the very best circles, you must pay more attention to

your own dress and behaviour. That slave you brought with you from St Just — Bathsheba — '

'Sheba is a freedwoman, Aunt Spurston. She could have stayed behind on St Just, but came with us because she can't believe we could manage without her,' Serena said, smiling.

'Well, whatever she is, she seems to manage to dress Lucy well enough. Why does she not do the same for you?'

'I suppose I don't ask her to!'

'Exactly so! At the moment you are careless, dowdy even, and there is altogether a want of ladylike formality about you. These colonial manners will not pass in London. Try for a little elegance. Learn what is acceptable behaviour for a lady. Lucy looks to you for her example, and never forget that you are on trial as much as she.'

Serena coloured, but forced herself to remain silent. Her aunt was probably right. If she only knew how hard it was, how Serena longed for the sunshine and freedom of her life on St Just! The weeks she had so far spent here in this damp, cold climate, hemmed in on every side by strictures on 'acceptable behaviour for a lady', had seemed like a year — a century. The trouble was that for too long she had been her own mistress. For years she had ranged the plantation in complete freedom, exercising the authority her father had given her. If truth were told she knew that the English inhabitants of St Just were not so very different from their London cousins. Her independent ways had more than once shocked them, though the Calvert name kept them silent. But at least there she answered to no one. Here she felt stifled — 'cabin'd, cribb'd, confin'd'.

'You are silent, Serena. I hope you are not indulging in a fit of the sulks.'

'No, no, Aunt Spurston. Forgive me, I was. . . I was thinking. You are quite right of course. I will try to mend my ways.'

Serena did her honest best in the weeks that followed to meet her aunt's exacting standards. Whereas before she had always hurried Sheba along when dressing, now she was patient with her maid's attempts to dress her properly. Together with Lucy, Serena stood docilely while they were fitted for morning dresses, walking dresses, carriage dresses, ball dresses; they learned to walk elegantly, sit elegantly, eat elegantly, converse elegantly; they practised the quadrille and the waltz, though Serena had no intention of dancing in London. They learned the subtle differences of curtsying, bowing the head and offering a hand, how to encourage welcome approaches and how to depress pretension. Lady Warnham proved to be as amiable as Lady Spurston had said, and Lucy struck up a most unexpected friendship with her daughter Isabella. In fact, Lucy seemed to be enjoying every minute, but to Serena the endless trivialities to be learned by a lady who aspired to Society's approval were stifling. She wanted to be alone, to feel free, to rid herself of her resentment in a burst of energy. At home on St Just she would have taken off on her horse for the day, but here that was impossible. A tame stroll round the dank gardens, a gentle trot with a groom round the park, were the only available forms of exercise. The very notion of a lady walking or riding out unaccompanied was unheard of.

But just when she was at her most desperate, salvation appeared — a course of action that was highly risky, unquestionably not 'acceptable behaviour for a lady', but all the same a perfect answer. It came in the unlikely form of Mrs Galveston, who one day brought with her a bundle of clothes which her grandchildren had outgrown.

'They're for your wretched charity, Dorothy. The Society for the Relief of Indigent Gentlefolk, or whatever you call it. Improvident, more like. However, Isabella hardly has room as it is for her clothes, and now Maria has ordered more for the chit. It's all quite unnecessary, as far as I can see. One or two pretty evening gowns and a presentation dress are all Isabella requires, but there, Maria was never noted for her common sense. Some of Michael's things are in the bundle as well. They're quite old, but too good to give to the villagers — they would not appreciate them. No, do not thank me. I am glad to find a use for them.' She turned to Serena. 'By the way, Miss Calvert, it is rumoured that the Cardoman necklace has been sold. Surely that was part of the Calvert heritage?'

Serena was ready with her answer. 'My father always disliked the necklace, Mrs Galveston. It is notoriously unlucky. But I wonder where it has been since he decided to get rid of it? I thought it had been sold in the West Indies, I must confess. Can you tell me more?'

Much to Serena's relief, Mrs Galveston was unable to enlighten her, for apparently the purchaser had remained as mysterious in England as he had in the West Indies. As for the clothes, they were taken to a closet in one of the unused bedchambers where such items were housed until they were bundled up and sent

away. But Serena sought them out, for an audacious
idea had formed in her mind as soon as she had seen the
boy's garments. She tried them on behind locked
doors — breeches, frilled shirts with one or two cravats,
a waistcoat, and a warm jacket. A large forage cap in a
military style successfully hid her hair, and there were
even some boots which almost fitted. She secreted her
treasure trove in the West Lodge — a cottage which had
fallen into disuse since the drive to the western side of
the park had been permanently closed after Sir George
Spurston's death.

When her aunt and Lucy next went visiting Serena
pleaded a headache. She waited till Sheba had stopped
fussing and had gone to the kitchens, then slipped out
to the stables. They were deserted, except for the stable
lad and Trask, the elderly hunter. Saddling him presented no problems, and she was soon in the cottage,
feverishly changing. She had left her petticoats in her
bedroom, and it was simple to replace her dress and
light slippers with shirt, cravat, breeches, jacket and
boots. One other thing she had brought from her
bedchamber — something which she had kept hidden
away in a special pocket in her valise, for her aunt, if
she had known of its existence, would have most
strongly disapproved. This was a small pistol. On St Just
she had carried it whenever she went any distance away
from the house, for the danger of poisonous snakes or
renegade slaves was very real. Now she slipped it into a
pocket in her jacket which could have been made for it.
She had no idea what dangers she might meet in
England — but it was better to be sure.

Once Serena's hair was bundled into the cap she
made a very fine boy, helped, no doubt, by the lack of

curves and the brown complexion so displeasing to Mrs
Galveston. She would be safe from detection in any
casual encounter, she was sure. And she did not intend
to meet anyone at all!

Half an hour later she was enjoying the wide views
and invigorating air of the North Downs. The ground
was too hard and Trask too elderly for her to let fly as
she would have wished, but the sense of freedom was
intoxicating. After a good run she paused on the highest
point for miles round. Far away to the north she could
see the smoky haze of the city, but up here. . .up here
the air was clean and the hills empty of any visible
dwelling. For the first time since leaving St Just she felt
happy. It was a far cry from the tropics, but it was
beautiful. Away to the south the slanting winter sun
exaggerated the folds and furrows of the land, and the
fields below formed a patchwork of black and brown,
russet and green. Something tugged at her mind, a line
of poetry she had recently read and not fully appreci-
ated till now. It was about hedgerows. . . '"Once again
I see these hedgerows——" she murmured slowly.
'"Scarcely hedgerows——" She frowned and tried
again. 'No, that's not right. "Hardly hedgerows. . .
hardly hedgerows. . ." but what comes next?'

'"Hardly hedgerows—little lines of sportive wood
run wild,"' said a voice behind her. 'And who the devil
are you?'

Serena nearly jumped out of her skin, and Trask took
exception to the sudden tug on the rein and took off.
After the initial surprise Serena knew she would have
no difficulty in bringing her horse under control—she
had dealt with horses of greater mettle than this. But
she allowed him his head for a while—she had no desire

for closer contact with the stranger, and she just might escape. It was annoying therefore to hear drumming hoofbeats behind her and to see a lean hand stretch out to take hold of the reins and bring Trask firmly to a halt.

'Let go! I don't need your help!' she said furiously.

'I think you do, you ungrateful whelp!' said the stranger looking at her in lazy amusement. 'And unless you express yourself more gracefully I'll take it upon myself to teach you some manners.' His voice was still amused but there was steel in it, and in the hand that held the reins. 'We'll start again. Who are you?'

She remained silent.

'Are you playing truant? Is that it?'

A fugitive smile touched the corners of her mouth and she nodded.

'You may safely tell me who you are. I'm no tale-bearer.'

She looked at him, unable to hide a lurking amusement in her clear amber-gold eyes. If he only knew!

The gentleman saw the amusement. His face was suddenly cold, the eyes diamond-hard. He tightened his grasp on the reins. 'I warn you — I intend to find out who you are, one way or another. What are you doing on my land?'

Serena tried to pacify him. 'How did you know what I was trying to say — about the hedgerows? You must be pretty clever. I've been trying to think who wrote it. . .?'

'Wordsworth — William Wordsworth. And I'm still waiting for an answer to my questions.'

He was not to be put off, it seemed. Serena realised that if she were not to be discovered on her very first outing she must satisfy him, somehow. She cleared her throat, and adopted the sulky tone of a schoolboy. 'I'm sorry. I didn't know it was private land. I didn't do any harm, just enjoying a ride. It was boring at. . .at home.'

'Gave your tutor the slip, eh? Where do you live?'

Serena waved her arm vaguely. 'Over there.'

'And what is your name? You shan't go till you've told me, you know.'

'It's. . .it's William.'

'Shakespeare or Wordsworth?' There was scepticism in the gentleman's voice. He wasn't so easily deceived.

Serena let herself look puzzled. 'Neither. It's. . . It's Blake. May I go now?'

The stranger laughed in genuine amusement — and Serena gazed in astonishment at the change in him when he did so. He was suddenly altogether more approachable, more human. 'You mean the "Tiger, tiger, burning bright" Blake? The golden tiger eyes match it, but I'm not so sure about the rest.'

'What do you mean, sir?'

'I mean that there's a whiff of poetic fishiness about you! Blake indeed!'

Serena said with dignity, 'My family is connected to the other Blake, sir —' which was no more than the truth '— Robert the Admiral, not William, the poet.' She hesitated, then pleaded. 'They'll soon be looking for me. Keeping me here is almost as bad as telling.'

'Very well, William Blake. We can't have the truant caught. But you will promise me not to do it again, if you please.' He held her eye until she reluctantly nodded. 'And in future keep your wits about you when you're riding. You could have taken a nasty toss. Off you go!' Serena was about to protest again that she had not needed his help, but he said softly, ' "Waste no time

in words, but get thee gone" — and that's by the other
William.'

She smiled impishly, replied, 'I believe the correct
reply is — "Sir, I go with all convenient speed" — that's
by Shakespeare, too!' and rode off followed by the
sound of his laughter.

For a short while Serena stayed circumspectly within
the grounds of her great-aunt's house. Much as she had
enjoyed her encounter with the strange gentleman it
had brought home to her the enormous risk she had
been running. She could not imagine what Lady
Spurston would say if her great-niece were discovered
to have been masquerading as a boy, but Mrs Galveston
would surely wash her hands of them all. Lucy's future
might be at stake.

So Serena contented herself with pleasing her aunt.
This was not always easy, for Lady Spurston had grown
so set in her own ways since the death of her husband
that the addition of two young ladies to the household
often made her irritable. She enjoyed talking of her
youth, however, and Serena would spend hours with
her great-aunt looking at old pictures and souvenirs of
the past. Lady Spurston was appreciative of her audience and one day said, 'You are a good girl, Serena.
And very good to Lucy. I dare swear the greater part of
your dress allowance for London was devoted to her.
Well, I have a surprise for you. In that bureau over
there you will find a small box. Be so good as to bring it
over to me, if you please.' Serena did as she was asked.
The box though small was heavy. 'Put it on the table
here. Thank you.' Lady Spurston opened the box and

took out a small picture. 'This is a portrait of your mother when she was Lucy's age. It is for you.'

Serena examined the heart-shaped face with its large blue eyes, delicate colouring and blonde hair wreathed in roses. 'I'm afraid I am not much like her. She must have been much admired.'

'She could have been a duchess. But, though your father was so much older than she was, she fell in love with him and his stories of the tropical islands, and nothing would move her.'

'Othello to her Desdemona,' murmured Serena.

'I beg your pardon?'

'It's a Shakespeare play, aunt. Desdemona fell in love with Othello for the same reason.'

Her aunt looked at her disapprovingly. 'You run the risk of being thought bookish, Serena, if you continue to quote Shakespeare on every occasion.'

'The Bible, my mother's edition of Shakespeare, and a few books of poetry were all we had to read on St Just, Aunt Spurston. I think I know most of them by heart! Did my mother ever come back to visit you?'

'No, we never saw her again after your father took her to St Just.' Lady Spurston paused, then said, 'We didn't want your mother to marry Lionel Calvert, you know—a widower with two boys not much younger than she was herself. The older one—Richard, wasn't it?—was a charming rogue. I don't remember the other one—he would be Lucy's father. What was his name. . .?'

'Rodney.'

'That's it, Rodney. He was a very quiet boy.' There was a short silence. 'She had always been so biddable, such a loving, obedient child. . .' said Lady Spurston, gazing into the fire. 'But she would not be dissuaded, and in the end your grandfather was forced to agree. And then she died when you were born. . .' Her voice faded away again. Then she suddenly raised her head and said sharply. 'There was some sort of scandal later, wasn't there? Not enough to damage Lucy's chances, I hope?'

'No, no. The scandal was all over long ago, Aunt Spurston. Thirteen years, in fact. And my father saw to it that the affair was all hushed up at the time. In any case, Rodney was not involved — he was already an invalid.'

'Good!' said Lady Spurston and then added, 'The other things in the box are also for you.'

Serena carefully put down her picture and looked inside the box. In it were some jewels and a fair number of gold coins.

'I haven't much to leave you, Serena. When we saw that there were to be no children of our own, Sir George arranged an annuity which will die with me. These baubles would have been your mother's had she lived. They are of more use to you now, I think, than after I am dead. And you may spend the money on clothes for yourself — yourself, mind, not Lucy.'

Serena got up and embraced her great-aunt warmly. 'I. . . I don't know what to say, Aunt Spurston. Thank you.'

Her aunt's expression softened, but she said sharply, 'Control yourself, Serena. A lady does not display excessive sensibility in public. Oh, if only my stupid disability did not prevent me from accompanying you in London. . .but there, Maria Galveston — or Lady Warnham, as I suppose I should call her, she's been married these twenty odd years — was a good girl, and I have no reason to suppose she is very different now. Her mother will see that she helps you. We still have a little time before the season begins, and I will spare no effort to see that you are prepared.'

Serena managed to amuse herself well enough with these conversations with her aunt and other rather tame pastimes, but finally the lure of another ride proved irresistible. It was for consolation, more than anything else. To Serena's mingled pleasure and regret Lucy, who had always been so close, was at the moment increasingly deserting her aunt in favour of her new companions. It was not surprising. For years Lucy had been denied the company of young people of her own age and class, and here in England she was not only learning the manners of the young ladies of English society — she was learning from Isabella and Isabella's brothers and sisters their amusements and interests, too. The preparations for their forthcoming début, which Serena found so tediously dull, were viewed by Lucy and Isabella with happy anticipation. Even Sheba seemed to have settled into an English household better than Serena herself, and spent much time in the kitchens, gossiping, regaling the other domestics with gruesome stories of voodoo and the like, and incidentally keeping warm. In short, Serena was lonely, and when she found that Lucy had apparently forgotten that it was her aunt's birthday, she grew very low in spirits.

Serena had always despised people who felt sorry for themselves, and she decided to take action. So once again she took out her boys' clothes and made her way to the top of the Downs. Here she dismounted, tied Trask to a tree, and walked to the edge of the ridge.

The weather seemed to reflect her mood, for the sky
was heavy with rain clouds and the fields looked dull
and grey. A most unaccustomed feeling of melancholy
overcame her in which the battle for Anse Chatelet
hardly seemed worth the effort and her own future
looked as drear as the fields below. With a heavy sigh
she turned to go back. The tall gentleman was standing
by Trask.

'Well, if it isn't my young friend William!' he said
genially. 'Which one are you today?'

'Sir,' said Serena, trying wildly to remember what she
had said her name was.

'Wordsworth, I think you said.'

'No, sir,' Serena replied in relief. 'Blake. My name is
William Blake.'

'Ah, yes, forgive me. My memory occasionally fails
me —— ' a slight pause ' — too.'

Serena could not resist it. She said gravely, 'I expect
it's your age, sir. My grandfather was very absent-
minded.'

He glanced at her sharply, but she managed to return
a look of limpid innocence.

'Hmm. I am not yet in my dotage, however. And I
clearly remember letting you go in return for your
promise that you would not do this again.'

Serena started to enjoy herself in spite of the risk she
was running. She looked injured. 'I am not sure what
you mean by that, sir. A Blake does not break promises,
I assure you.'

'Oh? So you're not playing truant again? Tutor
broken his leg, has he?'

'His arm, sir. A most unfortunate fall.' Serena looked
sideways at the gentleman, and what she saw caused her

to say hastily, 'I was only joking. I've been given a holiday — today is my birthday.' She lowered her head as the memory of Lucy's defection returned.

'That has the ring of truth. But why aren't you celebrating it at home? Where are your parents?'

'They're dead.'

'I see.' There was a pause. 'May I join you on your ride?'

Serena looked at him suspiciously, but he was serious. She eyed his bay mare, cropping the grass a short distance away.

'Could you ride her?' The gentleman's voice broke in on her wistful thoughts. She turned to him, her eyes glowing.

'Oh, yes!'

'Sure?'

'Oh, please let me try! I'll go carefully, I promise.'

He laughed at the eager face before him, and then he frowned.

'What is it? Aren't you going to let me, after all? I'm sure I can manage her.'

'I believe you can — and anyway, Douce is like her name, although she's so fast. I was just puzzled for a moment. . . Where have I seen those eyes? No matter. Come, I'll help you up.'

But Serena had already mounted the mare, who was pawing and nodding playfully. 'She's beautiful! Do hurry!'

The stirrups were adjusted and, while he was occupied in fetching Trask and mounting, she furtively checked her cap to make sure it was secure. They set off along the ridge. At first Serena was careful to hold Douce to a steady walk, getting the feel of the animal's

responses. But then they came to a piece of open land
and she gave way to temptation. She let the mare have
her head.

Serena had never experienced anything like it. The
mare fairly flew over the soft, springy English turf, and
the air rushed past, intoxicating in its cool, damp
freshness. For five minutes she was in heaven. When
she finally slowed down, Trask and the gentleman were
nowhere in sight. It was as well. Her cap was thoroughly
askew and her cravat was flapping wildly. Both had to
be restored to order before she returned, somewhat
apprehensively, to look for her companion. When she
came into view he pulled Trask up, and sat waiting for
her in silence. He was, quite understandably, very
angry.

'You deserve a whipping, my boy,' he said
unpleasantly. 'Get off that horse.'

'I'm. . . I'm sorry,' Serena faltered. She thought of
flight, but dismissed the idea. Riding off with the
gentleman's horse would only make bad worse.

He saw how her hand tightened on the reins, though,
and said menacingly, 'Don't even think of it.'

'I wasn't, not really.' Then, pleadingly, 'I'm truly
sorry, sir.'

He dismounted and came towards her. She quickly
jumped down and clutched his arm. 'Please don't be
angry! You've just given me the best birthday present
I've ever had. Don't spoil it!'

The gentleman looked down at the hand on his arm
with a frown, and then, surprisingly, stepped back. He
turned to mount Douce, but stopped with one foot in
the stirrup. 'Perhaps it is I who deserve the whipping,'
he said harshly. 'You might have broken your neck.

When you disappeared I was afraid for a moment that you had.'

'Oh, no! It was. . .it was magnificent! I cannot thank you enough! I felt as if. . .as if. . .as if I was "an angel dropp'd down from the clouds, to turn and wind a fiery Pegasus——"'

Once more he completed her quotation, '"And witch the world with noble horsemanship." So you're acquainted with the history plays as well. And I think you're right. You certainly know how to ride. Well, I'll overlook the fright you gave me — this time. Come, we must get back. It looks as if it will rain before long.'

The clouds were gathering fast as they rode back down into the valley, and by the time they reached the high road it was raining heavily. The gentleman was apparently absorbed in his own thoughts, and Serena was cold and wet, her elation of a short time before quite vanished. Suddenly he said, 'We'll stop here till the rain eases. Old Margery will give us shelter — and perhaps even something to eat — though it won't be quite a birthday feast. In here!'

They turned into a narrow lane, at the end of which was a tumbledown cottage. Serena was seized with apprehension.

'No, I. . . I must get back——'

'Don't be ridiculous, boy! You cannot go on in this downpour! What would your guardians say? The cottage may look decrepit from the outside, but Margery always keeps a good fire going. We'll be dry in no time.'

Nervously Serena dismounted and followed him inside. The cottage was empty, though a fire was laid ready.

'She must be working at the farmer's down the road.

She won't mind if I light this, however. We can reset it
before we leave. Now I'll get this going, and you can
fetch more kindling and wood from the shed. Then we'll
take our wet coats off and dry them. It won't take
long. . .'

He was busy with the fire. Serena slipped out, tiptoed
to Trask, and led him quietly to the end of the lane.
Then she leapt up and rode for her life along the
high road.

CHAPTER FOUR

THE fire was burning brightly. In a few minutes the cottage would be warm and they could get dry. Not before time — the rain had penetrated his thick riding coat and the boy must be chilled to the bone. He heard a step outside. 'You've been a time! Could you not find any?'

'Whatever are you doin', my lord? Oh, I beg y'r lordship's pardon. But if I'd a knowed y'r lordship was comin' I'd 'a made sure things was ready! 'Ere, let me do that!'

James Stannard, sixth Baron Wintersett, straightened up and surveyed the newcomer. 'Good day to you, Margery. We took the liberty of sheltering in your cottage while the rain was so bad. What were you doing out in it? When you weren't here I thought you must be at Rufford Farm for the day.'

'I 'ad ter go down the road a piece after the goat. She'd gotten loose, the bothersome thing. Y'r lordship's welcome to whatever 'e can find. There isn't much, though. I'll fetch some more wood in for the fire, shall I?'

'Where's the boy? He should have brought some in by now.'

'There's no boy 'ere, my lord — just the two of us.'

'What? Of course there's a boy!' He strode outside. The rain had stopped as quickly as it had started. Douce was placidly sheltering under the lean-to shed. Of Trask and the boy there was no sign.

'I see'd a boy ridin' off down the high road as I came up the lane,' offered Margery, who had followed him out. 'In a terrible 'urry, he were. Ridin' as if the devil 'imself were arter 'im.'

'In which direction?' Lord Wintersett's first instinct was to leap on Douce and ride in pursuit, but then he changed his mind. Let the ungracious whelp go! 'No, it's of no consequence. I expect he had to get back.' He looked at the cottage. 'I'll send someone round to repair this roof, Margery. It's leaking yet again. You should move into the village; this hovel isn't fit to live in.'

'I'll end my days 'ere, thanking y'r lordship,' said Margery, her face settling into obstinate lines.

'Very well. But if you should change your mind, let Rossett know. He'll find you somewhere to live.' And, slipping some coins into Margery's hand, Lord Wintersett mounted Douce and set off for home. As he rode his mind was puzzling over the boy's behaviour. An odd mixture, William Blake — if that was his name, which he doubted. It was strange to have this conviction of the boy's integrity, when so much of what he said was open to question. Whoever was teaching him had managed to instil a love of poetry, that was clear. But they were undoubtedly careless in their supervision. He was too often left to his own devices. The lad was probably lonely — he had certainly been unhappy when they had first met today. The slender figure standing at the edge of the ridge had had a melancholy droop to the shoulders. It had been that more than anything which had resulted in his own impulsive offer of a ride on Douce. James Stannard smiled grimly. He must have been mad! How his London acquaintance would stare if they had seen it! Frosty Jack Wintersett, for he knew what they called him, giving way to a kindly — and ill-considered — impulse! And then to be rewarded with such cavalier treatment. . .

In spite of his efforts to dismiss the boy from his mind, the thought of 'William Blake' continued to plague Lord Wintersett, and one particular aspect more than the rest.

That evening they were three at dinner, for his mother had appeared just before the meal had been announced. At first James had been delighted, but Lady Wintersett had acknowledged neither her son nor her daughter-in-law, and was now lost once more in a shadowy world of her own. Alanna Stannard sat between them, dressed in a very pretty lavender gown which enhanced her Irish colouring — black hair, speedwell-blue eyes and a wild rose complexion. It was difficult to believe that she had been a widow for so long, the mother of a child who had never known its father. James wondered briefly why she had never remarried. She looked very little older than the girl of nineteen who had most unexpectedly capti-vated his brother Tony — Tony, who had never looked twice at any woman before, Tony, who had always been immersed in his books and his plants, gentle, unworldly Tony, who had been a near genius. What had there been in Alanna to attract such a self-sufficient man? And what had Alanna found in Tony? It had been a most unlikely match, for behind her pretty face Alanna was an empty-headed butterfly — or so James had always thought. He had wondered at the time of Tony's marriage whether Alanna had made a mistake — had

she been seeking a rich young man who would give her
the social life she wanted? But he had misjudged her —
she had remained in retirement here at Wintersett since
her return from the West Indies, a widow with a tiny,
delicate baby, born prematurely after Tony's death.
James's face saddened as it always did when he thought
of his brother. He glanced at his mother, still sitting
silently. She had been a lovely woman, too. Now she
was like a ghost.

Alanna had kept up a flow of inconsequential chatter
throughout the meal, but she now interrupted it to ask
what was wrong. 'For I have asked you twice whether
you can obtain some French lace caps for your mama
and me, and you have made no reply.'

Lord Wintersett glanced at the figure at the other end
of the table. 'Would you like a new lace cap, Mama?'

A sweet, infinitely sad smile was the only response.
Lady Wintersett slowly rose and left the room. With a
little sigh Mrs Stannard got up to follow. 'I think you
should come down more frequently, James,' she said.
'You seem to be the only one of us who can get any
response from Mama.'

'A smile? Before she slips away?'

'It's more than anyone else gets, I assure you. She
spends hours at little Anthony's bedside, but her face
never changes. She is like a doll sitting there. I would be
so obliged if you could procure the lace caps.'

'Isn't my nephew any better? Why is he in bed this
time?'

'The winter is always bad for Anthony. He is very
listless, and his limbs ache, he says.'

A sudden picture of a face glowing with eagerness as
the boy on the ridge, who called himself William,

pleaded for a ride, an image of Douce and the boy flying off into the blue, poetry in motion, filled his mind. He dismissed it, and said, 'Well, of course Tony's limbs will ache, damn it! He never has any exercise! You'd do better to get him out and about instead of mollycoddling him. In a chair, if necessary.'

Alanna's blue eyes looked at him reproachfully. 'Your mama would not like to hear you swear, James; I am sure she would prefer you to keep your oaths for your club. And, forgive me, but how can you possibly judge what is best for my darling? You hardly ever see him! Dr Charlesworth ——'

'It is my considered opinion that Dr Charlesworth is a quack! All he does is echo your own wishes! What's wrong with Galbraith?'

'Oh, no! Dr Galbraith is impossible! I have tried him and he is quite unsuitable. He would kill little Anthony in no time at all with his fresh air regimes ——'

'Little Anthony! He is nearly thirteen, Alanna! You are far too protective of him ——'

'And why shouldn't I be? Is he not all I have left?'

Alanna's eyes were large with tears. James got up and went to the fireplace. He had lost interest in this argument. It was one which frequently occurred between them, and always ended in Alanna's tears. Since tears irritated him, and since he was in any case not prepared to stay at Wintersett Court to see any reforms carried through, discussion was fairly pointless. Mopping her eyes, Alanna made to leave the room.

'Wait! If you please, Alanna, we must talk. Come and sit down.' His sister-in-law came back to the table, her head drooping, and waited while James carefully closed the dining-room doors. Then he poured two glasses of brandy and, ignoring her shake of the head, put one of them in front of her. 'You might need it. I have something to tell you which might upset you.' He paused, then said abruptly, 'Sasha Calvert is coming to England.' Alanna's head jerked up, her hand at her throat. Her face was suddenly colourless.

'What did you say?' she whispered.

'Have a sip of brandy, it'll do you good. Sasha Calvert is bringing her niece to England. It seems that the girl is now of an age to be presented to Society.' His lip curled. 'The society of St Just isn't good enough for Miss Calvert's ambition.'

'She mustn't come to England, she mustn't!' Alanna's voice rose hysterically. 'James, you must stop her!'

'Oh, no, my dear. Even if I could, I would not dream of doing anything of the sort. It suits my plans quite well to have her four thousand miles from Anse Chatelet.'

'Be quiet, James! Be quiet! You don't understand!'

'Pull yourself together, Alanna!' he said coldly. 'It shouldn't matter to you whether Sasha Calvert is in England or in the Antipodes. You have no need to meet her. Indeed, it's better that you shouldn't. You never come to London, so any encounter is very unlikely. You could even spend the summer in Ireland if you wish.'

Alanna looked at him with haunted, terror-stricken eyes. He forced himself to speak more kindly. 'I do understand your feelings, believe me. I hate the Calvert name as much as you — and with nearly as much reason. Thirteen years have not diminished the memory of their infamy. But this time I will deal with its last member once and for all. Have confidence in me, Alanna.'

In spite of his reassurances she remained uncon-

vinced, pleading with him again and again to prevent
Sasha Calvert's journey to England, refusing to believe
he could not prevent it even if he wished. She became
quite distraught, and in the end he sent one of the
servants for her maid, saying that Mrs Stannard was
unwell and should retire to her room.

The thought of the boy continued to haunt him that
night and throughout the next week. Several times he
took Douce up on the Downs, and found himself
scanning the area for the slight, quaintly dressed figure
on horseback. 'William Blake' nagged at his mind like
the toothache. There was something elusively familiar
about him, and yet James was convinced they had never
met before. And then — he had to face it, to bring it into
the open — when the boy had put his hand on James's
arm, James had felt a totally unfamiliar sensation, one
which was strangely agreeable. He had been profoundly
shocked at the time, and had wondered if he was going
mad. The obvious explanation seemed so ridiculous
that he refused to entertain it for one moment. Nothing
in his past had ever suggested anything of that nature.
There must be another reason. He went over their
meetings again and again, recalling every detail. Slowly
an incredible suspicion began to take root. He grew
impatient to see the boy once more, so that he could
test his theory. But though James stayed at Wintersett
Court for much longer than he had originally intended,
the landscape remained empty of both boy and horse.

Serena had made up her mind that her excursions were
too dangerous to be repeated. She could hardly bear to
think of what might have happened in the cottage. What

excuse could she have found for keeping her soaking jacket on? What would have been the gentleman's reaction on finding out how she had deceived him?

Even after she reached the comparative safety of the Lodge her difficulties were not over. It took some time to remove her wet things and drape them over whatever she could find in the Lodge. When she arrived in the house, dressed but without her petticoats and with wet hair, Sheba was waiting for her.

'Where you been, Miss Serena? Your hair's all wet, and you got no petticoats! Shame on you!'

Serena hurried to her room with Sheba in close attendance. If her great-aunt saw her now she really would be in trouble. She was only halfway through changing when Lucy came in.

'Goodness, Sasha, where have you been? Out in the rain, I imagine — your hair's wet. I've been looking everywhere for you. What have you been doing, aunt of mine?'

Serena tried not to say anything, but Lucy would not be put off. Finally the fear that Lucy would continue questioning her in front of Aunt Spurston caused Serena to confess that she had been out riding on the Downs. The gentleman was not mentioned. Lucy was highly amused.

'And to think I thought you had become totally stuffy, Sasha! Oh, my dearest aunt, I do so love you!' She hugged Serena tightly, saying, 'And I will never breathe a word, I swear! Now, I have something for you.'

She ran out of the room and soon returned with a very pretty reticule, wrapped in silver paper. 'It's for your birthday!'

Serena was unable to speak. The reticule was exquis-
itely painted with poinsettias, delicate orchids and
ferns. The work must have taken Lucy hours to do.

'Serena?' Lucy's voice was uncertain.

'I. . .' Serena cleared her throat. 'It's beautiful.
Thank you.' She looked at Lucy's anxious face. 'Lucy,
it's the most beautiful thing I've ever seen! Thank you,
oh, thank you, my love.'

'That's all right, then. I thought for a moment you
didn't like it. Now tell me about your rides.'

'Not at the moment,' said Serena firmly. 'Great-aunt
Spurston will be waiting downstairs. I don't want her to
start asking questions—they might be difficult to
answer!' So Serena brought the boys' clothes back into
the house and put them with the other things for her
great-aunt's charity. She returned her pistol to its
special place in her valise and applied herself resolutely
to her duties, determined to forget her new acquaintance. In the days that followed this proved to be more
difficult than she had imagined. She was surprised how
sharply she regretted the thought that she would never
see him again.

One reward for Serena's concentration on improving
her behaviour was Lady Spurston's approval.

'You are growing more presentable by the hour,
Serena! I'll swear the lotion Mrs Galveston sent is doing
your skin a vast amount of good. You will never be a
beauty, but your complexion is much less sallow—and I
do believe you are filling out a little. Certainly your new
dresses are most becoming! And that woman of yours is
learning fast.'

Serena privately thought that it was lack of sun which
was causing her tan to fade, but in accordance with her

new mode of life she smiled, and when she next saw Mrs
Galveston she thanked her gracefully.

Alas for Serena's good intentions! Her great-aunt
forgot to have the charity clothes ready when the agent
next called, and they were left for another month. The
weather improved, and the fresh scents of an English
spring proved too enticing. Once again the clothes were
rescued from their storage place, the pistol was tucked
into the jacket, and, after a lively argument with Sheba,
Serena stole away to the stables. With the assistance of
a friendly stable lad, Trask was saddled and removed
unseen to the Lodge. Excited, her heart beating nervously, Serena set off through the country lanes towards
the Downs.

Trask himself also seemed to be feeling a springtime
renewal of energy. Together Serena and he had a good
run, until they both ended up on the ridge, panting. The
advancing season had turned the patchwork of fields
into a medley of greens. The air was brilliantly clear —
Serena could see for miles. Entranced, she slipped
down from Trask and stretched voluptuously, breathing
in the scents of the countryside. The tropics had their
own beauty, but this air was like champagne. She felt
quite warm, but did not open the jacket or remove her
cap. It was most unlikely that the tall gentleman would
appear again after all this time, but she dared not risk
it. . .

It was as well. Douce and her rider were emerging
from the trees, almost as if they had been waiting for
her. A warm glow of satisfaction spread through her
veins, astonishing her with its intensity. She suddenly

felt exhilarated. It was worth any risk to feel like this. 'Hail, Caesar!' she cried gaily.

His face was inscrutable as he dismounted and stood beside the horse for a moment.

'Hail to thee, blithe spirit! Bird thou never wert——'

Her eyes grew intent. 'I've not heard that. Where is it from? I don't think it's Shakespeare, is it?'

'Not Shakespeare. Nor Wordsworth. Nor Blake, my boy.'

He spoke with a curious inflection. What was wrong? He even looked menacing. For a moment she felt frightened and thought of flight, but he suddenly smiled and she was reassured. She must be imagining things! 'Then who, sir?' she asked.

'It's by Shelley—Percy Bysshe Shelley. Have you heard of him?'

'No.' He was now quite close. He was menacing—he seemed to loom over her, and she suddenly felt breathless.

'How. . .how does it go on?'

'Hail to thee, blithe Spirit! Bird thou never wert——'

His face and voice were hard as he added, 'Or should it be "boy thou never wert"?' He put out a long arm, pulled off her cap, and breathed a long sigh of satisfaction as her dark hair tumbled out over her shoulders. 'I thought so,' he said. He regarded her in silence while her face flamed and she stared back at him, mesmerised. Finally he smiled and, drawing her to him, he kissed her hard. 'I thought so,' he said again with satisfaction. 'You've been haunting me, my little changeling,' he murmured, covering her face in little kisses. 'I've had some sleepless nights over you. Now you must pay.' His fingers were undoing the buttons of her jacket.

Serena came to life. 'Stop! Stop it, I say!' She tried to get free, but he held her easily, laughing at her struggles.

'Don't bother to pretend. You've led me a pretty little dance, my dear, but it's over now. The game is over. I'm willing to admit you're an original. Unlike most of your sisters, you've at least succeeded in catching my interest.' He bent his head again, whispering against her lips, 'We'll discuss terms later.' He pulled open her jacket, took her even more firmly into his arms and started to kiss her again, more passionately than before.

Serena was in a state of panic. She had never felt so helpless. No man had ever kissed her like this before, held her so roughly, talked to her in such a manner. But soon her pride and spirit came to her rescue. She managed to kick Trask, who snorted and jibbed in surprise, and, taking advantage of a momentary relaxation in the man's grip, she tore herself free and backed away. Before he could catch her again she pulled her pistol out of her jacket pocket and cocked it. 'Don't take another step!' she said. He made to move, and she pointed the pistol at his knees. 'I mean it! I'll shatter your kneecap.'

They regarded one another in silence, Serena's eyes watchful and her hand steady.

'The devil!' he said then with a laugh. 'I believe you would, too.'

'You may count on it,' Serena said grimly.

'Hmm. Perhaps I was wrong after all. Does this mean — forgive me if I seem somewhat obtuse — that all this was *not* part of a plot to become — er — more closely acquainted with me?'

'I would rather have a closer acquaintance with a boa constrictor. Whatever made you think I would?'

'What the devil else was I to think? Oh, point that pistol somewhere else; I give you my word you're safe from me.'

'I'd rather keep it where it is for the moment. So far I have no reason to take your word for anything.'

'In that case we're quits, William Blake — or is it Wordsworth? What *is* your name, girl?'

She hesitated, then her lips began to twitch. 'It's Serena. But that's all I'll tell you.'

He gave a great shout of laughter. 'Serena! I refuse to believe it! You've made it up!'

'No, it's my real name.'

'Serena! Oh that's rich, that's really rich! Wait! Er. . .do you expect to ride Trask back?'

Serena turned her head to see Trask moving slowly out of sight. She gasped in dismay and moved to go after him, but before she had taken a step an iron hand had caught her wrist and forced her to drop the pistol. An exclamation of pain escaped her and she looked at him with a fear she could not conceal. But though he did not release her, he made no attempt to kiss her again.

'If you promise not to point it at me any more you may have it back,' the man said quietly, holding her gaze. 'I intend you no harm. Do you believe me? Will you promise?' Serena nodded and he picked her pistol up, made it safe, and handed it to her. She hesitated, then put it carefully away. Her wrist was aching and she furtively rubbed it. He saw the movement, and stretched out to take it. She backed away nervously. The gentleman raised his hands and smiled. 'I mean no harm. I'm sorry I hurt you, that's all. And I apologise for my behaviour a moment ago. I think we owe each other an explanation, don't you?'

'Trask?' she croaked out of a dry throat.

'Douce will soon overtake him. In fact, if you wait here I'll fetch him for you now.'

Trask was brought back and tied up, while Serena restored herself to order.

'Now, Serena!' His lips twitched and he said, 'A less suitable name would be difficult to find —— '

'Prudence?' suggested Serena. He burst into laughter. She went on, 'I may not be very serene, but I have been even less prudent, I'm afraid. But you have no notion how stifling it is to be a woman.'

'Tell me,' he said. 'Why did you have to turn into a boy?'

She looked at him uncertainly. How far could she trust him? He said, returning to a colder manner, 'I have given you my word, Serena. I do not in general force myself on unwilling females, once I am sure they are unwilling, that is. Not many of them are. But you have convinced me of your reluctance in the plainest possible way.'

She made up her mind. 'You misunderstand. I was wondering how much to tell you, not whether you were about to. . .to attack me again. I accept your word on that. Though why the discovery that I was not a boy should lead you to the conclusion that I would be. . . would be. . .a woman like that, willing to be treated in such a way, I am at a loss to understand!'

'Dammit, how could I think otherwise? Modest young females don't normally roam the countryside with no one to protect them! And modest young females don't normally dress like boys — or ride astride, if you'll forgive my mentioning it.'

'But why should you assume that I was doing all this just to attract you? Or do you take that for granted? I have to tell you that I find you guilty of a fault worse than any of mine.'

'What? What fault?'

'Your conceit!' She was pleased to observe that this remark had struck home. A faint pink appeared in his cheeks, but then he drawled,

'I have been pursued by the fair sex, Serena, ever since I was old enough to notice. But I am not so green as to believe that they loved me for myself. My family's fortune is famous. It's only too obvious where my attractions lie.'

'If your riches are your only attractive feature, that may well be true!'

'Is that your opinion? That my wealth is my only attraction?'

'We have agreed, have we not, that attraction is not a question between us?' said Serena loftily. She spoilt it by adding, 'In any case, I had no idea — still have no idea — who you are, so how could your riches appeal?'

He bowed. 'I am Wintersett.'

'Well, Mr Wintersett ——'

'Lord Wintersett. And my given name is James. So now we have settled the question of our relationship — or rather the limitations to our relationship, shall I say? — isn't it about time you told me why you had to be a boy? So far we have only established that being a woman is stifling.' He indicated a fallen tree-trunk at the edge of the track, and they sat down. Serena, in spite of his assurances, took care to keep her distance.

'Till recently,' she began carefully, 'I have led a less restricted life then I have to at the moment. Don't misunderstand — my former life was completely respectable, just more. . .perhaps "independent" is the word.'

'You're not old enough to be a widow! Are you?'

'You may speculate as much as you wish. I will not tell you anything more than I choose. But I was able to go much my own way.'

'And now?'

'Now I have to set an example to someone younger than myself.'

'You're a governess. I find that incredible, too.'

'Perhaps. Perhaps not. And sometimes, just sometimes, I cannot stand the restraints any longer. I have to get free.'

'But why the disguise?'

'You ask that! When you have just demonstrated — and so roughly, too — what happens to women who — what was your phrase? — "roam the countryside with no one to protect them".' Can you imagine the disgrace if it were discovered that the very person who should be setting an example was breaking every rule in Society's book? No,' she continued bitterly, 'I thought my disguise would give me the freedom I longed for without hurting people I —— ' she looked at his intent face — 'to whom I owe my loyalty. As for not riding side-saddle — have you ever seen a boy who did?'

'That's true! Yes, I can see that one followed from the other. And now?'

'And now I shall have to confine myself to "acceptable behaviour for a lady".' She sighed deeply. 'Walks round the garden, morning calls, which are *always* paid in the afternoon, polite conversation, in which one never, ever says anything worthwhile. Do you know that I am thought "bookish" because I enjoy Shakespeare? I shall probably finish by pressing flowers and painting on velvet.'

His laugh rang out again. 'May heaven preserve you from such a fate! I must confess, you intrigue me, Serena. It's clear that you are no governess — you occupy a superior position in society than those unfortunates — and I'm fairly sure you're no widow, either. What possible circumstances have combined to give rise to such a life as yours?'

Serena looked at him in alarm. He was too intelligent. Before long he would learn everything from her. 'I must go!' she said hurriedly, and went to pick up her cap, which was still lying where Lord Wintersett had dropped it.

'Oh, no!' he said and calmly appropriated the cap. 'You don't escape so easily. Like you, I spend much of my life with people who bore me beyond measure ——'

'I didn't say that! I love my ——' she stopped short. She had almost told him more. His face changed, and he looked like a stranger. His voice was icy as he said,

'Have I been mistaken yet again? Can it be that you seek relief from a boring lover in these. . .escapades?'

'No, no!' His face remained cold, so she said desperately, 'I'm. . .a kind of chaperon. The person I love is my charge.'

'You're not old enough!'

'I am seven and twenty.'

He looked flatteringly astonished. 'I will not express disbelief,' he said. 'You must know how old you are, and can have no reason to exaggerate your age. But I would not have guessed it.' Then a new thought occurred to him. 'If you are a chaperon, then you must be married — or a widow?'

'Neither. That is why I must be so circumspect.'

'Of course. As you are. Indeed. I have seen it myself.'

Serena chuckled. 'You, sir, have seen my alter ego. It is unkind of you to mock me. Now, if you will give me my cap. . .'

'I did not finish what I had to say, Serena.' He looked down at the vivid face lifted to his, the golden eyes half laughing, half anxious. 'I have found more amusement in half an hour of your company than in a year of most of my acquaintance. I do not intend to do without it.'

'But. . .but I cannot spend more time with you now!'

'Why not?'

'You must see it is impossible! Pretending to be a boy so that I can have some time to myself is one thing. Slipping out in disguise to an assignation is something very different — indeed, it would be shameful! And I will not do it!'

'I would never have thought you so poor-spirited. Or so conceited!'

'Conceited?'

'Yes, Serena. How can you be so quick to accuse me of conceit, when you suffer from the same fault yourself? What makes you think I want an assignation with you? Those I can have whenever I choose.'

'Of course,' she murmured. 'That wealth of yours. . . What would you want of me?'

'Companionship, friendship — call it what you will. I enjoy your company, and do not wish to lose it.'

'I'm afraid you must. I cannot agree to meet you clandestinely.'

'I fear, dear Serena, you will have to!' She started to

make an angry protest, but he overrode her. 'For if you do not agree to ride here in your boy's clothes, let us say once a week, when I am at home ——' he held her gaze '—I will seek you out where you live and reveal all. It would not be difficult to trace you if I really tried.'

Serena looked at him in horror. 'You wouldn't do such a thing!'

'I agree I probably will not. You will have seen reason before it becomes necessary.'

'But that's blackmail!'

'Quite. I am glad your understanding is so quick.' When he saw that she still didn't believe him he said slowly and clearly, as if speaking to an idiot, 'I will find out who you really are, and you will be disgraced, unless you agree to continue our acquaintance.'

It was obvious that he meant every word.

'You. . .you scoundrel!'

'Come, you are disappointing me, Serena. What am I asking you to do that you were not doing already? I have told you that I have no wish for an alfresco love-affair. And I would not suggest for a moment that we meet anywhere but here on this open ridge. No, it will be as if you are the boy I first thought you. I will even call you William if you desire me to.'

She looked at him uncertainly. 'But you know I am not a boy. It is. . .it is embarrassing to be in br. . . breeches, when you know I am a woman.'

His voice quivered as he said, 'I promise never to look at your br. . . breeches.'

'You will call me William?'

'All the time.'

'And not help me, or coddle me as you would a woman?'

'I will be as severe on you as on the toughest of the members of my own club.'

'And you won't think badly of me for this masquerade?'

'I'm beginning to think badly of you at this very moment, Serena ——'

'Ha!'

'I shall call you Serena while you continue to act like a woman. At the moment you are suffering from a totally feminine inability to face the inevitable. If you wish to be thought a man, then you must begin to think like one — logically and clearly.' He held up one hand and counted on his fingers.

'One: for no reason other than your own pleasure, you chose to dress as a boy and ride out on the Downs. Am I right?'

Serena nodded reluctantly.

'Two: at the risk of being accused of conceit, I will say that you have enjoyed our conversations as much as I. Correct?'

Serena nodded again and he looked satisfied.

'Three: if you do not agree to continue these very pleasant activities, you will suffer some very unpleasant consequences. Where is the choice?'

Serena was going down fighting. 'How can I possibly enjoy something I am doing under constraint?'

'Humbug! You want to, you know you do, constraint or no. But it's time to put an end to this unnecessary discussion. Are you to be Serena or William?'

'If I agree, you won't attempt to find out where I live or who I am? I can only carry this out if I feel my two lives are totally separate.'

'Hand on heart!'

'You'll let me ride Douce occasionally?'

His face, normally so cold, was transformed by his smile. 'Of course you may, my boy! Now, if you wish.'

Serena took a deep breath and said, 'Done!'

That was the first of several outings. Aunt Spurston, whose health improved as the weather got better, decided that she would visit Mrs Galveston every Friday in Reigate. Here Lucy could join Isabella in a dancing class with other young people of the district — all under strict supervision, of course — while Aunt Spurston herself renewed old acquaintances. Serena was excused from these excursions as the carriage was really only comfortable for two, and Aunt Spurston so much enjoyed the opportunity to gossip with her cronies.

'You will have time to yourself for a change, Serena. There will be little enough occasion for that once the season starts.'

It was as if everything conspired to smooth the way for Serena's meetings with Lord Wintersett. Sheba scolded, but helped her. Her great-aunt, naturally, always took the coachman and groom with her, and Tom, the stable lad, became one of Serena's staunchest allies. Trask enjoyed the exercise after several years of neglect. As for the outings themselves — they soon became the focus of Serena's week.

CHAPTER FIVE

SERENA'S life had till now been active and rewarding, but not really a happy one. Her childhood had often been lonely, in a household dominated by two strong-willed males—egomaniacs, both of them—her father and her brother Richard. Looking back, Serena could see now that Richard had always been selfish and unscrupulous, but she and her father had worshipped him, blinded by his charm and reckless courage. 'The looks of a lion, with a lion's heart,' her father had said of him. Richard and her father had both bullied Rodney unmercifully, and had at the same time despised him for allowing it. For a while Rodney had managed to escape them through his marriage with Lucy's mother. But when she died he had returned to Anse Chatelet with his little daughter, and in the end he had found another, more dangerous way to forgetfulness. Serena had been so anxious to avoid the same contempt that Anse Chatelet had been haunted by her tiny figure fiercely determined to win Lord Calvert's approval or Richard's admiration by acts of reckless daring. By the time she was fourteen she had learned to shoot, to ride, to sail almost as well as they did themselves.

Later, in a sadder and wiser time, she had worked unceasingly to keep Anse Chatelet out of the hands of the creditors. The work had been rewarding, but very demanding, and the consciousness of her twin responsibilities—for Lucy and for the estate—had weighed heavily on her.

Now, here in the heart of the English countryside, she learned what it was to be unreservedly happy. Together she and Lord Wintersett explored the hills, valleys, lanes and fields of Surrey. They seldom met anyone, for they kept to the unfrequented paths and byways. But her favourite place was still the top of the ridge, for there she could feel as if they were on the roof of the world, far removed from the restrictions of life below.

They explored each other's minds, too. The love of poetry they already shared, but Serena, conscious of her lack of other knowledge, listened avidly to her companion's accounts of his journeys in Europe, of the people he had met and the sights he had seen. New worlds were opening up before her, and she soaked up knowledge as a sponge soaked up water.

For his part, James talked more freely than he had ever done in his life before, and he waited with a quite unaccustomed interest for anything she might say or ask in response. She never disappointed him. Her quick intelligence, her strong sense of humour, the freshness of her views, were a constant source of pleasure to him. He delighted in the mobile features, golden eyes now sparkling with laughter, now wide with wonder, the generous brow wrinkled in concentration, the sensitive mouth soft with compassion or set in determination. Almost the only barrier between them was her fixed resolve to keep everything about her other life completely hidden. He sensed that this was her defence against any stirrings of conscience about her behaviour, and respected her wishes, never seeking to trap her into betraying herself. Any indications he gleaned from things she said he stored up in his mind, but he gave them little importance. He, too, liked the feeling of isolation from the rest of society, in the world which they had created for themselves on the top of the hill.

They had differences, of course. Serena had already experienced Lord Wintersett's ruthlessness in pursuit of something he wanted. She was occasionally repelled by his coldness, his indifference to the feelings of others — even of those he liked. And he soon found that Serena was touchy about her independence and very fond of her own way. Worse than that, she had a temper. He could see that years of discipline had taught her to control it, but once it was released it blazed like a furnace, leaving her with no thought for the consequences.

On one memorable occasion he actually had to use force to save her from catastrophe. They had wandered further afield than usual, and came upon an isolated cottage in front of which an ugly scene was being enacted. The cottagers — an elderly couple — were being forcibly removed from their home. Two men were throwing pathetic scraps of furniture out on to the grass in front of the cottage. The woman was wailing, and her husband had a bruise on his forehead — graphic evidence of the treatment they had received. Serena rode forward and said imperiously, 'What are you doing there? Stop what you're doing immediately!'

The two bailiffs looked round in surprise, but when they saw a mere boy confronting them they turned back to resume their activities.

'I told you to stop, you hog-grubbers!'

One of the men thus addressed turned round swiftly

and said, 'You saucy young buck! Be off and stop interfering with what don't concern you! This here lot has to be got out by tonight or else! We don't need you to teach us our jobs.' He turned round. 'Here, you!'

The old woman had scrambled to the pile of furniture and was trying to take it back inside. The bailiff went over to her and pulled her away so roughly that she fell into the mud. Serena, her eyes flashing molten gold, jumped down from Trask and ran to pick the woman up. This was the point at which James thought it prudent to intervene before "William" ran into disaster. He rode into the clearing and interposed Douce between the bailiff and the boy.

'What's the trouble?' he asked coldly.

The bailiffs took off their caps. 'Pardon, sir. We was just doin' our duty when this young gentleman appears.'

'And your duty consists of throwing a woman old enough to be your grandmother to the ground?'

The men flushed darkly, and one of them muttered, 'The old biddy must 'a tripped. She wouldn't do what we told 'er. Troublemakers, that's what they are.'

'Can't they pay their rent?'

'It's not that, sir. The master wants the land for another purpose. And the cottage ain't fit fer man nor beast to live in. They've been offered somewhere else.'

'But this is their home!' cried Serena. 'Why do they have to leave if they don't want to?'

'If the landowner wants the land and has offered them an alternative they have no choice,' said James. He turned to the men. 'But see that you go gently with the old people. Come — *William!*'

'I'm not going till I'm certain that they're all right,' said Serena hotly. 'Where is their new home?'

'In the work'ouse, young maister!' shouted the old man. 'And Sal and me are goin' to 'ave to live apart!'

'Well, what's wrong wi' that? You ain't much use to a woman at your age, old man,' jeered the other bailiff.

'That's monstrous! How dare you!' cried Serena. She dodged round Douce and kicked the unfortunate bailiff in the shins.

''Ere!' he roared, and grabbed Serena by the scruff of the neck.

James was there in a flash, almost breaking the man's arm as he knocked him clear. 'You,' he snarled, 'lay another finger on my nephew and you'll be the worse for it. Who is your master?'

'Sir Oliver Camden,' muttered the bailiff resentfully, picking himself up. 'You'd best be careful — Sir Oliver don't like interference with his concerns. And he's a magistrate, as well!'

'I know Sir Oliver. I don't believe he would wish this. I'll speak to him about it. Meanwhile leave the old people alone, do you hear? William — get on your horse. We're leaving.'

'But —' Serena started to protest.

'I said get on your horse!' When she would have argued James picked her up under one arm and carried her, kicking and protesting, to where Trask was patiently waiting. Here he threw her up on to the horse, called Douce to him, and they were soon riding away, with Trask's reins firmly held in James' hand.

Serena was furious. 'Let go! I said let go! You're every bit as bad as they are!'

James rode on in grim silence. Ignoring Serena's worst efforts, he guided them both until they were well clear of the wood. It was a superlative display of horsemanship. But as soon as he stopped Serena immediately wheeled Trask round and urged him back the way they had come. She was quickly overtaken, and this time James forced her to dismount. They stood facing one another in the quiet lane. Serena was still angry. 'How dare you treat me as if I were a child? Those people needed my help! I shall go back. You cannot stop me!'

James was every bit as angry as Serena, but he was in control of himself. He said coldly, 'You're a fool, Serena! Do you wish to make a public spectacle of yourself? You were within an ace of discovery back there! If I hadn't stopped him that bailiff would have found he'd got more than he bargained for when he held you by your collar! Pull yourself together!'

'But that old man—and the woman!'

'Forget them! Sir Oliver is within his rights, you know he is!'

'But he's going to separate them—after all those years together!'

James regarded her curiously. 'Why are these people so important to you?'

'It's not that—it's just that it's wrong to deprive anyone of their. . .their dignity like that. If you have people in your care you have to treat them with humanity. I've met people like them. Separate them and they'll die without each other; I've seen it happen.'

'They'll die anyway soon enough. Forget them!'

Serena looked at him in disgust and turned away. They stood in silence for a while.

'I'll speak to Sir Oliver,' he said finally. 'He can probably find some cottage in the village for them, though he might well wonder what business it is of mine. Still — will that satisfy you?'

In an instant she had turned round, her face glowing with gratitude. She came close and clutched his arm. For a moment James thought she was going to kiss him, and he experienced such a unexpectedly strong surge of feeling that, before he could stop himself, he had put his hand over hers, clamping it to his arm. 'Serena!' he said fiercely. She looked up, startled. For a moment they stared at each other, and then they both took a step back as if they had reached a sudden abyss.

'You. . .you promised always to call me William,' she said uncertainly.

James strove to regain mastery of his feelings. He knew that this next moment would be decisive. If Serena even suspected how powerfully she had affected him she would refuse to see him again, he was sure. If that happened. . .his mind shied away from the possibility. Her friendship and trust had become more important to him than he had realised. He must not lose them because of any transitory feelings of desire. Those could be satisfied cheaply. The value of this relationship with Serena was beyond price.

She was waiting for his response. He took a deep breath.

'As I think I've said before, when you behave as irrationally as you have just done with those men, I shall call you by your woman's name,' he said coldly. 'Act sensibly and you will be William again to me.'

Serena was reassured by this. In all their other meetings, apart from the one when he had discovered her to be a woman, Lord Wintersett had behaved impeccably. He had treated her and spoken to her like the boy she was pretending to be. If he had ever hinted at a warmer feeling she would have been forced to abandon her excursions, even if he carried out his threat to expose her. A moment ago she had been afraid that this might be the case, but his reply had hardly been that of a lover! She must have been mistaken. She was surprised how passionately relieved she felt, that she was free to continue with this strange friendship.

It was astonishing that such a brief moment could have such a profound effect on both James and Serena—the very opposite of what might have been expected. Each had recognised the danger of the moment. But each had also realised the value of their relationship, the importance of preserving it. So an incident which might have led to a reserve, a wariness between them, in fact served to draw them closer.

But the disadvantage of their precarious relationship was brought home to Lord Wintersett when Serena did not appear at her usual time the following week. The trust between them was now so absolute that he had no thought of carrying out his threat of finding her if she refused to meet him. But he was worried. Had she had an accident? Had she reached wherever she lived safely after the last expedition? Was she ill? He had no means of knowing without exposing her—the last thing he wanted. When she did not immediately appear for the second week he was so anxious about her that he was debating whether to set off to look for a clue—anything—as to where she might be. His relief therefore was enormous when she appeared over the hill, and he strode to meet her.

'Serena! What happened?'

'Last week? I must say I was quite relieved not to see

you riding up the drive to. . .the place where I live, like
Nemesis. I suspect you are a humbug, Lord Wintersett.
I should have tested your threats before now.'

'What happened, Serena? Did you have an accident?
Were you waylaid?'

'No, My. . .the person I live with was unwell. I could
not leave her.'

They suddenly realised that James was holding
Serena's hands, and she moved away self-consciously.
'You promised to call me William, Lord Wintersett!'
she said almost angrily.

'I know, I know!' he replied. 'It's sometimes damned
difficult to remember that. I've been worried about you.
You may dress like a boy, but you are a woman when
all is said and done. And vulnerable.'

Serena laughed as she flourished her little pistol. 'Not
while I have this, my friend.'

'Much good that toy would have done you had you
fallen off your horse and broken your leg.'

He was obviously seriously upset, and Serena, not
without some secret amusement, set herself to coax him
into a better mood.

The weeks flew by, and Serena was aware that she
would soon have to think of removing to London. She
had received a letter from Lady Pendomer saying that
Sir Henry's cousin, Lord Ambourne, was prepared to
sublet a small house in Dover Street at a very moderate
rent for Serena's stay in London. Serena had written to
Lord Ambourne, and had had a very civil reply offering
her the house, together with its staff, as soon as she
needed it. He regretted that he would unable to make
her acquaintance as early as he had hoped, since he and

his Countess were spending the early part of the summer on his estate in France.

Lady Warnham and her family were leaving Surrey within the month to open up the Galveston mansion in Portman Square, and Lucy was growing impatient to be gone. Her and Serena's wardrobes had long been ready. The small finishing touches, such as shoes, fans, shawls and the like, would be bought in the warehouses and shops of London. Little remained to be done in Surrey, and yet Serena lingered. She was sure she would meet Lord Wintersett in London, and was fairly certain that their friendship was secure enough to withstand the transition, but it would not be the same. In London she would be 'Miss Calvert', or 'Serena' — never 'William'.

When she mentioned her imminent departure to Lord Wintersett he seemed to feel regret, too. 'I take it you are going to London for the Season — your "charge" is no doubt to be presented? Oh, don't look at me like that, William! I have not pried into your affairs all this time, and you have no reason to suspect me of doing so now! Well, it is perhaps as well. This could not continue forever, much as I have enjoyed it. *Will* you be in London? Shall I meet you there?'

She nodded.

'It will seem strange,' he continued. 'I feel I know you better than anyone of my acquaintance, and yet we shall have to appear to be strangers. Do you realise that I have never even seen you in a dress?'

She looked at him doubtfully. 'Don't expect too much, my friend. Remember my position as a chaperon.'

'Now that really will be a piquant situation! The thought of seeing how William the Turbulent is transformed into Serena the Respectable Chaperon almost consoles me for the loss of our present meetings. Almost. But not quite.'

They had ridden up to the ridge and were looking down on bright green fields and sprouting hedges. "Hardly hedgerows. . ."' Serena murmured.

'"Little lines of sportive wood run wild". I shall miss William, Serena.'

'He has to go, Lord Wintersett. But he will always treasure the memory of how good you have been to him.'

'Serena——'

'No! I shall be Serena in London,' said Serena quickly. 'Wait till then. When do you plan to move to the town?'

'I live most of the year in London. My home here is not a very happy place, I'm afraid, and I am not often to be found there. This spring has been quite exceptional.' He smiled down at her. 'I think you know why, William.'

But Serena was thinking of what he had said before. Breaking her own rule, she asked, 'Why is your home not a happy one?'

'My nephew is confined to a wheelchair when he is not actually in bed. My mother is also an invalid, and recently she has been getting worse.'

'Can she be cured?'

'Who knows? Her illness is not physical, but the result of two shocks, the one rapidly following on the other. Both my father and my younger brother died within a month of each other. She has never been the same since.' Then he added abruptly, 'But don't let us spoil a beautiful afternoon with such gloomy thoughts.

It might be one of our last. Come — is Trask fit for
another gallop — or do you wish to ride Douce?'

Serena smiled. 'What an unnecessary question!'

Serena told James the next time they met that this was
their last meeting. He looked at the wide view below
and wondered why the devil it all had to look so bright.
Rain would have been more appropriate. He forced
himself to speak calmly.

'You told me last time that you were soon going to
London, so it comes as no surprise. And I will soon in
any case be unable to spend much time here in Surrey —
I have business of my own in London.' Serena shivered.
'You're cold?'

'No. Someone walked over my grave, I think.' She
looked at him with troubled eyes. 'Or was it because of
stories I've been hearing about a certain Lord
Wintersett?'

'Stories?'

'I haven't been prying. I respect your privacy as much
as you have respected mine. But now that our London
début is so near, my charge and I have been subjected
to a great deal of advice and gossip. . . I have heard
your name mentioned several times. The Lord
Wintersett I hear of then does not seem to be the man I
know.'

'No?'

'No. I hear that Lord Wintersett is cold, heartless,
indifferent to others. That any lady who attempts to
attract him runs the risk of a severe set-down. That even
his paramours — forgive me, I am still speaking in the
character of William, so I can mention these things —

never know when his interest will wane and they will be discarded.'

He said harshly, 'They are right, Serena — you see, I have already said goodbye to William, so you must now be called by your right name — I do not deny these stories.' Serena looked at him gravely and something in her eyes made him continue, 'You once said that I could have no notion how stifling it was to be a woman. But you have no notion of what it is like to be a very rich man. You once called me conceited because I assumed that you were pursuing me. My experience would never have led me to think otherwise. I will not bore you with other and different stories. But I think every trick known to woman has been tried to trap me — not my person, you understand, but my wealth. As for my paramours — they run the risks of their calling. They are well rewarded.'

Serena swallowed and looked away from him and down into the broad valley.

'What is it, Serena?'

'In one breath you excuse your lack of concern for others because you think they seek you only for your wealth. In another you use your wealth as a substitute for concern. "They are well rewarded," you said. It does not reassure me, Lord Wintersett.'

He took her by the shoulders and turned her towards him. 'The stories may be true. But one thing my critics have never been able to say. Look at me, Serena, for this is important to me.' She looked up, her golden eyes serious. 'No one has yet been able to say that I have broken any promises.'

'I suppose that is something. But it is not enough. I think you lack. . .'

'What?'

'I don't know. Kindness?'

'Is that important to you? Universal kindness, I mean?' he asked in surprise.

'I think it is.'

'Strange. It is not a quality I have sought to cultivate. One is kind to idiots or well-meaning fools. I have always avoided them where possible.' Serena was still looking troubled. He felt a sudden urge to remove the worried frown from her brow. 'Do you wish me to make promises to you? Is that it?'

'No!' she said vehemently. 'No! Now is not the time to be promising anything. This situation between us. . . is too artificial——'

'I sometimes feel it is the only real thing in my world,' he said whimsically.

'But the world you talk about is here, on this hill. It isn't real, either,' she said sadly.

'Serena, believe me, the world of London society is infinitely more artificial than any make-believe world we have here. You will be flattered and cozened, as I have been——'

'"Taffeta phrases, silken terms", Lord Wintersett?'

'Exactly! "Words, words, mere words, no matter from the heart." What a splendid thing quotation is! But please, Serena, don't change when you get to London.' A small frown creased his brow. 'I am strangely afraid that I am going to lose you. Can we not take some kind of vow? I am willing, if you are.'

'Lord Wintersett, if, when we meet again in London, you still wish to make a promise of any kind—for friendship, for loyalty or. . .of any kind—then I will listen to you. Not till then. And now I must go.'

'Then farewell till then, Serena. But first there's something I must do.' He drew her gently to him and kissed her, and was jubilant to feel her total response, untutored though it was. 'Whether you realise it or not, you have just made a promise all the same, Serena,' he said as they drew apart again. 'Serena, my "bright, particular star".'

Serena, still looking at him with wonder in her eyes, said nothing.

'Till London, then,' he said, holding her chin in his hand. She nodded silently. He kissed her once again, then let her go, and stood watching as Trask carried her away from him down into the valley.

As James returned to his home he had the unpleasant feeling that an idyll had just ended. What would take its place he had no means of knowing, but he feared the effect of London on their relationship. Serena had called their situation artificial and he supposed it was, but they were able to be more natural with each other here than in any conceivable situation in the city. Would Serena be different when she put her skirts on? He couldn't imagine her fluttering and twittering like the rest of society's vapid females, but she was almost certain to lose that wholly natural spontaneity which so delighted him. Especially as she was a "kind of chaperon". Who was her charge? Among the local families he rather thought the Warnham girl was of an age to be presented — but she had a perfectly adequate family, including the Gorgon figure of Mrs Galveston. Speculation was useless — he would find out soon enough.

Alanna's hysterical outburst when she had heard that Sasha Calvert was coming to England had not been

repeated, but she was pale and tense and feverishly
active. James had offered to send her to her parents in
Ireland for the summer, but she had refused, especially
when he told her that young Tony would stay in
England where he belonged.

'You would not separate us, James!' she exclaimed.

'I'm beginning to think it might be the best thing that
could possibly happen to the boy,' he said brutally.
'Tony will never make the attempt to be normal while
you are constantly hovering over him assuring him he is
delicate. Where is he now?'

'He's up today,' she said eagerly. 'In his room. He
has even been working with his tutor.'

James went along to Tony's room. It was a sunny
room on the ground floor, with a large window which
opened on to the garden. But the windows were always
closed, sometimes even shuttered, and the child often
lay in darkness for hours on end. James hated visiting
him. This boy was all that was left of his beloved
brother, yet he could see nothing of the older Tony
about him. Born at seven months, the infant had grown
slowly from a puling, sickly baby into a pale, lethargic
invalid. There was nothing of his father's gentle courage, none of Tony's eagerness to learn of the world
around him. He remained confined to his bed or a
wheelchair, watched jealously by an over-anxious
mother. Of all the casualties of the tragedy on St Just
this was the most pathetic.

Tony was sitting in his chair, but his tutor was
missing. The boy looked up as his uncle came in.

'I've been ringing the bell for ages. No one came.'

'Where's Mr Gimble?'

'He's gone to look for some book in the library.

Uncle James, would you pass me that box of comfits from the table by the bed?'

'The wheels of that chair—they can be pushed by hand, can't they?'

'Yes.'

'Push them, then. It's not far to the table.'

The boy opened his eyes in astonishment. 'But. . . but——'

'Go on. If you can do it I'll bring one of Flossie's pups to see you.' The boy's face brightened and he leaned forward to grip the wheels. His frail hands whitened as he pushed.

'It moved!'

'Of course it did,' said James, surreptitiously moving the chair a fraction further with his foot. But then Alanna, who for some reason could never bear to leave James alone with her son for long, came in. When she saw Tony straining to turn the wheels she shrieked in horror and ran forward to stop him.

'No, Mama! I must do it! Uncle James says he'll bring a puppy for me if I can.'

'A puppy! You must surely be mad, James! Anthony would be coughing and wheezing half the night if an animal came in here. Come, my darling, Mama will get you what you want. This box, was it?'

James gave an exclamation of impatience and left the room.

The next morning there was a note from Bradpole, requesting an interview with Lord Wintersett. Sasha Calvert was expected about the middle of April, and would be staying in a house rented from the Earl of Ambourne in Dover Street. James gave a twisted smile

at the thought. It was ironic that Ned should give shelter
to a Calvert, for Ned and he had been at school together
and the Earl was one of James's few close friends. Not
that Ned knew anything of the events on Anse Chatelet
so long ago, for the story of Tony's suicide in the West
Indies had remained a well-kept secret. Alanna had
wished it so for the sake of her son, and the Calverts
had had their own reasons for hiding the truth. The
world at large had been allowed to think that Tony had
succumbed to the tropical climate.

When they met, Mr Bradpole's manner was grave. 'I
have been unable to ascertain which packet boat Miss
Calvert and her niece took from the West Indies. The
passenger lists are most inadequate. But numbers of
people are arriving in London every day for the season,
and I have learned from Lord Ambourne's man of
business that he is expecting his tenants to move in next
week. Are you still as adamant, Lord Wintersett?'

James hesitated. In truth he had recently had
occasional feelings of distaste for this vendetta against
the Calvert family. But it was not in his nature to reveal
weakness or lack of decision, so he evaded a reply.
'What about affairs on Anse Chatelet?' he asked.

'News travels slowly between England and the West
Indies, and even more slowly between Barbados and St
Just. I do not expect to hear for some time.'

'Tell me when you do. I'll decide then what action to
take.'

Soon after that he tried to persuade Alanna to talk
about the past. 'Believe me, Alanna, I am far from
wishing to raise any ghosts. But the time is approaching
when I must decide what to do about Sasha Calvert, and
I need your help. I need to know what really happened.'

Alanna's blue eyes filled with tears. 'I have told you over and over again,' she whispered brokenly. 'It was a nightmare, James. Why do you force me to remember?'

'Try. Were you and Tony happy before you went to St Just?'

'Oh, yes!' she cried. 'We were deliriously happy! And on the island, too. Right up to the moment it happened. Yes, we were happy.'

'You were living at the house — Anse Chatelet?'

'Yes. Lord Calvert had invited Tony to stay there while he explored the island and sought out new plants.'

'Who else was living there at the time?'

'Let me see.... Lord Calvert was there, and Sasha, and Rodney — but he was an invalid. And the elder brother — Richard, I think he was called. And little Lucy.'

'And what happened?'

'That woman — Sasha. She hardly ever spoke to us in the house. But she followed Tony everywhere on his expeditions.'

'Where were you during these expeditions?'

'I stayed behind at the house, at Anse Chatelet.' She said defensively, answering his unspoken criticism, 'I suppose it would have been better if I had been able to go with Tony, but it wasn't what I was used to! I found the heat too much.'

'What about Tony? Surely the climate was new to him, too.'

'He was so fascinated by the plants out there that he didn't seem to notice it. Or me.' She added forlornly, 'He was always out.'

'When did you learn that Tony was having an affair with the Calvert woman?'

'She was so clever, James! She never went near him in the house. And when they were out everyone thought she was just guiding him through the forests. It never entered my head that she would appeal to him, for she wasn't at all like me. She was not at all feminine. But all the time. . . My poor Tony! My poor darling Tony!' She began to sob.

James set his teeth. 'I've nearly finished, Alanna,' he said as gently as he could. 'Tell me, if you can, what happened before Tony died.'

'I will, I will, James. But not now. I must go to see Anthony——'

'Mr Gimble is with Anthony. Tell me what happened, Alanna.'

She sat down again. 'I. . . I wasn't feeling well. I told Tony about. . .about the baby, and. . .and that's when he confessed. That he was in love with Sasha Calvert, and he wanted to leave me. There was a dreadful scene. I was distraught after it. Perhaps I should not have done what I did.'

'What did you do?'

Alanna paused and wiped her lips with her handkerchief. Then she continued, 'I went to Lord Calvert, to tell him how badly his. . .his daughter had behaved. He didn't believe me at first, but finally he said he would confront them. We were waiting on the terrace when they came in. When her father accused her Sasha just laughed.' Alanna was white to the lips, and she closed her eyes as she said, 'I shall never forget that laughter. It is still ringing in my ears.' She said this with such genuine anguish in her voice that James was moved to pity. He was about to suggest that Alanna should rest for a while, but she was already continuing,

'Can you imagine how Tony felt when she said. . .she said —— Oh, James, with such an expression of scorn! — she said she despised him, that she had no intention of taking him away from me, however besotted he might be. That one lover more or less made no difference to her, she had plenty, and any one of them was more thrilling than a tame little botanist. That I was welcome to him and could take him home with her good will.'

With an muffled exclamation James got up and brought his fist down on the mantelpiece. 'Go on!' he said harshly.

'Lord Calvert was beside himself with rage. He must have known what sort of a woman his daughter was, but he pretended to blame Tony. He swore to ruin him, to throw him off the island, and to see that he was never allowed back anywhere in the West Indies. I don't think Tony heard any of it. He was. . .he looked like a ghost, a zombie they call them out there. Then he went to our rooms. I followed him a few minutes later but. . .you know the rest.'

'And Richard Calvert?'

'Richard? What about Richard? What has Richard to do with this?'

'Didn't he die about the same time?'

'Later—after Tony. But the deaths were unconnected, I think.' Alanna swallowed. 'Richard fell off a cliff on his way back to Anse Chatelet. He was drunk. I believe he usually was.'

'They were a pretty lot! But now only Sasha is left. What shall I do about her? Anse Chatelet may be said to be mine if things go as planned. Is that enough?'

Alanna's pretty face showed her distress as she

pleaded, 'I don't want you to take Anse Chatelet! Leave Sasha Calvert where she belongs, where we will never see her again. Send her back, James! Don't even try to see her! Send her away!'

'You are talking nonsense! How can I send Miss Calvert away? And why should I?'

'You do not know her! She is a wicked liar — she casts a kind of spell over her victims till they do not know what to believe. They said on the island that she had learned the arts of voodoo. Look at the way she dazzled my poor Tony until he was driven to his ruin.'

'She is surely not such a Circe now! She must be well into her thirties.'

Alanna ignored him. She was becoming hysterical again. 'Send her away! Make it impossible for her to remain in England. She ruined our lives once and she will do so again unless you get rid of her!'

'I suppose that is one way,' said James thoughtfully. 'To disgrace her somehow in the eyes of society so that she has to leave England. It would be a kind of poetic justice, after her father's threats to Tony. But it would not be easy to do anything like that without involving the niece, too. And that must be avoided, for neither she nor her father were involved in this sordid affair.'

'Why are you so scrupulous about the niece? The Calverts are all the same.'

'Lucy Calvert is innocent and must be protected,' said James firmly. 'But have no fear, Alanna. Sasha Calvert will pay for Tony's sufferings — and yours.'

'I like your idea of poetic justice, James. If you destroyed the Calvert woman's credit in the eyes of the world, then no one would believe her stories,' said Alanna slowly. She smiled for the first time that evening. 'Oh, yes, James! I think that would be the best idea of all! If you wish, I'll help you in that. In fact I think I have the beginnings of a plan already. Why don't you leave it all to me!'

'Alanna, you are too impetuous! Sasha Calvert is not yet in England. When she arrives she should be given time to become known in society, and to establish her niece. Then we shall see.'

CHAPTER SIX

SERENA and Lucy, together with Sheba, were carried to London in a hired post-chaise. The chaise was comfortable, and the journey not long, so they arrived in Dover Street in reasonably good order. The Earl's agent was waiting for them. He introduced himself as Etienne Masson, and they found to their surprise that he was French. 'Though I prefer to describe myself as Norman, *madame*,' he said with a smile.

He introduced the footman, John, and the housekeeper, Mrs Starkey. Mrs Starkey curtsied and said in a soft, West Country voice, 'Your rooms are ready, ma'am. Shall I lead the way?' While John supervised the unloading of their many valises and had them carried up to the rooms, Masson gave them the directions for the best shops and the sights he thought they would like to see.

'John knows London very well, madame. He will accompany you anywhere you go.'

'Always?' asked Lucy in astonishment.

'It is the custom, *mademoiselle*,' the agent replied apologetically, with the smile that Lucy always seemed to attract.

'And I for one am grateful for it,' said Serena. 'From what I have seen of it so far, the size and bustle of London appals me.'

'Forgive me, *madame*. You have only just arrived. You will soon see that London is in fact very small — the

93

part of it which you will need to know, that is. Er. . .
Lord Ambourne seemed to think that since you are a
small household Mrs Starkey might combine the ser-
vices of steward and housekeeper. She is experienced in
both kinds of work. She has a number of domestics to
help her in the house, but if you would prefer to engage
maids for yourself and Miss Lucy Calvert I will arrange
it.'

Serena was secretly relieved that the household
expenses would be so much lighter, but simply replied,
'It is kind of Lord Ambourne to take such trouble. We
have brought our own maid with us from St Just, and I
think she will be enough, but I will let you know a little
later what we decide.'

'Then I will take my leave. I hope you will enjoy your
stay here.'

After Monsieur Masson left, Serena and Lucy
explored the house. It was delightful.

'How can Lord Ambourne bear to let it out? Does he
not use it himself?' Serena asked.

'The Dowager Countess occasionally stays here when
she is on her own. But when the Family are in London,'
said Mrs Starkey, and Serena could hear the capital in
her voice, 'they stay in Arlington Street — at Rotherfield
House. They are all in Normandy at the moment, but I
believe they will be here later in the season.'

'I hope so,' said Serena, 'for I should like to thank
Lord Ambourne in person for his kindness.'

Mrs Starkey smiled. 'It's probably her ladyship you
ought to thank, Miss Calvert. Very particular, Miss
Perdita is, about her house. Lady Ambourne, I should
say. She lived in it before she was married, you see, and
his lordship kept the lease on because she likes it so

much. But I'm forgetting my duties. Would Miss Lucy or yourself like a refreshment?'

Serena had wondered somewhat apprehensively about the domestics in Lord Ambourne's establishment. The servants at Anse Chatelet had all known her since she was a child. Betsy, the housekeeper there, had been Serena's nurse, and Sheba had been Lucy's. For many years Serena had relied on all of them to help her in keeping Anse Chatelet viable, so the relationship between household staff and mistress had been more informal than was usual. She had heard dreadful stories from Mrs Galveston and her friends of maids who were more conscious of position than their mistresses, of footmen who despised anyone who did not know his place. It had been impressed on her that she must always keep her distance with London domestics, otherwise they would 'take advantage'. Another source of worry had been Sheba's position in the household. Would London domestics accept Sheba? But the stories were all proved false as far as the servants in Dover Street were concerned, and Sheba, with her tales of magic and her warm grin, quickly made herself as popular in the servants' quarters here as she had been in Surrey. Mrs Starkey had known Lady Ambourne before her marriage and admired her enormously. Indeed, she was devoted to the whole Ambourne family, and was prepared to extend her good will to any of their friends who happened to be staying in Dover Street. It was impossible not to like her, for she was a sensible, kindly woman, who soon took the interests of both her young ladies to heart. 'But Mrs Starkey,' cried Serena when she heard herself thus described, 'You mustn't call me a young lady! I am supposed to be Miss Lucy's chaperon!'

'If you'll forgive my saying so, Miss Calvert, it's hard to believe that, when you're looking so handsome.' She regarded Serena admiringly. They were standing in front of the cheval mirror in Serena's bedchamber, where Mrs Starkey had been helping Sheba with the final touches for her two ladies' first appearance in society. Whether it was Mrs Galveston's lotion, or the new wardrobe, or something quite different from all of those, Serena was blooming. Her dark hair was now fashionably cut and arranged, her dark-fringed, amber-gold eyes glowed with well-being, and her skin was pearl-like. A conventional beauty she would never be, but she was striking. Too striking. With determination Serena took off her topaz-yellow silk dress, undid her hair and, while the bewildered housekeeper looked on, ordered Sheba to plait it into a tight chignon on the back of her head. Mrs Starkey might have disapproved of the freedom with which Sheba voiced her objections, but she heartily agreed with her sentiments.

'Sheba, that is enough! You have had your say, now do as I tell you!' said Serena. 'And fetch the green dress, the one with the high neck, if you please.'

Still grumbling under her breath, Sheba brought out a dress in a dull, greyish-green, and helped her mistress put it on.

'Sasha! What are you doing?' cried Lucy when she saw her.

'Looking like a chaperon,' said Serena grimly. 'We came to England to give you a London Season, Lucy, not to make a spectacle of me. It's you who must shine.'

'But I do!' said Lucy, twirling gaily round. 'Apart from you in your yellow dress, I'm the most beautiful thing I've ever seen! I'll swear this creation by Maria is

more exquisite than any to be found in London! Lady
Pendomer is a trump!'

'Lucy! Wherever did you pick that up?'

'Oh. . .' Lucy blushed. 'I beg pardon, Sasha. It's
something Isabella's brother says.'

'Good God! About you?' asked Serena, looking at
her niece in amusement. Growing even redder, Lucy
nodded. 'Well, I'm sure the sentiment is admirable. But
the word itself should not be any part of a young lady's
vocabulary!'

'I'm sorry, Aunt Serena. I should have said that Lady
Pendomer possesses the attributes of a very good
friend!' She laughed and danced away, then came back
to ask mischievously, 'Is it all right to say "Good God"?'

Lucy and Serena joined Lady Warnham at Mrs
Galveston's mansion in Portman Square, prepared for
the culmination of all Serena's plans — Lucy's introduction to London society. Lucy was nervous, but this
merely gave a sparkle to her eyes and a becoming colour
to her cheeks. At the rout party which followed Serena
sat firmly with the chaperons, and only with difficulty
did she disguise her pride. The daughters of most of the
best families in London were there but, in Serena's eyes
at least, not one of them could hold a candle to her
niece. She noticed with some amusement that there was
at the party a sort of magic circle of Lucy's Surrey
friends, who tended to regard intruders with uneasy
suspicion and were ready to see them off. But Lucy
handled them all as if born to it. The girl was a credit to
her training. When the two Misses Calvert returned to
Dover Street that night they were both extremely
satisfied with the evening.

Serena had not looked to see Lord Wintersett at Mrs
Galveston's. The party had been specifically for the
younger section of society, with the purpose of giving
Isabella and Lucy some experience before they were
launched into the deeper waters of a full-scale ball. It
was hardly an occasion which would be graced with his
lordship's presence! But he was never far from her
mind. However busy she was, matching silks, trying on
shawls, walking in the parks, occupied in the hundreds
of activities which made up the London Season, she was
always aware that he might suddenly appear round the
next corner. She grew increasingly nervous of seeing
him again. What would he think of her? Each time they
went to a ball or some other grand affair she took out
the topaz silk dress, wondering whether Lord
Wintersett would be there. But each time she put it
away again and put on something more modest. She
was Lucy's chaperon.

   It was Lucy herself who was instrumental in persuad-
ing Serena to change her mind. Lucy's nature was
sunny, and here in London she was having the time of
her young life. But one day she came in from a walk in
the park with a face like a thundercloud. Serena was
unable to find out what was wrong, but was even more
concerned when Lucy refused an invitation to spend the
next afternoon with Isabella. When she finally extracted
the cause of Lucy's displeasure she didn't know whether
to be relieved or annoyed.

   'I've quarrelled with them,' said Lucy.

   'Why?' asked Serena in astonishment. 'You've
always been such friends with Isabella. Whatever was
it about?'

'It wasn't Isabella. It was the other girls. They were being unfair.'

'To you.'

'No, about someone else.'

It was clear to Serena who this was. There was only one other person who could rouse Lucy to this passionate defence. 'About me?'

'They called you a dowd, Sasha! They said you had spent all your money on me, and had none left for yourself. They started to make fun of you. It's not true, is it?' Lucy was worried.

'Of course it isn't! I have lots of dresses, you know I have.'

'Well, why don't you wear them?'

Lucy was seriously upset. Serena remembered that Great-aunt Spurston had told her that Lucy would be judged by Serena's appearance as well as her own, had even given Serena money and jewels for this purpose. Had she been selfish to ignore her great-aunt's advice? Was it protection that she had sought among the quietly dressed chaperons? Serena started to get angry not only with herself, but with those who had made her darling niece unhappy.

'Spend the afternoon with your friends, Lucy. Try not to let what they say about me make any difference. They don't understand. But just between ourselves — just between ourselves, Lucy, my love — I think they might be in for a surprise. . .'

So that night Serena put on her topaz silk dress, together with the diamond drop earrings and bracelet which her great-aunt had given her. Her black hair was swept into a knot on top of her head and secured with a diamond pin, and loose waves and curls framed her face. Her slender throat rose proudly from the low-cut neckline of her dress. Sheba's face was one big grin, and Mrs Starkey was very impressed. Lucy was ecstatic. 'You'll eclipse everyone there, Sasha! Oh, indeed they will be surprised!'

'Tonight, Lucy, I want you to exert yourself — as I shall. You will call me Aunt Serena, and we shall both remember all our lessons in the manners of the ton. We shall be very grand — true Calverts of Anse Chatelet. Do you agree?'

'Oh, yes,' breathed Lucy, her eyes shining.

The occasion itself was also grand — a ball at the Duchess of Stockhampton's, no less. Serena was aware of curious eyes on her as they mounted the huge, curving staircase, but she put her chin up a touch higher and ignored them. Her blood was up, and generations of Calverts marched with her. A chaperon she might be, but Lucy's aunt was no dowd!

Mrs Galveston greeted her in typical manner. 'Good evening, Miss Calvert! How well you look! I was beginning to wonder whether you would have been happier left in Surrey, but now I see I was mistaken. We may well find you a match, after all. Indeed, I doubt a respectable widower would have a chance with you tonight! Perhaps we should look higher?'

'I am not,' said Serena coolly, 'in search of a husband, Mrs Galveston. But I am touched by your compliments. May I return them? Town life obviously suits you.'

Mrs Galvston almost smiled. 'Your great-aunt would be proud of you. She always said you'd repay dressing, and there's no doubt you have an air about you tonight.'

Serena smiled and moved on. One of Lucy's beaux, a

handsome, well set-up young man who was looking rather nervous, came up to ask if Lucy would stand up with him for the country dances.

'Thank you. May I first introduce you to my aunt? This is Michael Warnham, Aunt Serena. I believe you are acquainted with his mother?'

Serena hastily disguised her involuntary laugh with a cough and inclined her head slightly. As the young man took Lucy off with a sigh of relief, that maiden gave her aunt a very arch look.

Serena was soon besieged by various ladies with requests to be allowed to introduce Lord This and Sir That. She smiled charmingly at her admirers, and answered their eager questions willingly enough, but refused all requests to dance.

About halfway through the evening Lord Wintersett came into the room and gazed casually round. His eye lighted as if by accident on the chaperons' corner, and then moved on. Serena was not there. He surveyed the scene before him. She was not dancing, either. He had hardly expected it. Perhaps she had gone with her charge to the supper-room. He was about to leave the ballroom when an animated group on the other side of the room caught his attention, and he glanced at the central figure. She was surrounded and her head was bent. But he knew instantly who it was, and at that very moment Serena looked up and their eyes met. His widened as he saw the proud lift of the head and recognised the sparkle of diamonds in her ears. He looked briefly in the direction of the winter garden, and she closed her eyes once. No more was needed. A few minutes later he was standing at the end of the path, half hidden by the lavish arrangement of plants, when he saw Serena coming towards him.

James had not known what to expect — he had imagined everything from a sedate, quietly dressed ladies' companion, to a girl/woman uncomfortable in society and ungraceful in skirts. But he had never imagined anything like this cool, poised beauty. The diamonds in her ears and at her wrist, the pin in her hair, the exquisite dress — these were merely the trappings of a most unusually lovely lady. He was almost afraid to speak to her, almost afraid that he would find that his Serena had gone forever. Then she smiled, her eyes glowing with happiness, and he knew he had not lost anything. Nothing at all. He had gained more than he could ever have imagined.

'Lord Wintersett? You are shameful, sir! We have not been introduced, and yet you invite me to an assignation in the Duchess's winter garden!' Her amber-golden eyes were brimming with laughter. 'I dare swear you will even say I took it upon myself to follow you!'

'Serena! I am overwhelmed!' He took her hands in his. 'William was never as lovely as this!'

'Alas, poor William in his hand-me-downs! No! I am wrong. Fortunate William!' She gently released herself. 'At least in the short time allowed him he was free from observation and criticism — except by you, of course. Here in London it is very difficult to escape at all.'

'From your admirers, no doubt.'

'From my critics, rather! I must not stay long. The chief function of a chaperon is to prevent her charge from behaving as I am doing at this very moment! I must not be found out!'

'You! A chaperon? I know you said you were, but I

find that impossible to believe. How can you possibly look after someone else when you so obviously need protection yourself?'

Serena looked at him mockingly. 'What, Lord Wintersett? "Taffeta phrases, silken terms" from you, of all people? You have no need to pay me pretty compliments, sir. I know you for what you are.'

'Do you, Serena? Do you? Then I must congratulate you, for I no longer know what that is myself. I know what I was in the past.'

A faint rose appeared in her cheeks. 'I must go,' she said. 'I have already been out here too long.'

'William was not so cowardly.'

'William was an invention, a dream. The reality is Serena, and Serena is bound by the conventions of society. I hear you have always avoided situations like this in the past, Lord Wintersett—indeed, that you have severely punished the poor ladies who have enticed you into them. Why do you wish to prolong this one?'

'You ask that? After our. . .tacit vow?'

The colour rose in Serena's cheeks, and she said hurriedly, 'I must return to the ballroom.'

'What if I refuse to let you go?' He took hold of her hand again.

She shook her head. 'Oh, no! Here in London you cannot blackmail me or force me to do your bidding—I have too much to lose.'

He tightened his grip and said softly, 'I think I could persuade you.'

'But you will not attempt to do so. It would not be kind. And who knows? The great Lord Wintersett might suffer a reverse. I might prove adamant!' She took her hand away and moved towards the door. The orchestra was striking up a waltz.

'Dance with me, then!' When she hesitated he swept her into the ballroom and on to the floor. He put his arm at her waist, and at her warning look he laughed and said, 'Strict propriety, I swear, Serena!' Decorously they circled the room, but there was that about them which drew all eyes. The young bloods admired Lord Wintersett's conquest, the young ladies envied Serena for her daring capture, for the duration of the evening anyway, of society's most eligible and most dangerous bachelor. The matrons and chaperons whispered behind their fans and shook their heads. Wintersett was beginning another of his flirts! It was a pity that it should be quiet Miss Calvert. Perhaps her success tonight had gone to her head.

But the two who were dancing were oblivious to all this. They were lost in each other. James held Serena with the lightest of touches, but they could not have felt closer if he had embraced her. A curious feeling of certainty mixed with a dangerous excitement ran between them, surrounded them, isolated them from the rest of the room. Watching their mutual absorption, society wondered and gossiped.

At the end of the dance Serena made to return to her seat, but her partner refused to let her go. 'No! Come to the supper-room—I want to give you champagne, Serena. I wish to discuss a promise.'

'A promise?' she echoed, flushing again.

'You would not listen to it in Surrey. You told me to wait until we met in London. Now we have met, and I will not wait any longer to claim what you must know is mine.'

'Aunt Serena!' Lucy's voice broke the spell. 'So this is where you are! You decided to dance after all?' Lucy looked curiously at Lord Wintersett.

'Lucy!' Serena was blushing in real earnest now. 'I. . .I. . .' She glanced at Lord Wintersett and took hold of herself. 'Lucy, I wish you to meet an. . .an acquaintance of mine, Lord Wintersett. Lucy is my niece, Lord Wintersett. And my charge,' she added with a warning in her voice.

Lucy's eyes were huge. 'Wintersett?' she asked. 'Lord Wintersett? But Aunt Serena ——'

'Lucy ——'

'What your aunt means to say, Miss Lucy, is that it does not do to believe all the stories you hear. Am I right?' James was enjoying himself. He had little doubt that this charming girl would discover in a very short time what sort of acquaintance he intended to have with her aunt, but was content to leave it for the moment. 'May I escort you both to the supper-room? We might discuss these stories over supper.'

Still looking slightly puzzled, Lucy allowed herself to be ushered to the other side of the ballroom. Here they were met by Michael Warnham.

'Lucy! Oh, good! You've found your aunt.' He looked curiously at Serena and Lord Wintersett, but decided to continue. 'Have you asked her yet? No?' He turned to Serena, with a charming smile. 'Isabella and some of the others are making up a party to go to Hampton Court tomorrow. We should like Lucy to come.' Lucy's expression made it clear how much she would like to go. 'Do say she may, Miss Calvert! My mother has agreed to act as chaperon.'

Serena was distracted as Lord Wintersett narrowed

his eyes and turned his head swiftly towards the young man. She hesitated.

'Oh, Sasha, do say yes!' pleaded Lucy.

'*Sasha*!'

Serena smiled at Lord Wintersett's interruption. 'It's what Lucy calls me when we're alone,' she explained. 'A pet name from my own childhood. Very well, Lucy, my love. I'll see Lady Warnham later and arrange things with her. It's very kind of her.' She glanced at Mr Warnham and added, 'I suppose you wish to join Isabella now, Lucy? Perhaps Mr Warnham would escort you to her?' Lucy nodded, and Mr Warnham bowed and took her off.

'*Sasha*! That cannot be your name! But she called you Sasha. And he. . .the boy — he called you *Miss Calvert*! *Sasha Calvert*?'

Serena looked at Lord Wintersett in some concern. He was very pale, and he spoke jerkily.

'I had forgotten that we had not been formally introduced! How shocking!' smiled Serena. 'But if you don't like "Sasha", I am happy to answer to Serena. In fact, I prefer——'

'Why did you tell me your name was Serena?' he rapped out.

'Because that's what it is! Serena. But Lucy has called me Sasha since she was a baby.'

'Why did you not tell me this before?'

Serena looked at him as if he had suddenly become deranged. 'Why should I? My proper name is Serena. And you forget that until recently I was always "William" in Surrey.' She put a tentative hand on his arm. 'Are you not well, Lord Wintersett.'

'I am perfectly well, thank you,' he replied. As if to

bely this he put his hand to his head and ran it through his hair. 'Sasha Calvert,' he murmured. 'You're Sasha Calvert!' He looked down with distaste at her hand, resting on his arm. 'Your solicitude is excessive, I assure you,' he said coldly.

Serena flushed, then grew pale. 'Forgive me,' she said withdrawing the offending hand. A thought seemed to strike him.

'Where do you live, Sasha Calvert?'

Serena looked at him in amazement. He seemed to be speaking against his will, and his tone of voice was peremptory, even angry. He might have been able to speak to William like this, but not to Miss Calvert of Anse Chatelet! She replied stiffly, 'I fail to see why that should concern you, sir, but while in London I live in Dover Street. My home is in the West Indies.'

He turned away from her, and she thought she heard him say 'Oh, God!' but could not be sure.

Serena began to feel she was in some kind of nightmare. Though no one else was near enough to overhear their conversation, she could see that they were arousing a great deal of speculation. She said quietly, 'We are being observed, so it is difficult for me to speak. I am not sure what I have said or done to offend you, Lord Wintersett?' She paused a moment, looking up at his averted face with a plea in her eyes. When he remained silent she took a step back and said, 'Forgive me. I must have misunderstood your feelings. Or perhaps you are as capricious as your reputation would suggest. I will bother you no longer.'

He seemed to pull himself together at this, and turned again to face her. She was astonished at the change in him. His eyes were empty of feeling and his face was

like stone. He eyed her up and down with a curl to his
lips, then cast a glance round the room, 'You are right,
Miss Calvert. We are being observed.' He smiled and
raised his voice as he drawled, 'No, it is you must excuse
me. I must admit I can hardly tear myself away—
especially after the idyll in the winter garden, which you
so. . .hopefully arranged. But, alas! I must. However,
you look so delightful that I am sure there are many
others here who would be only too glad to take my
place. Your servant, ma'am.' He bowed and strode out
of the room.

By exercising every ounce of self-control Serena
pulled herself together and kept her head high as she
walked back to the bench where Mrs Galveston and
Lady Warnham were sitting. She would not give the
assembled company the satisfaction of seeing the extent
of her shock or of watching her scuttle to some convenient alcove or cloakroom to hide herself like a hurt
animal. When one of the Warnham sons offered to
fetch her some refreshment she accepted gratefully, and
took care to drink the champagne he brought slowly
and with appreciation. After a short while the trembling
in her limbs stopped, and she began to grow very angry.
Her pride would not have allowed her to cut the evening
short, but it was this anger which helped her to endure
it.

It was obvious that the massive snub Lord Wintersett
had delivered her so publicly was the chief topic of
conversation among the mothers and chaperons present, and though some of them regarded her with
sympathy there was a certain amount of head-shaking
and shrugging of shoulders. They all knew that Lord
Wintersett was a dangerous man to tangle with, and, in

the opinion of some, Miss Calvert had been foolhardy
in showing her feelings so openly. They had all watched
that waltz.

Criticism and sympathy were equally intolerable to
Serena, and, since she did not lack partners, she
escaped both by accepting every invitation to dance.
She dazzled them all. The diamonds in her ears glittered
with no greater intensity than Serena herself, but she
could not have said afterwards who had danced with
her, or how long they had danced with her, or what they
talked about while they were dancing. At some time in
the evening Lucy joined her, obviously having heard
some of the gossip, but Serena said softly but fiercely,
'No, Lucy, not now. Tell me of your outing tomorrow,
tell me what you had for supper, or what Mr Warnham
was saying, or anything you like, but do not, I pray you,
mention. . .' She stopped. She found it impossible to
say Wintersett's name.

The evening eventually came to an end and Serena
was at last able to escape to the haven of Dover Street.
She could not avoid Lucy's anxious questions, but told
her very little. She did not know herself what had
happened to cause Lord Wintersett to change so rapidly, so how could she explain it to Lucy? After a short
while Lucy gave up asking questions and set herself to
restoring her aunt's spirits. For perhaps the first time in
their lives Lucy was the one who gave comfort that
night, and Serena was the one who needed it.

Serena's behaviour in the next week did much to re-
establish her in the eyes of society. Mrs Galveston had
arrived in Dover Street the day after the ball and,
though she gave Serena a hard time herself — harder
than she realised — she also gave her some excellent

advice. After this Serena went about her usual visits and outings with composure, warding off all impertinent questions and comments by admitting, apparently frankly, that she had roused Lord Wintersett's anger and had had to pay for it. 'As a colonial,' she would say with a disarmingly rueful smile, 'I'm afraid I still have to learn what is done and what is not done. I think the gentleman in question——' she still could not say his name — 'took my lack of formality for something more than I intended. Tell me, is he always so concei. . . er. . .so quick to assume that the ladies are in love with him?'

While there were still some who looked knowing when they heard this, most people were so impressed by Serena's quietly confident manner that they began to think that Lord Wintersett had indeed been too hard on a newcomer from abroad, that his well-known aversion to being pursued had in this instance misled him, and soon Serena was generally held to have been treated ungallantly. All the same, society looked forward with interest to see if there was to be another encounter between Lord Wintersett and Miss Calvert.

It was a week before this happened, and in the meantime Serena made a new acquaintance. Lord Ambourne's mother had returned earlier than expected from France, and had arrived in Rotherfield House the day after the Duchess of Stockhampton's ball. She called on Serena soon after that. When she was told that the Dowager Countess of Ambourne was in the carriage outside and wished to know if she were at home, Serena's heart sank. Of course she must receive her — it was very gratifying that the Countess should take the trouble to call. But another Mrs Galveston was not a pleasing prospect, and this high-born lady would be even worse, she was sure. Serena was due for a surprise! John ushered in a tiny figure in a pelisse and bonnet in the very latest mode, who came forward saying in a charming French accent, 'My dear Miss Calvert! How agreeable to meet you! Forgive me for calling on you so early, but Lady Pendomer's letter was written in such terms that I felt I had to see the paragon she described as soon as possible! And my son asked me to visit you, also.' She surveyed Serena. 'But *alors*, you are much better than I expected!'

Serena smiled her first genuine smile since the ball as she indicated a chair and they sat down. 'It's very kind of you to call, Lady Ambourne, but I'm afraid Lady Pendomer is over-partial. I am no paragon. Paragons are perfect, and I am far from that!'

'That is just what I meant! Perfection is very boring, don't you agree? Now you must give me news of Lady Pendomer, and then tell me about yourself. I wish to know everything!' The Countess settled comfortably in her chair, accepted some refreshment from a beaming Mrs Starkey, and proceeded to delight Serena for the next half-hour. Though Lady Ambourne had the indefinable air of a great lady, she was not at all haughty or reserved. She talked freely of her son and daughter-in-law, of whom she was clearly very fond, and had Serena laughing at her descriptions of her grandsons' antics. 'You will think me a doting grandmother, Miss Calvert—but how can I help it when the children are so clever and so good? Well, perhaps not "good" exactly— but so charmingly naughty!'

At the end of the visit the Countess asked Serena to

call on her soon in Rotherfield House. 'Bring Miss Lucy Calvert with you — I am sorry not to have met her. Perdita and Edward will not be back from Normandy for a few weeks yet and I miss them very much, so you will be doing me a kindness. In fact, I should like to arrange some kind of evening party for you both, for it's time we had something to brighten up the family mansion — a barn of a place, Miss Calvert, but it does very well for balls and the like. Living in it is less agreeable.' She departed, leaving behind a faint breath of a perfume and a strange feeling of comfort. Though Serena had said nothing, of course, about Lord Wintersett, she had found the Countess warm and sympathetic. She would be a good listener if Serena ever needed one.

CHAPTER SEVEN

FOR a week after the Duchess's ball Lord Wintersett was not seen at any of the drums and assemblies held in the evenings, nor was he observed riding in the parks or walking in the gardens of London during the day. This surprised no one. It was said that he had recently been in the habit of disappearing to his estate in Surrey for days at a time. Though Serena secretly gave a wry smile at this, she was grateful for the respite. When she and Lord Wintersett next met she wanted to be in command of herself. Keeping composed in company in general was one thing. Coming face to face with a man she could have loved — for, lying awake in the hours of darkness, she had faced that fact — and a man who had treated her so inexplicably was quite another. However, they were both present in the Assembly Rooms exactly one week after the ball. Though Lucy was not there, having gone with Lady Warnham to another gathering, Serena stayed by Mrs Galveston, for she took care nowadays to behave with utmost circumspection.

He came in late with a lady on his arm, a ravishing blonde with a startlingly good figure. It was a pity, perhaps, that the lady was wearing pink, thought Serena critically; blondes should not wear pink. Nor was it perhaps in the best of taste to choose a dress which, in spite of its elaborate trimmings, so clearly revealed the lady's ample charms. Serena's own dress of pale blue zephyrine caught up over a slip of white sarsnet silk, which she had thought so pretty, suddenly seemed very tame.

'The devil!' exclaimed Mrs Galveston, startling Serena into turning round to her. 'Look at them! His lordship, looking as cool as you please, and Amelia Banagher. I thought that connection was finished some time ago, I must say.'

'Who is the lady, ma'am?'

'It is better for you not to know, Serena.' This was said with pursed lips. 'Indeed, if Miss Lucy were with us I should most certainly take you both home immediately.' Then, as her love of gossip got the better of her, she leant forward and said confidentially, 'Amelia Banagher comes of a highly respected Irish family. She married Lord Banagher when she was seventeen, but they haven't lived together for years, and her mode of life since has shocked everyone — though not quite enough to have her totally ostracised. Everyone knows that she was Wintersett's mistress last year, though they were discreet enough about it. They say she took it very hard when he discarded her. I wonder how she persuaded his lordship to bring her tonight? And how did she wheedle that magnificent necklace out of him?' The couple had been advancing up the room and both Serena and Mrs Galveston could now see them more clearly. 'He paid a fair penny for that, I dare say, if those rubies are real.'

The sight of Lord Wintersett had given Serena an unhappy pang, but now the anger which had never been far below the surface since the night of the ball began to burn again. 'They are real, and he did indeed pay a pretty penny, ma'am. I fancy you will recognise it when — if — they come any closer. The lady is wearing the Cardoman necklace.'

Mrs Galveston looked suitably shocked, and turned to Serena with an expression of sympathy. When she saw Serena's face her look changed to one of apprehension. Her young friend was flying flags of anger in her cheeks, and her eyes were glowing like those of a cat. 'I think we should leave now, Serena,' said Mrs Galveston, sounding nervous for the first time in years.

'I would not think of it, ma'am,' said Serena between her teeth. 'That would carry the flavour of retreat. And I am in no such frame of mind.'

It was too late in any case. Lord Wintersett was upon them and at his most urbane.

'Mrs Galveston, your servant, ma'am. I believe you know Lady Banagher?' Unsmiling, Mrs Galveston inclined her head by no more than a millimetre. Lord Wintersett turned to Serena. 'Amelia,' he said, without taking his eyes, which were glittering with malice, from Serena. 'May I present Miss Calvert of Anse Chatelet? Miss Cardoman Calvert.'

The two ladies exchanged what hardly passed for a curtsy. Lady Banagher raised an eyebrow. 'Cardoman? Isn't that the name —— ' She fingered the ruby hanging in the cleft of her breasts and gave Lord Wintersett a slow smile.

He took her fingers and kissed them lingeringly, then with a sideways look at Serena said, 'I believe it is called the Cardoman necklace, my dear. Miss Calvert, was it not at one time a valued possession of the Calvert family?'

'Hardly,' drawled Serena. 'It belonged to us, certainly, but the family has wanted to sell it for years.

Like so many other things, Lord Wintersett, its history is somewhat. . .tarnished.' With totally spurious concern she asked, 'Oh, dear, am I to understand you were the mysterious purchaser?'

Lady Banagher looked startled. 'But I thought it was a gift from a king? From King Charles?' She turned to her companion. 'You said——'

Serena swept on. 'King Charles had it made for his mistress, Lady Banagher. But there have always been so many of those, have there not? However, I think the necklace looks charming on you. Just right.' Mrs Galveston made a strangled sound and Lady Banagher at first looked uncertain, and then her brow clouded as she began to wonder whether Serena's compliment might not be all it seemed. It was clear that Lord Wintersett was in no doubt. His face, which had been somewhat pale, darkened, and he said curtly, 'Come, Amelia. It's time we danced. Mrs Galveston will forgive us. Miss Calvert.' He bowed and removed Amelia, who was still looking puzzled.

Mrs Galveston regarded Serena with admiration. 'Your great-aunt was always telling me what a spirited girl you were, Serena—I hope you will allow me to call you Serena?—but I must confess that when I first met you I was disappointed. But no more. I have never seen Lord Wintersett at such a loss. My felicitations. I think you may consider his unkind behaviour at the Duchess's ball well returned.'

Serena, still angry, said, 'I'm afraid it was ill done to involve Lady Banagher, however.' Mrs Galveston said something regrettable, which Serena ignored. Instead she continued, 'But you are wrong to think I was taking revenge for Lord Wintersett's behaviour at the ball,

Mrs Galveston. That would have been better forgotten.
I am convinced that for some reason which I cannot
fathom Lord Wintersett means to injure me in any way
he can. I believe he bought that necklace and put it on
his mistress in order to bring the Calvert name into
disrepute.'

'Oh, come, Serena. The necklace is too expensive a
bauble to play with like that! It must be worth five
thousand pounds at least! You must not let your
imagination run away with you!'

But Serena remained unconvinced, and her suspicions were confirmed later in the evening. During one
of the country dances she found herself partnered with
her adversary — for that was how she now regarded him.
She faced him across the set. He was pale again, and she
saw now that he was thinner than he had been in Surrey.
But his eyes were diamond-hard and his mouth set in
ruthless lines. She remembered that she had once
accused him of a lack of kindness. Now he looked. . .
pitiless. They joined together to move up the room.

'I congratulate you on your rapier wit, Miss Calvert.
But, for all your brave words, I think you did not enjoy
seeing a necklace worn by your mother and grandmother round the neck of a harlot for all London to
see,' he said.

'Conceited, mad, and no gentleman, either! Fie, fie,
Lord Wintersett!' she replied mockingly. 'Have you
forgotten that the lady is your partner for the evening,
sir, when you call her such a name?' They swung away
from each other, then as they returned she added, 'But
you may hang the necklace round all such ladies in
London for all I care; it makes little difference to me.
My mother died when she was not much more than

twenty, so I never knew her. As far as I am aware she
never wore the necklace.' She smiled sweetly as they
parted again, then said, as they came back together to
move up the set, 'So if your ambition was to cause me
chagrin, your ruse has failed. An expensive mistake.
Oh, but I was forgetting — the *rich* Lord Wintersett does
not consider such things.'

'By God, ma'am,' he said in a voice of suppressed
fury, 'if the necklace is to be worn by a harlot, then it
should be round your own neck!'

Serena was so shocked by the term he had used and
the very real animosity in his voice that she stumbled
and nearly fell. With relief she realised that they had
come to the end of the set and she could escape.

In bed that night she lay awake asking herself over
and over what had provoked that last remark. It had not
been idle abuse, she was sure. For some reason Lord
Wintersett regarded her as a Jezebel. But *why*?

James returned from the Assembly Rooms to Upper
Brook Street with his mind in a most unaccustomed
state of turmoil. He had planned the evening knowing
that Sasha Calvert would be at the Assembly Rooms
that night. He had relished the thought of Sasha's
humiliation when the world realised that the Calverts
were being forced to sell their most prized possessions.
How her Calvert family pride would resent seeing the
precious Cardoman necklace paraded before the world
on such an unworthy neck! For this he had engaged the
help of his former mistress, Amelia Banagher, who had
now become notorious for her numerous affairs. She
was always hopelessly in debt, and a suggestion that her
ex-lover might settle some of her more pressing bills

had been enough to persuade her to accompany him, and to wear the necklace. Indeed, after the evening was over and James had escorted her back to her rooms, there had been an awkward moment when she had made it clear that she was ready to do more — for love. James was relieved that he had managed to extricate himself without offending her, for he had found the idea surprisingly repugnant. And, for all his planning, the evening had been a failure. He had no sense of triumph, felt no satisfaction.

He knew why. In spite of the discovery that Sasha and Serena were one and the same, he still felt a strange kinship with Serena. He had such a strong sixth sense about her that he was sure that his insults tonight and on other occasions had struck home. But only once had she lost her self-possession and revealed her distress — when she had stumbled in the country dance. And instead of being triumphant he was ashamed. His savage outburst to Serena during that dance had not been planned. It was the result of an unexpected surge of anger at her steady refusal to be daunted. Since his was a nature which needed to remain in command of himself as well as others, he was furious at this loss of control. And then, worse still, when she had nearly fallen he had experienced an overwhelming desire to catch her, to protect her. It was enough to drive a man mad!

He sat now in his library, looking at the necklace. Its huge cabochon rubies gleamed dully in the firelight — a pool of blood in his hands. He smiled reminiscently as he thought of Serena's reaction to the sight of the necklace. It was impossible not to admire her. Few women would have responded with such spirit and wit

to his insults, his attempt to diminish her in the eyes of
society. She had never allowed herself to be diminished.
Far from becoming discredited, she had gained society's
sympathy and admiration, including his own. But what
was he thinking of? How the devil could he possibly
admire Sasha Calvert?

In the days that followed James was no nearer to
finding peace. The thought of Serena/Sasha was like a
canker, a goad, which kept him awake at night, and
unable to rest during the day. He hated Sasha for her
treatment of Tony, and he hated Serena for being
Sasha. He despised himself for being so confused, for
wishing to punish Sasha, while taking pride in Serena
when she frustrated his efforts.

He went back to Surrey, thinking that his determination to discredit Sasha Calvert would be strengthened
if he had another talk with Alanna, if he reminded
himself of the unhappiness the Calvert woman had
caused his family. But in Surrey he found himself going
for long rides on the Downs, taking Douce on to the
ridge, where he was haunted by the memory of
'William', of their talks, their arguments, their shared
laughter. He remembered with bitterness his fears that
he would lose Serena in London. As he had. He was
tormented by the two contrasting pictures — on the one
hand Serena, a woman of intelligence and compassion
with an integrity he had never questioned, and on the
other Sasha, the destroyer, the wanton. And this visit to
Surrey, far from strengthening his determination,
seemed to be undermining it, for doubts began to creep
into his mind. In his initial shock and blind anger at
discovering that Serena and Sasha were one and the
same he had not attempted to set one against the

other—Serena's good against Sasha's evil. But was it *possible* for the Serena he had known to have done the things Sasha was said to have done on the island? Perhaps she had changed? Perhaps Tony's death had caused her to reform? She must have been very young . . .in fact, *very* young! He must talk to Alanna again. But he could not bring himself to mention Serena to Alanna—only Sasha.

'Sasha Calvert told me recently that her mother was only twenty when she died, Alanna. However I try, I cannot reconcile this with the age of her brothers. Surely Richard Calvert was older than Tony?'

'Yes. Yes, he was.' Alanna's voice was nervous. 'Did I not tell you? I thought I had. Lord Calvert was married twice. The Sasha woman was the daughter of the second marriage.'

'So how old was she when you were on the island?'

'Why are you asking me? What are you trying to do, James?'

'Merely to establish some facts. How old was she?'

'I don't know! What does it matter?' said Alanna petulantly. 'Old enough! Sixteen or seventeen, I think.'

'She once said she was now twenty-seven. That would make her fourteen.'

'Fourteen, fifteen, seventeen! Am I a mathematician? You've been spending too much time with Miss Calvert! I told you what would happen. She's such a liar, she will bewitch you as she bewitched Tony. . . Oh, Tony, Tony!' Alanna burst into loud sobs.

James waited until she was quieter, then said, 'Fourteen is not much more than a child, Alanna. I find it difficult to imagine Tony deserting you in favour of a child.'

'You don't know what they're like in the tropics, James!' Alanna said between further sobs. 'The women mature at a ridiculously early age. Many of the natives have children at thirteen or even less! And she — Sasha — ran practically wild all over the island — she must have had her morals from them.' She burst out, 'Why are you asking these questions? I tell you she never left him alone! Poor Tony had no chance. Dear God, why do you remind me?'

Alanna was now very distressed. She clutched at James, pleading, 'Get rid of her for me, James! Have nothing more to do with her, but get her sent back to where she belongs, I beg you!'

Disguising his distaste for her melodrama, James said patiently, 'Be calm, Alanna. It takes time.'

With an exclamation of despair Alanna ran out of the room, leaving James with the feeling that, if she had enacted these tragedies thirteen years before, he for one did not blame his brother for seeking consolation elsewhere. He told himself that women were often temperamental when they were breeding — had Alanna chased Tony into the arms of Sasha Calvert by her own irrational behaviour? With an exclamation of impatience he realised that even now he was seeking excuses for the unhappy business. Alanna was probably right. Sasha Calvert had power to make a man believe anything!

Before the incident in the Assembly Rooms, Serena would have been content to go through the rest of the season accepting that Lord Wintersett no longer wished to continue their friendship, and learning to live without it. She had reluctantly concluded that the fact that she came from the Colonies, and her irregular conduct at the outset of their acquaintance — dressing as a boy and roaming the countryside — had caused him to have second thoughts when they met in more formal circumstances. The explanation was not completely satisfactory. The charm with which he had first greeted her, his compliments in the winter garden — these had seemed real enough. And that dance. . . Her thoughts shied away from the dance. But his behaviour afterwards had been so extraordinarily cruel! Then she heard more stories of Lord Wintersett's summary dismissal of females who pursued him, his heartlessness in other matters, too, and she finally accepted his treatment of her as not untypical. What she found impossible was to reconcile the man in London with the man she had known in Surrey.

But now the situation had changed. That he or anyone else should dare to insult her by calling her a harlot was not to be borne! Not without some action on her part. She had no male protector to call on — the nearest approach to that was Lord Ambourne, and not only was her claim on him too slight, but he was also on the other side of the Channel. Besides, she had no wish to create further scandal by calling on an outsider for protection. However, the thought of Lord Ambourne brought the Dowager Countess to her mind. She would see if she could consult Lady Ambourne.

Accordingly Serena took the Countess at her word and called on her in Arlington Street. As Lady Ambourne had said, Rotherfield House was imposing rather than homelike, but Serena was led through the huge state-rooms to the back of the house, where there was a small garden-room. Here her hostess was sitting on a comfortable sofa and she insisted that Serena should sit by her side. They talked for a while, but finally the Countess sat back and, putting her head on one side, said, 'I have enjoyed our chat, Miss Calvert, but you shall now tell me what is exercising your mind. If I can be of any assistance to you, you have only to ask.' Serena looked amazed and the Countess laughed. 'You look just like my daughter-in-law!' she said. 'Perdita swears I have second sight. But it isn't so. It was obvious to me that you were not entirely happy when we last met. Today you are angry, too. What is it, child? Begin from the beginning.'

Serena found to her astonishment that she was telling Lady Ambourne everything—her restlessness in Surrey after the freedom of her life on St Just, her expeditions to the Downs disguised as a boy, and her meeting with Lord Wintersett. She took care not to mention his name for she had decided that no purpose could be served by revealing it. And she had, besides, this ridiculous inability to say it! Her voice, which had been soft and warm as she had talked of her relationship with the gentleman in Surrey, grew more agitated as she went on to describe the gentleman's behaviour since. She omitted to say anything about the necklace, but told her listener the substance of the insult during the country dance. 'I am at a loss to explain it, Lady Ambourne. The gentleman's animosity is real. But he called me. . . called me. . .'

Lady Ambourne said the word for her. 'A harlot.'

'And he has no reason to suppose that I am anything of the kind!' cried Serena angrily. 'Our relationship on the Downs was totally innocent—more that of a boy and his mentor. I just don't understand! What am I to do?'

Lady Ambourne sat in thought for a moment. Then she said gravely, 'It is obvious to me that there must be more behind Lord Wintersett's behaviour than you have told me.' When Serena gasped she added, 'Please do not misunderstand, Miss Calvert. I do not believe for a moment that you are wilfully hiding anything of substance from me.'

'It's not that,' said Serena faintly. 'How did you know I was talking of. . .' She exclaimed impatiently as she once again found herself unable to say his name.

The Countess smiled. 'My dear child, I have known London society these past thirty years or more.'

'I suppose everyone is talking about us.' Serena's voice was bitter.

'There is naturally some gossip, yes. But I have heard nothing of what you have told me this afternoon—of Surrey and so on. And on the whole, you know, opinion in general is in your favour—if that is any comfort. Lord Wintersett is not universally liked.'

'Do you know him?'

'I'm afraid he is a great friend of my son's. They were at school together.'

In some confusion Serena started to gather herself together. 'In that case, you must forgive me, Lady Ambourne. I am sorry to have caused you embarrassment. I. . .I must go.'

'What are you thinking of, child? Edward's friendship with Lord Wintersett does not mean that I am blind to that gentleman's faults—any more than I am blind to Edward's faults. In some ways they are very similar. Oh, yes. I assure you they are! They can both be completely ruthless when it suits them—and they can be cruel. But Edward has been more fortunate than

James. He was surrounded in his youth by a loving family, and he now enjoys a very happy marriage. James, on the other hand, had a tyrant for a father, and his family circumstances since his father's death have been most unhappy.'

'Is there no one he loves?'

'There are, or were, two. One is his mother, whose devotion was divided between her husband and her younger son. I have always thought that it says much for the basic soundness of James's nature that the other person he loved was this same younger brother. But he is now dead.'

'What happened to him?'

'He died abroad some years ago at about the time James came into the title. His mother has never properly recovered from her double loss.'

'Do you like him, ma'am?'

'I think I do. Edward is a good judge of men, and though James is generally held to be coldhearted I think this is not really so. But it would certainly not be easy to find out. Of one thing I am certain. He is a just man.'

'Then why is he so cruel to me?'

'I do not know, but there must be some reason which he thinks justifies his behaviour. Are you sure, quite sure, you cannot think of anything?' Serena shook her head. 'No. Well, I shall do my best to find out. Will you allow me to make some discreet enquiries?'

Serena took her leave a little later, after arranging to call on the Countess again in three days' time.

When Serena called at Rotherfield House again three days later she found the Countess in an unusually grave mood.

'Miss Calvert, I think I have at least found a previous connection between your family and Lord Wintersett. If you remember, I mentioned a younger brother who died abroad some time ago.' She looked penetratingly at Serena.

'Yes?' Serena was puzzled.

'I am somewhat surprised that you do not seem to know that he died on St Just.'

'Oh, no! Forgive me, Lady Ambourne, but that cannot be so. If it were true I would have known of it. Nothing ever happened on St Just without my knowledge!'

'His name was Tony,' Lady Ambourne continued. 'Tony Stannard.'

In a voice that was almost unrecognisable Serena said, '*Tony Stannard* is — was — Lord Wintersett's brother?' Lady Ambourne nodded. 'Oh, God!' Serena buried her face in her hands.

There was a silence. Finally Serena lifted her head and whispered, 'I had no notion. . .I simply did not connect the two names.'

'That is obvious, my child. However, the link is as yet slight. There is little in the fact that Mr Stannard died on St Just to account for Lord Wintersett's enmity.'

Serena drew a long shuddering sigh and said, 'What have you learned of his death, Lady Ambourne? What does London say?'

Lady Ambourne was still grave. 'It was reported that he fell victim to a tropical disease.'

Serena got up and moved restlessly about the room. 'Tony Stannard! Poor, poor Tony! And a Wintersett! Oh yes! I understand now.' She stopped in front of the Countess, who was looking as if she had more to say.

'What is it, Lady Ambourne? Why do you look like that?'

'There are rumours that the circumstances of Tony Stannard's death were not as reported.' Serena turned away, but the voice with its charming French accent continued relentlessly, 'Rumour says that the young man killed himself. No one seems to know why, however.'

Serena remained silent.

The Countess appeared to be choosing her words carefully as she said, 'You came to me for help and advice, Miss Calvert. I would not normally press you to reveal anything you do not wish, but it seems to me that the cause of Lord Wintersett's enmity must lie in his brother's death. You have already confided a great deal of your story. Do you feel able to tell me anything more? I think I have no need to assure you of my discretion.'

Serena thought for a moment. 'I cannot discuss Tony Stannard's death, Lady Ambourne — not even with you,' she said slowly. 'But if it will not weary you, I will tell you something of the events which led up to it. They might well go towards explaining Lord Wintersett's enmity, for they reflect little credit on the Calverts. Though I should have thought it would be directed rather towards my family than to me. . .'

'My memory is very accommodating. I shall remember only what I need to know in order to help you. I should be extremely surprised if there is anything to your detriment in the story.'

'There is one aspect of which I ashamed. But I will tell you, all the same.'

The Countess sent for some tea and told Purkiss that

she was not to be disturbed for an hour. Serena was soon launched into the unhappy story of the Stannards' visit to St Just.

'My father had heard through a Cambridge friend that Tony Stannard wished to study tropical plants, so he invited the Stannards to St Just, and offered them the hospitality of Anse Chatelet. Tony Stannard was newly married when he came to stay. His wife, Alanna, was quite young and very pretty—I think she was Irish—and at first they seemed to be devoted to each other. But after a while she started to complain—she didn't like the heat, she didn't like the insects, she was afraid of what the sun would do to her complexion. It wasn't what she had been used to, I suppose. Perhaps even more, it wasn't what she had looked for in marrying Tony Stannard. I gathered that the family was quite rich, and she had hoped to play a leading role in society.'

'It was natural, I suppose. A young girl, pretty, married to a rich man. Surely she could reasonably expect a fashionable life?'

Serena shook her head. 'I was still quite young at the time, but even I could see that the study of plants was Tony's life. He was a brilliant botanist, you know. It was obvious that the fashionable world was not for him. But Alanna Stannard was not really at all interested in Tony's work, and she soon gave up accompanying Tony on his expeditions into the rain forest. I must confess I was secretly glad.'

'Why?' asked the Countess, opening her eyes wide. 'What had it to do with you?'

'I used to guide Tony on his expeditions. I knew the island better than anyone. If Mrs Stannard came with us we were constantly having to stop — to rest, to help her across a stream, to clear a wider path. . . . And we had to carry all sorts of extra supplies — creams and lotions, cushions and rugs, water, wine. We were always having to stop for picnics. You can imagine how impatient a child would get with all this.'

'So Alanna stayed at home?'

'Yes. She remained all day on the veranda, feeling, no doubt, that she was being treated very ill. You will observe,' said Serena with an apologetic smile, 'that I was not particularly fond of the lady.'

'I had noticed,' said the Countess with a smile. 'But tell me — now that you are older and have more understanding, do you not feel some sympathy for her?'

Serena thought for a moment, then said, 'I don't know. What happened afterwards makes it impossible to judge.'

'Pray continue.'

'First I need to digress a little, to give you some background. What do you know of the West Indian islands, Lady Ambourne?'

'Not very much. St Just is one of the smaller ones, is that correct? As you know, Henry Pendomer is a second or third cousin of Edward's, so all my knowledge comes from him. He's the Governor of St Just. But doesn't he look after some other islands as well?'

'Yes. Sir Henry governs a number of the smaller islands together. In fact, he only spends about four months a year on St Just.'

'And?'

'Thirteen years ago, when the Stannards came to stay at Anse Chatelet, my father was still strong and active. The Calverts have lived on St Just since the days before

there was a Governor there at all, and until very
recently they have always regarded the island and its
people more or less as their own. The islanders looked
on my father as a sort of uncrowned king, and my. . .
my. . .brother Richard regarded himself as the Crown
Prince.' Serena was finding this more difficult than she
had thought, but the steady, sympathetic gaze of the
Countess encouraged her to carry on. 'We all loved
Richard. We were dazzled by him. I was his shadow, his
slave, always trying to ride as well as Richard, to shoot
as well as Richard. . . I had no other friend, wanted no
other companion.' She sighed. 'He was always causing
trouble, yet he would charm his way out of it all. He had
such an infectious smile — you would find yourself
laughing when a minute before you had sworn you
would never speak to him again. And women. . .they
were fascinated by him. It's difficult to explain. . .'

'You have no need. I have met someone quite like
him, Serena.'

Serena looked doubtful, but carried on. 'It ruined
him. The adulation, the feeling that he could do
anything. . .anything at all, the lack of any restraint. . .
I think that if he had had to struggle for what he had, if
there had been a war he could have fought in, a cause
he believed in, he might have been saved. But there
wasn't. And finally he was overtaken by his demons. . .
Even my father rejected him in the end. . .' Her voice
faded and she paused. Then she squared her shoulders
and said in a clearer voice, 'I was telling you about the
Stannards. About Alanna Stannard. A pretty, new face
on St Just was just the sort of challenge Richard
enjoyed. He was never satisfied until he had conquered,
and Alanna Stannard was instantly an object of desire.'

'And she. . .?'

'I think you must know the answer to that, Lady
Ambourne. Mrs Stannard was lonely, bored, and feeling resentful towards her husband for his neglect of her.
She spent long hours alone. Whenever Richard set out
to charm anyone he was irresistible. In this case the end
was inevitable, I suppose.'

'Was there no one to stop them, to talk to Alanna?'

'No one. The Pendomers had just left St Just for their
tour of the other islands. By the time they returned it
was all over.'

'And no one else? What about your father?'

'Until the final, dreadful end, my father could never
see any wrong in Richard. And I was a child — I didn't
even realise what was going on until father told me
later, when he thought I was old enough. Apart from
that, I was out most of the time with Tony Stannard. I
knew the island and its inhabitants so well, you see. I
knew where the interesting plants were.'

'Poor Alanna!'

'Why do you say that? Alanna at least returned alive
to England. Richard and Tony are both dead.'

'But Alanna's baby was born prematurely, and the
child is still an invalid even now. Alanna never sought
the gaiety of London life, but has lived in retirement in
Surrey, looking after her son, ever since she returned.
But you say your brother Richard died, too?'

'He fell two hundred feet from a cliff path near Anse
Chatelet. We found his body the next day on the rocks
below.' Serena shut her eyes and when she opened
them again they were full of anguish. 'I blame myself
for his death,' she said in a whisper.

The Countess put a sympathetic hand out and would

have spoken, but Serena continued, 'Did you. . .did you say that Alanna had a child, Lady Ambourne? After she came back from the island?'

'Of course. He is Wintersett's heir.'

'But ——' Serena stopped abruptly. 'No. No matter.' She got up again and looked out at the gardens. Then she added bitterly, 'I wish I had never come to England! If it were not for Lucy I would return to the West Indies tomorrow!'

'Come, come, this is no way to talk!' The Countess led her back to the sofa. 'We have now accounted for Lord Wintersett's unfriendliness. It is, I suppose, natural that he should dislike the name of Calvert, but I think I can talk him into a more reasonable frame of mind. He might even call later this afternoon.'

Serena said slowly, 'I am not sure we have quite accounted for it. What he called me was specific, not a slur on my family as a whole.'

'Then he must explain himself,' said the Countess briskly. 'Unless. . . No, he is surely not such a fool! Can he believe perhaps you. . .er. . .consoled Tony for his wife's disloyalty? You were with him a great deal, were you not? No, no! It is too absurd!'

'Indeed it is, I think — even for him! I was fourteen years old — a child! Probably even younger than most girls of that age. I regarded Tony simply as a wonderful source of knowledge — no, of marvels. He was a born teacher, and I was thirsty for anything he could tell me about the plants and trees of my own home.'

'Of course, of course. There must be another explanation.'

CHAPTER EIGHT

WHILE Serena's conversation with Lady Ambourne was taking place Lord Wintersett was making his way to Rotherfield House in response to an invitation from the Countess. He had arrived in London two days before and had found Lady Ambourne's note, together with a letter from Bradpole requesting an interview. The lawyer had arrived the next day with a folder of documents and the news that the substitute manager on Anse Chatelet had indeed defaulted on the payments, and that the agent in Barbados had foreclosed as ordered. 'I have the documents here. They only require your lordship's signature.' He spread some legal papers out on the table. 'Er. . .Norret, the manager, has pleaded that he was unaware how important it was to get the quarterly payment in on the exact day, and further, that unfavourable winds and tropical storms delayed his journey to Barbados. He is supported in his plea by Lord Pendomer, the Governor of St Just. I am aware that I risk your anger in saying this, Lord Wintersett, but I will say it just the same. It can do you no credit to foreclose on what is in effect a technicality. I hope you will consider changing your instructions to the agent, and restoring Anse Chatelet to its former owners.' He waited, but James was deep in thought. The lawyer sighed and continued, 'However, if you remain obdurate, the documents are here.'

James was in a quandary. For years he had sought

possession of Anse Chatelet with the sole aim of evicting the Calverts. The estate was now his, if he insisted — but he could not quite bring himself to let the axe fall. He thanked Bradpole brusquely for his news, and told him to come back in a week for his decision. Bradpole's face, which had been very serious, lightened when he received this indication that his client might be reconsidering his course of action.

James was still pondering this question as he made his way to Rotherfield House. But as he drew nearer to Arlington Street he began to speculate on the reason for Lady Ambourne's invitation. Ned, he knew, was still in France, so it was not to meet him. Strange! He was however very willing to visit the Dowager Countess, for he had always found her a sympathetic and amusing hostess. He arrived promptly at the appointed hour and was received by Purkiss.

It was at this point that Purkiss, the Ambournes' elderly and experienced butler, made his worst mistake in all his years of service. The lapse occurred when the visitor presented himself at the door of Rotherfield House, gave Purkiss his hat and cane, and said easily, 'You needn't bother to announce me, Purkiss. Is Lady Ambourne in the garden-room? Right, I'll go through.'

Normally the butler would have frozen such informality on the spot, but Lord Wintersett had been a familiar figure in the house since he had first arrived in an Eton jacket many years before. Purkiss also knew that her ladyship was expecting him, and that she wished her two visitors to meet. It was true that she had told the butler when he had taken refreshments in earlier that she was not to be disturbed for an hour, but that had been almost an hour and a half before. So Purkiss

allowed Lord Wintersett to carry on, without first
making sure that her ladyship was ready for him. . .

James strode confidently through the state rooms, but
went more slowly as he drew nearer to the garden room.
He could hear voices—the Countess had a visitor, it
seemed. He stopped short, astounded, when he realised
that the voice was Serena's. What was the Countess up
to? She had been in London for some time now—she
must know something of the situation between Serena
and himself! Was she trying to effect some sort of
reconciliation, perhaps because of Ned's position in
this? Was that why he had been invited?

Then he heard Serena say, 'It's true that I pursued
Tony Stannard relentlessly. All over the island.' There
was a smile in Serena's voice. 'I suppose I had a bad
attack of hero worship! At first he didn't take much
notice of me. I was just an importunate child, a
nuisance! But then, as time went on, he learned to
tolerate my company and even to enjoy it! In the end
we became surprisingly close. I think you could even
say that I loved him, after a fashion.'

James's first impulse was to turn on his heel and stride
back the way he had come. His second was to continue
into the garden room and demand to know why his
brother was being discussed. He was on the point of
doing this when he stopped abruptly. The Countess had
just asked 'I suppose you were missing Richard's
company?'

'I suppose it might have begun like that. But at one
time Tony seemed as important to me as Richard.'

'You haven't yet told me why you felt responsible for
his death?'

James found himself holding his breath. What would Serena say?

'It was what I said to him shortly before. . .before he d. . .died. I was in a rage — I've always had a hot temper and this time I was in a fury. I told him. . . I told him I despised him. That he'd be better dead.' Her voice dropped so that James had to lean forward to hear. 'And he was dead, very soon after that.' There was a silence. Then Serena said unevenly, 'Why did I say such things to him?'

There was a rustle of silks, and Lady Ambourne's voice was soft as she said, 'But you were little more than a child! How were you to know that your words would have such a catastrophic effect?'

'He no longer saw me as a child. What I said affected him mortally. He had heard my father telling him he had no future on the island or anywhere else, and he looked to me, sure that I would comfort him. We had been so close! But suddenly I felt I hated him and wanted him to know it. It is my belief that my rejection of him that night caused his death.'

'My dear! How can you blame yourself? You surely did not really wish him dead!'

'Lady Ambourne, please do not misunderstand me. I regretted his death and still regret it — the Calverts do not seem to have had a happy hour since that dreadful time. But even now I cannot feel that there was any other way out for him. I only wish that I had never uttered the words which drove him to it. I think they will be on my conscience forever!'

James turned and went back the way he had come. When he reached the entrance hall he gave Purkiss a message to deliver to Lady Ambourne, something

about urgent business elsewhere. The message was
confused, for his mind was on what he had just heard.
Sasha Calvert was a self-confessed adulteress, a woman
who had driven Tony to his death, and whose chief
regret was that this had made the Calverts unhappy!
That and her uneasy conscience! It was enough to
remove any doubt about Anse Chatelet — and more! He
sent for Mr Bradpole that night.

Alanna Stannard sat in the window of the drawing room
and gazed out resentfully at the green lawns and flower-
filled rosebeds of Wintersett Court. The London season
was now at its height. How she would have loved to be
part of that colourful parade! For thirteen weary years
she had lived here in retirement, miles away from any
kind of amusement. She had devoted her energies to
looking after her son, with only a half-witted mother-in-
law for company and an occasional visit from her
formidable brother-in-law to enliven the monotony.
She sighed. At first it had been easy, for it had seemed a
suitable atonement for her sins. Then she had grown
discontented. She still was, but now she was feeling
more nervous with every day that passed.

For years she had lived with the lies she had told of
her sojourn on St Just, and, though she had never been
really happy, she had at least felt secure. Her word had
never been doubted by her husband's family. Not only
were the West Indies thousands of miles away — far
enough to discourage casual communication — but it
had been in the interests of both families to hide the
truth as each had seen it. The Stannards had believed
they were protecting Tony's memory from the shame of
betraying his pregnant wife, and the Calverts had

probably wished to protect their own family from the scandal of Richard's seduction of a guest. The facts surrounding Tony's death had therefore been well concealed by both families. All this had worked to Alanna's benefit.

But now, with the advent of Sasha Calvert in London, Alanna's world was suddenly threatened. She was living on a precipice. She had done her best to prevent any meeting between James and the Calvert woman, but her efforts had failed. James had clearly been talking to her in London, and had recently shown signs of doubt, had even come down to Wintersett Court to question Alanna further. Any day now he might ask Sasha Calvert directly about the events on St Just thirteen years before, and what would happen then? Alanna shifted in her seat uneasily. Surely he would take the word of his own sister-in-law, the mother of his heir, against that of a Calvert? Of course he would!

Alanna got up, fetched her hat and parasol, and went outside. But though the sun was warm, she shivered. What if James didn't take his sister-in-law's word? Her old friend from Ireland, Amelia Banagher, had told her how well society regarded Serena Calvert, as she now called herself, in spite of James's efforts to discredit her. Amelia, who had not enjoyed the débâcle with the necklace, had also hinted that James was more impressed than he admitted. How stupid men were! These small tricks with necklaces and suchlike were useless! Something outstanding was needed, something to ruin Sasha Calvert once and for all! Then no one would believe her, whatever she said, and she would go back to her West Indian island and be forgotten! Alanna already had a half-formed plan in her head. It required a little more thought, for failure would be disastrous, and then she would see what could be done. But she would need help. . . Alanna decided to write to Amelia.

While Alanna Stannard was plotting to do mischief to Serena, Serena herself was doing her best to promote Lucy's interests. She had never before put into words her feeling of anguish and guilt about her brother's death. Now, though Lord Wintersett's dislike was still only half explained, she felt better for having unburdened herself to the sympathetic ear of the Countess, and felt ready to put her own problems aside for a while and concentrate on Lucy. Michael Warnham had become most particular in his attentions, and Serena was taking pains to get to know him. He was certainly an eligible candidate — twenty-three, heir to a barony, and certain to inherit a large share of his grandmother's considerable fortune. Isabella, his sister, was Lucy's great friend, and the Warnhams appeared to approve of a possible match. Serena found him pleasant and amusing, but she was not yet certain that he had enough strength of character to retain the respect of her high-spirited niece. If he had not, it would be a sure recipe for an unhappy marriage. So for the moment Serena was keeping an open mind. Lucy seemed to find much to admire in Mr Warnham, and Serena was amused to see how willing her niece was to defer to his judgement. There might be more to this young man than she had thought!

Her efforts on Lucy's behalf had led her into attending more balls, concerts and assemblies than she would otherwise have wished. She had always intended to keep in the background, leaving Lady Warnham and Mrs Galveston to chaperon the two girls. But in order to meet Michael Warnham, to observe him in company with Lucy, she had to take an active part in society. She was aware that Lord Wintersett's eyes were frequently turned on her, sometimes brooding, sometimes with an unaccountable gleam of satisfaction, but she never allowed herself to be put off. Serena was proving to be a minor success.

One evening, at a reception given by the French Ambassador, Serena was delighted to see the Countess of Ambourne approaching. The Countess was accompanied by an extremely handsome man in his thirties, dark-haired and grey-eyed.

'Ah, Serena!' she cried. 'I have such a pleasant surprise for you! I wish you to meet my son Edward.'

Lord Ambourne smiled quizzically as he bowed. 'My mother has her own quaint way of putting things, Miss Calvert. You must forgive her. The pleasant surprise is mine, I assure you!'

Serena laughed and curtseyed. 'Lord Ambourne, I would forgive your mother anything. She has been so kind to me — as you have, too. I find your house in Dover Street delightful.'

'The house belongs to my wife. I am pleased you like it.'

'Then I must thank her. Is she with you?'

'She is in London, but not with us tonight. She was a little tired after the journey.'

'I am sure Perdita would wish to meet you as soon as possible, Serena. I shall arrange it,' said the Countess. 'But have you yet spoken to the Ambassador? Come, let me take you to him — he will be intrigued to meet

someone from the West Indies. He has estates on
Martinique, you know.'

'Ma'am,' protested Serena. 'His Excellency surely
has more important people to speak to tonight?'

'That shows you do not know him! Now me, I have
known him since we were children, and I assure you he
will always take time to talk to a beautiful woman.' The
two ladies, escorted by Lord Ambourne, made their
way through the crowded rooms into the Ambassador's
presence. His Excellency received the Countess with
cries of pleasure, and they talked rapidly in French for
several minutes. Then he turned to Lord Ambourne
and asked most kindly after his family and his estate in
Normandy. Finally he turned to Serena, who was
amused to find that the Countess could perform rigor-
ously correct introductions when she chose.

'Miss Calvert,' said the Ambassador, 'I am
enchanted. Is it too much to hope that you will dance
with me? We could talk about Martinique and St Just.'

Serena looked somewhat apprehensively at the
Countess, who nodded encouragingly. 'I am honoured,
Ambassador,' she replied with another curtsy.

The Ambassador proved to be an excellent dancer
and an amusing companion. Serena was enjoying herself enormously when halfway through the waltz an aide
came up to him and said something discreet. The
Ambassador pulled a face. 'Miss Calvert, I am desolate.
Duty spoils my pleasure. But do not worry, I shall leave
you in good hands.' He looked round to the gentleman
who had been standing by them. 'Ah yes! May I present
the gentleman who has been described to me as the best
dancer in London, Miss Calvert? Lord Wintersett! You
are more fortunate that you deserve, milor'!' With a

smile and a graceful bow the Ambassador was gone. Serena and James were left facing one another on the edge of the floor.

James bowed. His face was cold. 'Miss Calvert?'

'Please forgive me, Lord Wintersett,' said Serena, equally coldly. 'It was kind of the Ambassador to think I wanted to carry on dancing. But I find I am tired, and I must return to my companions. They will be looking for me ——' She turned to go, but was held firmly.

'I think you do not understand, Miss Calvert. A request from an ambassador is the equivalent of a royal command. You must dance with me, however repugnant the idea is — to either of us.'

They set off in silence. For a while they circled the room carefully, avoiding anything but the slightest contact, but as time went on they each relaxed. They drew imperceptibly closer, James's hand more firmly at Serena's waist, Serena's hand resting more confidently on his shoulder. Serena shut her eyes. It was like the first time she had danced with this man — the same strange mixture of excitement and certainty, the same feeling of wordless communication. What James Stannard thought about her she could not begin to guess. But whatever it was, it had no effect on what she, deep down, had come to feel for him when they were in Surrey. It was astonishing, but nothing that had happened since had changed that. It seemed to have become part of the fabric of her being. Unwilling to continue with this melancholy train of thought, Serena opened her eyes. James was looking down at her with a bemused look in his eyes, as if he, too, was remembering their idyll.

Encouraged, Serena smiled, tentatively at first, then

as his gaze softened she said hesitantly, 'Our friend William—Blake the poet, not Blake the boy from the hill—has words for this situation, I think. Will you listen?'

'What are they?' he said, still looking at her with a smile in his eyes. She began, '"I was angry with my friend, I told my wrath——"' But she was interrupted before she could go any further.

'"My wrath did end"?' The smile vanished. His face changed once more to that of an implacable enemy. His hand gripped hers cruelly as he said softly, 'I think not, Sasha! You do not escape so lightly, for all your wiles! And recalling our relationship in happier times will not help you, either. You deserve no privilege of friendship.'

'But *why* do I not deserve it? Why will you not discuss it with me?' In spite of herself her voice had risen.

'I suggest that you control yourself, Sasha Calvert. Unless you wish us to be the subject of yet more gossip? That would suit me better than it would you, I believe.'

The waltz came to an end, and the other dancers started to leave the floor. Serena began to follow them, but then stopped, turned to Lord Wintersett and said with determination, 'I *will* have it out with you! Here, if you will not find a more suitable place!'

He looked at her with a twisted smile on his face. 'Why is it that you can rouse my admiration, even though I know you for what you are? You are unique!' He took her arm and led her off the floor. 'Come!' he said, and opening the door of a small salon he ushered her into it. Serena just had time to see Lady Ambourne's troubled gaze before Lord Wintersett shut the door. 'Now?'

FREE BOOKS CERTIFICATE

Yes! Please send me **Four FREE Temptations** together with my **FREE gifts.**

Please also reserve a Reader Service subscription for me. If I decide to subscribe, I shall receive four superb new titles for just £7.80 each month postage and packing FREE. If I decide not to subscribe I shall contact you within 10 days. Any free books and gifts will remain mine to keep. I understand that I am under no obligation whatsoever - I may cancel or suspend my subscription at any time simply by contacting you. I am over 18 years of age.

7A4T

Ms/Mrs/Miss/Mr _____

Address _____

_____

_____

Postcode _____

Signature _____

A FREE GIFT

Return this card and we'll also send you this cuddly Teddy Bear absolutely FREE.

A FREE GIFT

We all love mysteries, so AS WELL as your FREE books and Teddy Bear we've an intriguing gift for you.

MILLS & BOON READER SERVICE

FREEPOST
PO BOX 236
CROYDON
CR9 9EL

Offer expires 31st January 1995. The right is reserved to refuse an application and change the terms of this offer. One application per household. Offer valid in UK and Eire only. Offer not valid for current subscribers to Temptations. Overseas readers please write for details. Southern Africa write to IBS, Private Bag X3010, Randburg 2125. You may be mailed with offers from other reputable companies as a result of this application. Please tick box if you would prefer not to receive such offers ☐

MAILING PREFERENCE SERVICE

Serena turned and faced him steadily. 'Lord Wintersett, I will not refer again to our "relationship in happier times". That period of my life shall be forgotten. I claim no "privilege of friendship", either — indeed, when we first met in London, and you behaved so. . .in such an ungentlemanly manner, I believed that my behaviour in Surrey had given you a disgust of me. I could not account for the sudden change in your conduct towards me in any other way! But there must be more to it. This antipathy, no, it is much more than that — this personal animosity puzzles and distresses me. I cannot account for it. I wish you to tell me its cause!'

'Bravely said! If a little disingenuous. You already know why.'

'You hold the Calverts responsible for your brother's death?'

'The other Calverts are all dead themselves. I hold you responsible, you alone, Miss Calvert.'

'But this is prejudiced nonsense! I loved Tony! I never meant him any harm!' When he turned away from her with an expression of disgust, she cried desperately, 'Help me to understand! They call you a just man — hard, but just. Why are you going to such lengths to punish *me*?'

'You do not yet know to what lengths I am prepared to go, Sasha Calvert!' The expression in his eyes as he turned back to face her was so malevolent that she took a step back.

'You hate me!' she whispered. 'I believe you really hate me. Oh, God! How could I be so deceived? To think I once imagined I could actually love you!'

'Love! I would sooner be loved by a loathsome toad!

What could you possibly know about love? I've heard
you talk of the kind of love you offer! A love that tells a
desperate man that he is despised! A love that drives a
man to his death!'

For a moment Serena was taken aback. The words
were so familiar. Then it came to her. 'You were there!
At Rotherfield House. You must have been eavesdropping! Eavesdropping on my conversation with Lady
Ambourne. How dare you?' Serena was fast losing her
temper. The thought that this man had listened unseen
to the confession of her deepest, most painful feelings
about her brother's death outraged her.

She lost control altogether when she heard him say,
'This moral stance sits ill on a harlot, Sasha!'

Something inside Serena exploded and she slapped
Lord Wintersett with the full force of her arm behind
the blow. He instantly grabbed her to him and kissed
her hard. She tried to scream, but he held her mouth to
his, so that she could hardly breathe. Her struggles to
escape were futile, for his arms trapped her in an iron
grasp. She felt sick. This kiss was worse, much worse
than the first embrace on the hill, for though that had
lacked any respect, this had not the slightest element of
more tender feelings in it. Anger, a desire for revenge,
a primitive lust, but no regard for her, not the slightest
hint of any feeling for her as a person. When he finally
released her she was so dizzy that she was unable to
stand, and he had to hold her again to save her from
falling. She stood rigidly, staring at him in horror,
unable to hide her fear and revulsion. His face was
white to the lips, a dazed look in his eyes.

'I. . .I. . .I don't know what to say, Serena. I don't
know what came over me. . .'

She managed at last to move away from him, to walk to the door like a sleepwalker.

'Serena!' She stopped, but did not turn round. 'Serena, it was never my intention to attack you in that barbaric manner. I am sorry, deeply sorry.'

'I believe you,' Serena said harshly. 'You would rather kiss a loathsome toad, you said. But you k. . . kissed me just the same. Do you think that saying you are sorry can wipe it from my memory?' She put her hand on the doorknob.

He continued desperately, 'If you go out of the room now, looking as you do, the whole of London will be scandalised.'

Serena turned round then and looked at him ironically. 'Do you not think London should be scandalised at the punctilious Lord Wintersett behaving like a savage, a wild beast?'

'I am ashamed of my behaviour, Serena. I deserve your scorn and theirs. But even you must agree that I was provoked. Do you not think London would be equally scandalised at Miss Calvert using her fists like an untamed gipsy? No, wait! I am not concerned for myself in this instance. It is you I wish to spare. Wait a short while, please. Give yourself time to recover. You cannot wish to arouse the sort of comment I am sure would otherwise follow.'

She looked at him incredulously. He meant it! 'What are you at now, Lord Wintersett? I was under the impression that that was precisely what you wanted!'

'Not in this instance. This was no part of my plan. I. . .I do not know what came over me. I will say once again that I deeply regret what I did, and ask you to forgive me ——'

He stopped as Lord Ambourne and his mother came into the room, leaving the door open. The Countess went quickly over to a door in the wall on the right and unlocked it. A maid entered. Then Lady Ambourne took Serena by the hand, and said in a slightly raised voice, 'Gracious, Serena, you look ill, child. How thoughtful of Lord Wintersett to bring you in here when you felt faint! I am sure Marie was a help until I managed to come. I am only sorry that Lord Wintersett's message did not reach me sooner. I have informed Mrs Galveston that I will take you home, and she will stay with Lucy and her friends. Thank you, Marie, you may help Miss Calvert to her feet.' She whispered, 'Forgive the French farce, Serena! It's the best I can do to prevent scandal. You have been closeted with Lord Wintersett for some minutes, and the tongues are wagging outside. We need not tell them that Marie has only just arrived! I've told her to swear she was here all the time.'

Lord Ambourne was giving his friend a long, straight look. As the little party made its way to Lady Ambourne's carriage he said coolly, 'Shall you be at home tomorrow evening, James? May I call on you? I think we have things to discuss.'

The next day was sunny, but there was a cool breeze which sent the remaining blossom on the trees in Green Park drifting over into the garden of Rotherfield House. The Ambourne family were sitting in the garden room. The window doors were wide open to let in the air, while those sitting on the pretty sofas and chairs were protected from the wind. The younger Lady Ambourne was laughing up into her husband's face as he spread a shawl over her knees.

'Stop, Edward!' she protested. 'I am not cold, not in the slightest. Nor am I any longer tired! There is no reason on earth why I should not visit Miss Calvert as soon as I am respectably dressed! I wish to meet her!'

Serena heard this as she followed Purkiss through to the garden-room and she thought what an attractive picture they made. Lord Ambourne's dark head was bent over the sofa on which his wife was lying, and she was stretching her hand out towards him. The expression on his face belied his next words.

'Perdita, I am already angry with you for coming downstairs while I was out! Dr Parker expressly forbade it.'

'Pooh! You are tyrants, you and Dr Parker both, and it will do neither of you any good to be pandered to. Do you not agree, Mama?'

'Yes, but you know Edward will have his way, Perdita. Except. . .'

'I knew it! What are you plotting?'

'I believe my plot is already here. The mountain has come to Mahomet,' said the Dowager Countess, rising with a hand stretched out in welcome to Serena. She dismissed Purkiss with a nod and brought Serena forward to her daughter-in-law's couch.

'My mother surpasses herself. The metaphor is not even apt yet for Perdita. But now you may have the pleasant surprise of meeting my wife, Miss Calvert,' said the Earl with a grin. Serena looked down at a woman of about her own age with eyes of the darkest blue she had ever seen. The younger Lady Ambourne was as beautiful as her lord was handsome, and together they made a

striking couple. It was easy to see the reason for the
Earl's concern, for Lady Ambourne was clearly in what
was usually called an interesting condition.

'Surprise? What do you mean, Edward? The surprise — and the pleasure — are mine, Miss Calvert,' said
Lady Ambourne, adding as her husband gave a laugh
and even Serena smiled, 'What have I said? Why are
they laughing, Mama?' When they explained, she said,
'Well, the thought may not have been original, but it is
none the less true. Welcome, Miss Calvert. As you see,
I find it a trifle difficult to get up at the moment ——'

'You will not attempt to do so, Perdita,' said the Earl
firmly, and when she looked rebellious he smiled and
added, 'Please?'

'Then, Miss Calvert, you must sit down next to me
and amuse me,' said Lady Ambourne. 'You see how I
am beset with despots and conspirators. Now, I have a
hundred things to ask you. You must tell me what you
think of London, you must tell me about Miss Lucy and
her début — I hear that Michael Warnham is growing
most particular in his attentions, by the way — and you
must tell me about Lady Pendomer and her family.'

The Dowager Countess left them together, and Lord
Ambourne soon excused himself too. Serena spent a
very pleasant half-hour at the end of which she could
see that Lady Ambourne, in spite of her brave words to
the contrary, was getting tired. She rose to go.

'I hope you will come again, soon,' said Lady
Ambourne. 'We are not here in London for long.
Edward has some affairs in London to see to, but we
shall return to Ambourne as soon as he has finished. I
miss my children, and, though I wouldn't say so to

Edward, I must own that I find London tiring. But I should like you to come again before I go.'

'You are very kind, Lady Ambourne. And so is Lady Ambourne. . .er. . .the Countess. . .I mean your mother-in-law.'

'Confusing, is it not. Well, the Ambournes do not stand on ceremony when it is inconvenient to do so. I think you had better call me Perdita. I notice Mama calls you Serena, and I propose to do the same. We may not have known each other in person for very long, but Lady Pendomer's letters have made me feel you are an old friend. Bring Lucy with you when you next come. I should like her to talk to me about young Mr Warnham, if she will. I am glad to hear you say that you quite like his grandmother. I enjoy Mrs Galveston myself, but there are many who find her a tartar! Goodbye, Serena!'

Lord Ambourne appeared as Purkiss was ushering Serena through the state-rooms. 'May I speak to you, Miss Calvert?'

They went through to a study. Here the Earl gave her a small glass of wine and saw her comfortably seated.

'I hope you will not consider me impertinent, but I am curious to know a little more of what happened last night. Do you wish me to take the matter up with Lord Wintersett?'

Serena grew pale. 'I. . .I think it is better forgotten, Lord Ambourne. No harm came of it, I think, and. . . and. . .' Once again she had this curious inability to say Lord Wintersett's name. 'The gentleman had already apologised to me before you came in.'

'For what?'

Serena pulled herself together. She raised her chin.

'It is kind of you to concern yourself, Lord Ambourne, but I consider the matter settled. Lord. . .Lord W. . . Wintersett embarrassed me, but, though I am ashamed to admit it, I had provoked him.'

'You are sure that you are satisfied?'

'Yes. Quite sure.'

'I must confess I am relieved to hear you say so. James is an old friend of mine, and I am not anxious to pick a quarrel with him.'

'Oh, you must not think of it!' Serena cried. Then after a pause she said, 'Lord Ambourne, you say you are old friends. Has he ever spoken to you about his brother?'

'Tony? Not a great deal. I never really knew him. He was younger, of course, and rather a quiet person. James used to talk a lot about Tony's work — he was very proud of it. Tony was already making a name for himself even before he left Cambridge, and we all thought he was sure to go into academic life. He was a bit of a monk at Cambridge and his marriage took everyone by surprise, James most of all, I'd say. Why do you ask?'

'What was. . .your friend's reaction to his brother's death? Was he unbalanced by it?'

'What an odd question!' Lord Ambourne stared at her, but though Serena grew pink she said nothing. He shrugged his shoulders and went on, 'He was certainly not unbalanced by it. I've never met any man saner than James Stannard. But it did have a strong effect on him, and he never mentioned Tony afterwards.' He sat thinking for a moment. 'I suppose he became more. . . inaccessible, though he was always a bit cool, especially to anyone he didn't know. They called him Frosty Jack at Eton, you know. He was never so to me — we have been very good friends for years.' He eyed her curiously. 'Why are you asking me all this? Is there more to Tony Stannard's death than the world knows? Did he in fact die of a fever? Or is it true that he committed suicide?'

'I. . .I cannot tell you that. I was a child at the time.' She began pulling on her gloves, and they both rose. Then almost involuntarily she added forlornly. 'He blames the Calverts for it all, and I suppose there's some justification for that. But I find it strange that he blames me in particular. I really don't know why.'

'Are you asking me to find out, Miss Calvert?'

Serena's thoughts raced. The idea was a tempting one, but the two men had been friends for many years. What if that friendship was destroyed because of her? Lord Wintersett's apology the evening before had seemed sincere — she doubted he would attempt more tricks. Also, the season was more than half over, and Lucy was now so well established in society that Serena could reasonably take the less prominent role that she had always wished for herself. If she could avoid meeting Lord Wintersett for the short time left he would forget her. Quite soon she would leave England to return to the West Indies, and after that it was most unlikely that they would ever meet again. No, the mystery was better left alone.

She sighed and said, 'Thank you again, Lord Ambourne. You are very kind. But I think not. Instead, I shall try to avoid meeting your friend. Goodbye.'

That evening over dinner Lord Ambourne asked his ladies what they thought of Serena Calvert.

'She's a lovely woman, Edward. Not altogether in the usual manner. . .but those eyes! They are quite extraordinary — such a clear golden amber.'

'I would like an opinion on her character, Perdita, not her appearance. I can see her beauty for myself, and I agree with you. She is not completely to my taste — my preference is for sapphires, as you are no doubt aware — but very lovely.'

'She is unhappy, I think. Her face is sad in repose.'

'That is hardly surprising!' said the Dowager Countess. 'Serena's family history is far from being a happy one. She is quite alone in the world except for Lucy. And she has worked like a Trojan to keep the family estate going. Alicia Pendomer's letters have been so ecstatic on the subject of Serena's dedication to duty and other boring things that I was not at all looking forward to meeting her. But she is absolutely charming. I am quite baffled by James Stannard's behaviour — and very disappointed in him.'

'How can we judge, Mama? We hardly know anything of the matter. You tell me Serena Calvert is charming, but what value has that? She may even have been hardworking — but is she honest?'

Both ladies were quite clear on this point, and were incensed that Edward should think it necessary to ask.

After Perdita had gone to bed the Countess sought out her son. 'I don't want to worry Perdita with this matter, Edward, but I heard you tell James last night that you would like to see him.'

'Yes, I thought I would go in a few moments.'

'You wish to speak to him about his behaviour, I suppose? Are you and James about to fall out over this matter?'

'You may rest your mind, Mama. Miss Calvert has said that she has no wish for me to take the matter further, so I am not about to challenge him, thank goodness. I'm glad she's so sensible. I cannot say I understand James's behaviour, but I shouldn't wish to lose his friendship over it. However, I think I would like him to be aware that Miss Calvert is a friend of the Pendomers and so entitled to some protection from me. I shall do it tactfully, so you need not look so worried. Do you know more than you have said about the affair?'

The Countess then related as much as she thought she could about the Stannards on St Just. It wasn't easy. She had given her word to Serena, so much of the story remained untold.

CHAPTER NINE

JAMES was not looking forward to this forthcoming meeting, any more than Lord Ambourne. He was not so rich in friends that he could afford to lose one, and Ned and his family had been very good friends indeed. During the dark days of his schooldays, when nothing James did ever pleased his father, when his mother treated him with indifference, and Wintersett Court was like a prison to him, a visit to Arlington Street or Ambourne had been like coming into light. Damn Sasha Calvert! Wherever he looked she was there, destroying everything he had ever valued.

When Lord Ambourne was announced the two men greeted one another cautiously, like fencers. But, to James's astonishment, it gradually became clear to him that Ned was not there to challenge or condemn. Unlikely though it was, Serena seemed not to have told Ned what had actually happened. It had been obvious the night before that his friend was willing to take on the role of protector, but Serena had apparently not desired him to do so. With a sigh of relief James produced a bottle of wine, and the two men sat down to chat more easily. One bottle led to another, until the candles were guttering in their sockets and the fire was almost dead. Ned asked idly, 'What *did* you do to Serena Calvert, old fellow?'

'She didn't tell you?'

'No, she said you'd apologised and that she had

provoked you, and that she wished the matter to be forgotten. I'd give a lot to know what you did, though. It's my belief that Serena Calvert is a cool enough character, but she was certainly in a flutter last night.'

'I kissed her,' said James abruptly. 'And you're wrong about her being cool. She has a fiendish temper.' He fingered his jaw.

'Well,' said Edward, with a large gesture which betrayed how much wine the two friends had consumed. 'Well, the ladies often make a fuss about a kiss, but it can be a pleasant experience for all that. No harm done. She said so.'

'She said it had been a pleasant experience? I don't believe it.'

'Not that, no. But she said no harm had been done.'

'I wish I could believe that was true. I frightened her, Ned. And I'm ashamed of myself.' He burst out, 'That woman seems to bring out the worst in me. Sasha, I mean. Not Serena. No, not Serena.' He filled his glass and drank deep.

'You're foxed, James! Who's this Sasha woman?'

'She killed my brother.'

Edward sat up, reached for the bottle and poured some more wine into James's glass and some for himself. 'You're wrong, James, old fellow. Your brother killed himself, unless I'm much mistaken.'

'Who told you that?'

'Never mind. He did, didn't he?'

'Yes. Yes!' James got up and stood by the fire, kicking it with his boot. 'But *why* did he? You cannot imagine what it's like to live with that question, Ned. I don't suppose we shall ever know the answer now. I try to forget — I even succeed for a while, and then I go

back to Surrey and see my mother and Tony's boy, and
the question returns to plague me, together with the
sense of waste, the bitter waste! You know what he was
like, curse it! Why did he have to kill himself over a
confounded woman?' James turned away from the fire
and roamed restlessly about the room. 'He had his
work — the Calverts couldn't have kept him out of it for
long! God knows, the Wintersetts are a match for any
damned colonials. And for Tony — Tony of all people —
to do that to my mother. . . The devil take it! *Why*?'

'What makes you so sure that he killed himself over a
woman?' asked Edward carefully.

'What else could it possibly be? Anyway, I have
proof. I've even heard her admit it. Oh, for God's sake,
let's leave it!' James looked moodily down at his glass
and drank again.

Edward said slowly, 'I'll tell you something you might
like to think over, James. A while back I almost made
the biggest mistake of my life, just because I was too
blind to see the truth. I could have lost Perdita because
of it. Mind you don't fall into the same trap. Now tell
me exactly what it is that you have against Serena
Calvert?'

James stared at Edward and then he started laughing
helplessly. 'Nothing at all, Ned, nothing at all!' Then he
dropped down on his knees beside Edward, and whispered solemnly, 'But Sasha — now that's another question. Oh, what a surprise I have for her!' He slipped
slowly down the side of the chair to lie in a heap on the
floor.

Edward saw with regret that nothing more could be
got from James that night. He called that gentleman's

valet, and walked, somewhat unsteadily, back to Arlington Street.

The next morning Edward took one look at Perdita's wan face, called Dr Parker, ascertained that his wife would be able to withstand the relatively short journey to Ambourne if it was taken in easy stages, and declared that he and his wife would leave London that afternoon. The Dowager regretted their departure, but agreed with her son. Her daughter-in-law smiled ruefully, wrote numerous notes, including one to Serena, and then lay back thankfully in the chaise and was carried away.

Thus it was that Lord Ambourne was unable to pursue the mysterious question of Sasha Calvert and the surprise in store for her. His overriding concern for his wife caused all such thoughts to vanish from his mind.

The following day James sat for most of the morning gazing moodily into space. The meeting with Ned had gone better than he had hoped. James was aware that, had she wished, Serena could have caused a rift between Ned and himself which would have been difficult to heal. If Ned had heard the whole story of James's behaviour at the French Ambassador's reception he would have been obliged to tackle his friend about it. But Serena had not told him the whole story. Why not? She had no reason to spare James. He had insulted her, had attacked her, had even frightened her. He frowned at the memory of the look in her eyes when he had held her after that shameful kiss. She was usually so dauntless, so spirited — the golden eyes did not often hold such a look of fear, he was sure. He got up impatiently. Why was he worrying? For whatever reason, his friendship with Ned had been preserved, and if all went well Sasha Calvert would soon be out of Anse Chatelet and out of his life. So would Serena. The thought did not make him feel any better.

James was relieved when a visitor in the form of Mr Bradpole came to distract him from his gloomy thoughts. But the damned lawyer brought with him the papers which completed Lord Wintersett's possession of Anse Chatelet. Neither gentleman felt particularly cordial. There was no comfortable chair for Mr Bradpole, no glass of Madeira, nor did the lawyer seem to wish it. Instead he gave the impression that he saw no cause for celebration.

'What do I do with these now?'

'The copies should be delivered to Miss Calvert, Lord Wintersett. Does your lordship wish me to retain the originals?'

'Of course. I'm not sure why you ask, Bradpole. Nor do I understand why you have brought the copies here instead of delivering them to Miss Calvert. You have her address.'

The lawyer said colourlessly, 'I thought your lordship might wish, even at this late stage, to reconsider your decision. Or, alternatively, you might wish to deliver them in person.'

'What the devil do you mean by that?'

'The acquisition of the Calvert estate has been an object with you for some time, Lord Wintersett. I believe the reason to have been personal rather than a matter of business. But if your lordship wishes me to deliver the papers I will, of course, do so.'

'Then do so, Bradpole' said Lord Wintersett curtly. 'Now, if you please — and damn your impudence!'

Mr Bradpole bowed and went out. James threw himself into a chair and wondered why the devil he was feeling so out of sorts. His head was aching, but that could easily be accounted for by the amount of wine he had drunk the night before. He had had hangovers before now. It was not that. He smiled sourly. Bradpole never gave up. 'Even at this late stage'! Perhaps he should have ignored the lawyer's implicit criticism and taken the papers round to Dover Street himself? But truth to tell, he had been afraid. After the scene at the French Ambassador's he could well believe that Serena would refuse to see him again. He got up and walked restlessly about the room, reminding himself of the events on St Just, holding them like a shield against the wave of desolation which swept over him at this thought. After a while he managed to subdue this ridiculous feeling and sat down again to consider the lawyer's visit. Serena would soon have the papers about Anse Chatelet. How would she react to its loss? She would probably be devastated, a thought which gave him surprisingly little pleasure. This was Sasha's loss, Sasha Calvert's loss, he reminded himself fiercely, but it was no good. Thoughts of Serena were filling his mind — regret for the pain he was causing her, a wish that it had not been necessary. What the devil was wrong with him? This was the culmination of years of planning and waiting, and he should be feeling pleased that they had borne fruit, not jaded and weary! The trouble was that he seemed to be living in two worlds at once, neither of them happy. He sat there brooding for a while and then decided that a good dose of fresh air would clear his head and possibly raise his spirits. A ride in the park was called for.

On his return he found a note requesting him to call on Miss Calvert in Dover Street at his earliest convenience. He was astonished at the sudden feeling of elation. The reason for her request mattered not at all. What was important was that Serena was at least prepared to face him again!

Serena was pacing up and down in the drawing-room of the house in Dover Street. The fateful papers lay where she had thrown them, scattered over the table in the window. Lucy sat wide-eyed and pale on the sofa.

'What does it mean, Sasha? We've always lived at Anse Chatelet; it's our home! He cannot take it from us! Can he?' Lucy's lip quivered as she spoke, and Serena stopped her pacing to take Lucy in her arms and attempt to comfort her.

'Don't cry, Lucy! Hush, my love! I'll get it back, I swear! Come, dry your eyes. He might come at any moment, and we must not let him see any weakness. He's a no-good——' Here Serena used some island patois which shocked Lucy out of tears and into laughter.

'Sasha! Whatever would Lady Pendomer say?'

Serena grinned at her niece. 'She wouldn't say anything, Lucy. She wouldn't know the words. I'm surprised you do!'

'I was brought up on the island, Sasha. You can't play with Joshua and the others without learning some of the things they say. How I miss Joshua and Betsy and the rest! Oh, Sasha, are we never going to see Anse Chatelet again?'

Lucy's mercurial spirits were descending once more. Serena said hastily, 'Of course we are! But Lucy, if you marry here in England, St Just would surely be less important to you than it has been till now. You like it in England, don't you?'

'Oh, yes, I love it! In fact, I'd miss Isabella and. . . and the others even more than I miss my friends on St Just. It's not that I don't love the people on Anse Chatelet, Sasha! I do, still! But. . .it's different here. Some of the people here are very important to me.' Serena looked quizzically at her niece, who blushed and added, 'I think I'd miss Isabella's brother most of all. He. . .he's fond of me, too, I think. But what would you do if he. . .if I. . .were to marry?' Serena saw that Lucy was thinking for the first time what marriage in England would entail, realising for the first time that it would mean parting from her beloved aunt. Lucy's face brightened. 'I know, Sasha! When I marry we can live in England together!'

Serena smiled wryly. Now was not the time to point out that she had no intention of living with her niece once Lucy was married. From the beginning Serena had made up her mind that she would see Lucy safely established, and then return to St Just to spend her energies on Anse Chatelet. Now, it seemed, this consolation was to be denied her. But she would not give up without a fight!

One result of this conversation was that Lucy was able to face the arrival of Lord Wintersett with composure. He came in dressed in impeccable linen under a dark green coat and riding breeches tucked into shining Hessians, his face impassive as usual. He gave a cool bow. Serena greeted him in an equally businesslike fashion and said, 'You know my niece, I believe, Lord W. . . Wintersett.'

'I do indeed. Your servant, Miss Lucy.' Lucy got up, curtsied modestly and sat down again. He went on, 'Though I am surprised to see her present on this occasion. I thought it was to be a business meeting, Miss Calvert. I assume you have had the papers concerning Anse Chatelet?' He took his glass and eyed the chaos on the table. 'Yes, I see you have.'

'It *is* a business meeting, Lord W. . .Wintersett,' Serena was glad that she could at least say his name, though she wondered impatiently why she couldn't say it without stumbling! 'The estate is Lucy's home, as well as my own. And you can hardly blame me for wishing for a companion in your presence.'

A faint red darkened Lord Wintersett's cheeks, but he drawled, '*Your* home, Miss Calvert? I think not.'

'That remains to be seen,' replied Serena swiftly. 'The manner in which you acquired my estates was doubtful, to say the least.'

'It was legal, Miss Calvert.'

'A minimal claim, I should have thought. Most men of honour would not have stooped to such measures. And though I am fully aware that an appeal to your sense of honour would be like asking a hyena to stop scavenging——' There was a gasp from Lucy, which she hastily suppressed. Serena ignored it and continued, 'I am persuaded that the courts might view an appeal with sympathy—especially as the Governor of St Just would support it.'

Lord Wintersett smiled mockingly, '"A hit", William, "a very palpable hit"!'

'Then may you be "justly killed with your own treachery"!' said Serena, her voice full of feeling. 'And we will omit further quotation, if you please. I enjoy that game only with my friends.'

'Well, then, my case might be destroyed, though I doubt it. But it will certainly not be destroyed by you! Believe me, your weapons are puny. Anse Chatelet is mine by every law in the kingdom, and I defy anyone to take it from me.'

'Of course! I had forgotten. The *wealthy* Lord W. . . Wintersett can afford the best lawyers in England!'

'I haven't won Anse Chatelet with my wealth, Miss Calvert, but by your own family's prodigality in the past. If I hadn't taken up the mortgage, someone else would have!'

'Pray do not attempt to defend yourself——'

'I am not,' said Lord Wintersett grimly, 'trying to defend myself. I see no necessity to do so, not to a Calvert. God's teeth, you squander a handsome and profitable heritage and then come whining to me when it is taken from you——'

Lucy jumped up and faced Lord Wintersett, her cheeks scarlet.

'How dare you? How dare you talk to my aunt in such a way? What do you know about it? Sasha has worked hard and gone without for years—all to save Anse Chatelet! She has never squandered a thing in her life——'

'Except my brother's life.'

Lucy swept on, ignoring the interruption '—and she has something you will never have, not for all your money. She has the love of everyone who knows her. You can keep Anse Chatelet! Sasha will live with me when I am married!'

His icy gaze swept Lucy's face. 'Married? That is

good news indeed, Miss Lucy. May I ask who the
fortunate young man is?'

A cold shiver went down Serena's spine at this
question. Lord Wintersett was a dangerous and vindictive man and he must not be allowed to threaten Lucy's
happiness. She put a hand on Lucy's arm. 'You may
not, sir. It is none of your business. Lucy, thank you for
your defence, I am touched. I think Lord Wintersett's
visit is almost over, so would you now leave us?'

Lucy looked doubtfully at them both, but Serena
forced a smile and nodded her head, 'It's all right, Lucy,
really! I wish you to go, please.' Lucy gave their visitor
one of her best curtsies, every line of which conveyed
disdain, and went out. When the door was shut once
again Serena said urgently, 'She is young. And devoted
to me. You must forgive her.' She was aware that she
was pleading with him, but could not help herself. 'Her
father was already a sick man when your brother and his
wife were on St Just. He took no part in their affair. Do
not. . .do not spoil her life.'

'You think I would harm a girl who can't have been
more than five years old when my brother died?'

Serena said spiritedly, 'I could well be forgiven for
thinking so! You have just annexed her home!'

'Not hers, Serena. Yours. I understand that Miss
Lucy has a fortune of her own, and that you intend her
to marry in England. Losing Anse Chatelet should
mean nothing to her.'

'Nothing? Nothing! Why, you heartless, vindictive
scorpion, how can you judge what a home means to a
child. The feelings of love and comfort, the happy
memories of childhood!'

He grew white and turned away from her. After a

pause he said harshly, 'Lucy is fortunate if she has such happy memories of her home. But she is about to be married, she said, and she will soon forget the loss of Anse Chatelet when that happens. I repeat, I mean her no harm. You may believe me, Miss Calvert.'

Behind his words she sensed a feeling of unhappiness, of deep loneliness, and angry though she was it gave her pause. She said uncertainly, 'Though I have not experienced it, everyone says you are a just man. Hard, but just. It would not be just to punish Lucy.'

He said abruptly, 'If your niece marries in England, will you in fact live with her?'

Serena shook her head. 'No.'

'What will you do?'

'I had always intended to return to St Just in order to run Anse Chatelet. It was my ambition to carry on building it up again.' She looked up defiantly. 'It still is!'

'And if your appeal fails? As it will.'

'I. . .I might return to Surrey. But it would be hard, I admit. My aunt is elderly and set in her ways. . .'

'You might be forced to seek refuge with William!'

He seemed to regret the words as soon as they were spoken, as did Serena. They were both reminded of the companionship they had known and lost. He frowned, then seemed to come to a sudden decision. 'Miss Calvert, if you will promise to go back to St Just immediately I shall accept Sir Henry's word that the payment should have arrived on time and cancel the foreclosure. Anse Chatelet would be returned to you on the old terms. But you must leave England and not come back again, not ever.'

Serena was suddenly aflame again. '"You must not"! "You must promise"! Who the devil do you think you are, Lord Wintersett, to suggest that I should never visit Lucy in England — or even come for my own pleasure? I am a Calvert of Anse Chatelet, and would not be one of your pensioners — not for the world! If I cannot win my estates back with my own efforts, you may keep them! I am damned if I will accept your charity or your restrictions!'

He gave a reluctant smile. 'Forcefully, if not conventionally expressed. That temper of yours will dish you one of these days, Serena. You know, I find you an enigma. You would almost persuade me of your integrity, except that I have heard you condemned out of your own mouth.'

'Integrity? How could you possibly judge integrity? Where is the integrity in the low, cheating ruse you have employed to steal Anse Chatelet? And how can I have condemned myself out of my own mouth? I simply don't understand what you mean. Why did you say I had squandered your brother's life?'

'Because you drove him to his death, that's why!'

Serena looked at him blankly. '*I*? I drove him to his. . . But that is nonsense!'

'"I loved him", you said.'

'Yes, but —'

'"I pursued him relentlessly", you said.'

'Yes, but —'

'"I told him I despised him, that he'd be better dead", you said.'

'No! That I did not say! Not to Tony!'

'Then to whom?'

Serena was about to answer him, then she stopped short. Why should she betray Richard to this monster? 'I will not tell you,' she replied. 'But it was not to Tony.'

He raised a sceptical eyebrow, but she ignored him. 'You are wrong about me, Lord Wintersett. I loved Tony, and I would never have willingly harmed him.'

He looked at her, confident of his case, scornful of her attempt to plead her innocence. 'It had to be you,' he said. 'There was no one else.'

Serena's eyes widened as the implication of what he was saying hit her. 'I. . .I. . .' she stammered.

'Please continue!' he jeered. 'Tell me that Tony did not kill himself! Or that if he did, it was not because of a woman!'

'It was not because of me,' she said quietly. 'And that is all I will say. You must believe what you will. You have done your worst to the Calverts. It is now time to forget. But I warn you, I will fight for Anse Chatelet. And if you harm a hair of Lucy's head I will cause you more anguish than you have yet known, Lord Wintersett. Goodbye.'

When Alanna heard that Sasha Calvert had been taken up by the Ambournes and was enjoying a modest success in society, her fears for her own safety reached breaking point. She had to rely more and more on Amelia Banagher for her information — a not altogether satisfactory source, for Amelia was no longer received in the very best houses. Though James had paid them frequent visits in the earlier part of the year, he seemed now to have tired of the country and was spending much more of his time in town. There was a greater risk, therefore, that he would become more friendly with the Calvert woman than was healthy, and Alanna was in daily expectation of a visit from an irate James demand-

ing to know the truth about St Just. She bestirred
herself to complete her plans.

It was towards the end of June and Alanna was
holding a council of war. To a casual eye this was a tea-
party in the garden, given by Mrs Stannard for some
Irish friends — a natural enough occasion. But the lady
sitting gracefully by the sundial was one of the most
notorious courtesans in London, and the distinguished-
looking gentleman who had brought her was Fergus
O'Keefe, an Irish soldier of fortune and a man of parts,
all of them bad. Alanna was anxious to disgrace Sasha
Calvert, and the other two were eager to get what
money the rich Mrs Stannard would pay them to help
her — though in the case of the lady there was a certain
amount of personal ill-will as well. Amelia Banagher
had not forgotten Serena's remarks at the Assembly
Rooms.

'But how can you be sure that Sir John and Lady
Taplow will be staying at the Black Lion, *acushla*?'
asked Captain O'Keefe.

'Don't be stupid, Fergus! Do I not know where all of
them have their favourite inns? Have I not seen the
Taplows many a time at the Black Lion at Hoddesdon
when they've been on their way back to London from
Huntingdon? They haven't seen me, mind!' Amelia
gave a rich laugh. 'They take good care not to. They
might soil their disapproving eyes!'

'I dare swear you are seldom alone.' Captain O'Keefe
accompanied this remark with a wink.

Amelia's laugh was scornful. 'Hardly! I've even been
there with one of the Taplows' closest acquaintances.
That was a lark! They almost twisted their heads off

their necks in their efforts not to see either of us that time!'

'But Amelia, how will you see that word about Miss Calvert's fall from grace spreads through society? From what I've heard the Taplows are so upright that they don't believe in scandalmongering either, do they?'

'Alanna, pray stop worrying! I've set up an assignation myself in the same inn on the same night with Harry Birtles. He's the most notorious rattle in the town. I'll make sure he sees what he needs in order to make a juicy tale. It will get round, never fear. So with Harry to spread it, and the Taplows to confirm it, the plot can hardly fail. Be easy!'

'Very well. But I hope you are right. And the plot will only succeed if the rest goes well, too. Captain O'Keefe, what about your part?'

'Well I still think it would have been better for me to use my charm on the lady — it doesn't often fail, eh, Amelia? But you said not to try, so I've hit on the idea of hiring a coach and putting the Ambourne cipher on the panels for the night. Then I can have a message sent, supposedly from Lord Ambourne himself, asking her to visit him.'

'No, no! You must ask her to visit the Dowager, not Ambourne! She would never come out at night to meet him.'

The gallant captain pulled a face. 'She sounds a damned dull fish to me — I can't see much fun for myself in this business, and that's a fact!'

Alanna said coldly. 'You are not being paid to have fun, Captain O'Keefe. The woman is not to be harmed while she is in your power, do you hear? It's her reputation I wish to be damaged, nothing else.'

'You may rest easy, Alanna,' said Amelia. 'I'll make sure he behaves. We'll be together most of the night. He'll just appear when it's necessary in the morning.'

'What about Sir Harry? Won't you be occupied in. . .er. . .entertaining him?'

'Not if I slip a little something into his wine. He drinks like a fish. No, I can manage both of them. Miss Calvert's virtue will be safe, if that's what you want — though I think you're being a mite overscrupulous.'

'I will not pay either of you if Miss Calvert is harmed, Amelia.'

'Well that reminds me, Alanna, my dear,' said Amelia. 'When will you pay us, and how much?'

'We agreed five hundred pounds ——'

'Each?'

Alanna looked at the faces before her. They were suddenly hard and watchful. She nodded. 'Each. I will pay you each a hundred and fifty pounds beforehand, a hundred and fifty immediately afterwards, and two hundred when Sasha Calvert is finally disgraced. But pray finish telling us what you plan to do, Captain O'Keefe.'

'Once the lady has entered the coach she'll be taken to the inn. The landlord has been primed — you did say you'd pay expenses, didn't you, Mrs Stannard?'

'Reasonable expenses, yes. Afterwards.'

'Beforehand,' said the Captain softly.

'Very well. Carry on.'

'She'll not like being abducted, of course. Amelia here will give her some womanly sympathy, and offer the lady something to drink. Miss Calvert will be out for the night after she drinks it.'

'You're sure you can gauge the dose accurately?'

'Mrs Stannard, once she has it in her, I could tell you to the second when she'll wake up again! Was I not once assistant to a doctor?'

Alanna looked doubtfully at Amelia, who nodded reassuringly. 'It's all right, Alanna. I've known him do that kind of thing before.'

Still looking doubtful, Alanna asked, 'And when she wakes up?'

'Before she wakes up,' Captain O'Keefe corrected her. 'When she's still half asleep, I'll make sure she's on display to the world through the open door of the bedchamber. If Amelia does what she's supposed to the world will include the Taplows and the chatty Sir Harry. By the time she wakes up properly her reputation will be like the seeds on this dandelion head.' He blew on the dandelion clock in his hand, and the seeds vanished on the wind.

After they had gone Alanna was uneasy. Necessity was driving her into this plot, but she did not enjoy the association with Fergus O'Keefe. He was charming enough, but she felt he could be dangerous. She must consider her plan a little more carefully, for she had a lot at stake. If O'Keefe did misbehave and the plot were discovered then nothing would save her, not even her relationship to the Wintersetts. The Ambournes would see to that, especially as they were to be involved, however indirectly.

Serena was busy during the next few days. She was disappointed that the younger Ambournes had returned so unexpectedly to the country, but was consoled when she found that the Countess was intending to stay on for some time. She sought the lady's advice on a suitable lawyer.

'Our family lawyer is Bradpole. He is very good, but I believe the Stannards use the firm as well. But Perdita had an excellent lawyer. Let me see. . .the name was Rambridge, I think. I shall send one of the men to make some enquiries at Lincoln's Inn tomorrow, Serena!'

Mr Rambridge called at Dover Street almost immediately. He was cautious on the question of Anse Chatelet, saying, 'The firm of Bradpole, Chalmers and Bradpole is highly respected, Miss Calvert. I would find it hard to believe that they would be involved in anything of a dubious nature.'

But after Serena had explained the circumstances, including the role played by Sir Henry Pendomer, the lawyer promised to look into it. Serena thanked him, gave him the papers and various addresses, and stressed how urgent the task was. At this he smiled and said, as all lawyers did, that one could not hurry the processes of the law, but then he became more human and assured her that he would not waste any time.

Serena also went down to Surrey to visit her great-aunt. Lady Spurston demanded to know the whole story, which was impossible. But Serena told her enough to rouse her indignation at the injustice, and she promised to give Serena all the help in her power.

Feeling she had done as much as she could for the moment Serena then devoted herself to Lucy's interests. It was now more important than ever that Lucy should be established, and though Serena still had private doubts about Michael Warnham she suppressed them. Lucy seemed to have made up her mind in his favour. She spent some time with the Warnhams, who were obviously pleased with their son's choice. Considering how modest Lucy's fortune was, this was a great compliment. They were a pleasant family, and Serena rather thought that her niece would be happy with them. She willingly agreed to allow Lucy to go down to Reigate with them for a few days. London was getting very hot and dusty, and Mrs Galveston had expressed a wish to spend some time in the country.

Serena felt quite lonely when Lucy and the Warnhams had gone. The depression which was never very far away these days came down like a black cloud on her spirits. What if she did not succeed in her attempt to save Anse Chatelet? What would she do with her life? The prospect of living with Aunt Spurston was not an alluring one, and she suspected that her aunt would not view it with much joy either. After the death of her husband the old lady had become used to living alone. She had been willing to support her great-niece for a few months, but after Serena and Lucy had gone to London Lady Spurston had returned to her quiet life with relief.

Serena decided to try to forget her problems for the moment, and kept herself busy. Always with John, the footman, as her faithful follower, she paid calls, went shopping, buying small unnecessary things in order to cheer herself up, and visited the galleries and museums for which she had never till now seemed to have time. She went walking in the park, admiring the phaetons, the curricles and various other strange vehicles as they bowled along. The horses were beautiful. With a sigh she thought of Douce and Trask and the wonderful rides on the Downs.

'Good afternoon, Miss Calvert.' With a start she

looked up. Douce's master had just drawn up in a dangerous looking high perch phaeton with a pair of extremely handsome greys.

'Sir,' Serena said coldly.

'You are alone? That is a rare phenomenon. Where is Miss Lucy?'

His tone was so affable that she regarded him with suspicion. 'She is spending some days with friends,' she said as curtly as good manners would allow.

'Come, a drive round the park will do you good. John will help you up.'

'Thank you, but I would not dream of putting you to the trouble. . .'

'It's no trouble, Miss Calvert, I assure you. Are you afraid of the vehicle? There's no danger. John?'

John came forward, and before she quite knew what was happening Serena was high in the air on a narrow seat. With a word to John to wait where he was till they returned, Lord Wintersett drove off at a sedate trot. John was quite happy with the situation. Lord Wintersett was a friend of the Ambourne family, there could be no objection to him.

The two in the phaeton drove in silence for a minute or two. Serena was surprisingly at ease, and was enjoying the view of the park from her elevated position. She began to feel more cheerful. Suddenly Lord Wintersett spoke.

'Are you comfortable, Miss Calvert?'

'Thank you, yes,' she said stiffly. 'Why did you insist on taking me up? I find it very odd.'

'I hardly know myself,' he replied with a curious smile. 'I saw you standing there — you were looking as you did on your birthday, on. . .on the hill. Miserable. I suppose I wanted to cheer you up. Why, I cannot say!'

'I am perfectly happy! Your sympathy, if that is what it is, is misplaced, I assure you, Lord W. . .Wintersett.' She bit her lip in vexation. Curse that stammer! 'But perhaps your reason is less charitable? Perhaps you wished to taunt me, to find out if I have changed my mind and am ready to accept your conditions?'

'I've withdrawn the offer,' he said. 'I've reconsidered, and have made other plans. But no, you misjudge me, Miss Calvert. I'm not here to talk about them. When will you manage to say my name without stuttering?'

'I don't know. But I'd prefer not to have to say it at all,' she replied. 'Pray set me down.'

'What, here? I'm afraid that is impossible. You must wait till we are back with John — London is a dangerous place to a lady on her own. By the way, that's a fetching little bonnet. It suits you.'

Serena was growing angry. She resented being forced to sit quietly while he said what he pleased. And she resented her enjoyment of this ride even more! 'I cannot imagine why you think I wish for your compliments. Do you enjoy having me in your power like this? Please take me back! Immediately!'

He smiled — a long, lazy, utterly charming smile. 'Well, you know, I rather do. But I shall take you back when you say my name again, Serena.'

'Will you release me if I do? And my name is Miss Calvert.'

'Only if you say it without stammering.'

'I have your word? Not that that serves any purpose.'

'You have my word.'

Serena took a deep breath. 'Then I wish that wealthy

. . .witless. . . .weaselly. . . Lord Wintersett would stop
wearying me!'

He laughed. 'What a woeful whopper, woman! I beg
your pardon — I should have said "Miss Calvert". That's
better — you almost smiled! I think I'll surprise you and
keep my word. I have things to do. Good day to you!'

He drew up by John with a flourish, saw her safely on
the ground, nodded and drove off, leaving Serena
completely mystified. What was Lord Wintersett up to
now? What were his mysterious plans? Whatever they
were, they seemed to have made him look more
favourably on her. For a moment he had almost been
the man she had known on the hills of Surrey.

CHAPTER TEN

SERENA had visited Lady Ambourne at Rotherfield House once or twice since the lawyer's visit. The Countess had seemed somewhat absent-minded, almost worried. So when Serena received a note from her that evening asking her to come immediately, and begging her to stay the night in Rotherfield House, she paused only long enough for Sheba to pack a small bag with necessities. Sheba was uneasy at letting her mistress go without her. She argued and wailed and prophesied doom until Serena became really annoyed. But Serena was determined to stick to what the note had asked. She could do no less for the friend who had been so kind to her.

The matter is urgent and confidential, Serena. If I could impose on your discretion, I should prefer you not to discuss this visit with anyone. You will, of course, have to tell Mrs Starkey you are spending the night with me, but say no more than that, I beg you. *Bring no one else*. Yours in haste, etc.

When she got to the door John was at her side, but she waved him away. 'Look, the Countess has even sent the carriage for me. Stay here, John.'

There was a maid in the carriage, but it was dark inside, and Serena couldn't see the woman's face. The groom helped her in and then they set off. Serena sat down and turned to the maid. 'What is it? What is

179

wrong with the Coun——' Suddenly she was seized,
then two people swiftly gagged and blindfolded her.
One of her assailants was powerful and rough, and
when she at first tried to kick him he twisted her arm
behind her back and threatened to break it. The
woman, presumably the one who had pretended to be a
maid, helped to tie her bonds more firmly, but the only
voice she heard was that of a man.

The journey seemed endless. They were travelling at
a reckless pace, and she was thrown all over the seat by
the jolting of the carriage, unable to save herself
because of her bonds. She felt sick and faint—the gag
was uncomfortable and it was almost unbearably hot.
She must in fact have fainted for a while, for when she
came to they were in the country, travelling swiftly
along a turnpike road. Turnpikes had toll houses! She
would listen for the next one. The keeper would surely
hear the commotion she would make. But her captors
had thought of that. As they approached the gate
Serena felt the man in the coach pull her hood over her
face and take her in his arms. The coach stopped. The
driver and the gatekeeper exchanged a few pleasantries
as the toll was paid.

'I shouldn't disturb the gentry inside, if I was you,'
said the coachman. 'They're 'avin' a rare old time in
there.'

Serena heard with despair how the tollkeeper turned
away and went back into the toll house.

The nightmare journey continued, but eventually
they pulled up. From the scents and the absolute quiet
Serena guessed they were deep in the country. Her
captor removed her gag, but not the blindfold. 'You
wish to make a call of nature? The maid will go with

you.' Serena hesitated but her need was urgent. 'Betty! Take Miss Calvert behind the bush. I'll whistle, my dear, so you can hear that I'm keeping my distance.' He roared with laughter, but while Betty led Serena a little way off, he continued to whistle and talk loudly to the other men. Betty whispered hoarsely, 'Make haste! The Captain's a devil when he gets annoyed.'

'What does he want with me?' croaked Serena. Her throat was dry and her head ached abominably.

'Don't ask me! I do know it's not what you might think, though. Are you rich? Does 'e expect to get a ransom?'

Serena shook her head. 'If he does, he's in for a disappointment. Can. . .can you untie the blindfold? If I could only see. . .Betty, won't you help me escape? I have jewellery at home I could let you have. . .'

'It's more than my life's worth, miss! Come on!'

Back at the carriage Serena could hear Betty having an argument with the man she had called the Captain.

'Oh, go on, Captain! Let 'er 'ave a drink. She can 'ardly speak! Jest a little brandy won't do any 'arm! It's not 'uman to leave 'er to die of thirst. I could do wif one meself!'

'All right, all right. Not too much, mind!'

Betty returned. Serena could smell the brandy. The maid said, 'There y'are! One fer me, and one fer you. I've put a drop of water in it, 'cos I expect yer thirsty.' The cup was held to Serena's lips and she drank greedily. She heard the man say,

'Right! Off, my bonny fellows!' The last thing Serena remembered was being bundled into the coach again.

* * *

Serena opened her eyes slowly. The sun was slanting through the window. Was it evening or morning? She yawned. She was so sleepy. . . There was a horrible taste in her mouth, and her head felt thick. She wanted to close her eyes and sleep again but something told her that she must keep awake. Where was she? She tried hard to focus her eyes on the room. It was a bedchamber, but not her own. She looked down. She didn't remember undressing, but she was wearing her night shift. That maid. . .Serena had a dim memory of the maid helping her off with her clothes. Not very expertly. She tried to sit up. Her head! She must ignore it — she must get up. She would get up in a moment. . .

Suddenly the door burst open, and a tall man came in, leaving the door wide behind him. He was half dressed, his shirt undone and hanging outside his breeches. Serena struggled out of bed and tried to run to the door, but she could only manage a few steps before she staggered. There were people outside, staring in, and she opened her mouth, ready to scream to them, for help. But the man was too swift. He held out his arms as if he were expecting her to run into them, and then caught her tight to him, her face hard against his chest. She couldn't say anything, indeed she could hardly breathe.

'There, there, my darling,' he said loudly. 'I was only away a few minutes. See? I'm back already. Oh, Serena, my love! Have you missed me all these months? St Just was never like this, was it? There, there, Serena, be calm now!'

Serena's head was pounding. She tried to pull herself away, but his grip, in sharp contrast to his tender words, was cruelly tight. Her senses were swimming and she

felt herself falling. From a great distance she heard him
say, 'Wait, Serena! I'll carry you back to bed, shall I?'
Then he shouted, 'What are you all staring at, damn
you!'

The door was kicked shut and Serena was thrown on
to the bed and held there, the man on top of her, his
hand over her mouth. She was terrified. The man
grinned, showing white teeth in a swarthy face. His eyes
were black — he looked like the pictures of pirates she
had seen in Jamaica. He whispered, 'I've done you no
harm, and will do none, though the temptation is very
strong, me darlin'. You're a charmin' little bundle, for
all your prim outside! But if you say a word, I swear I'll
lose my control. Understand? There isn't a soul in this
inn that doesn't believe you're willing, so none will
come in unless I invite them. Now, if you wish to come
out of this safely, all you have to do is to drink this drop
of cordial. You'll fall asleep and when you wake I'll be
gone. No, don't shake your head. You're going to drink
it whether you will or no, so better to do it without
getting hurt.'

He stretched out, picked up a small glass, and put it
to her lips. Most was spilled, but some of the bitter
liquid passed through and was swallowed. It was enough
to put her into a half-sleep. Some minutes later she
heard him talking. There was someone else in the room.

'Stop your jangling, woman! None of your friends
suspected, did they? How was I to know she'd come to
as soon as that? However, all's well that ends well. My,
but she's a brave one! It's a shame to do this to her, and
that's a fact!' She heard them go out, and as the door
was shut behind them she sank into unconsciousness.

When she next came to there was a chambermaid in

the room, with a tray. It wasn't the girl from the night
before. Serena's bag was on the chest by the bed, her
clothes neatly folded beside it and on top was a note.
The girl was looking at it. When she saw that Serena
was watching her she blushed in confusion.

'Good morning, ma'am. I brought you breakfast.'

Serena sat up. 'Where am I?' she asked. The
chambermaid burst into a volley of giggles.

'At the Black Lion, ma'am.'

'But where?'

'At Hoddesdon, ma'am. Shall I fetch your shawl?'

Serena looked down. She had been mistaken. The
night shift was not one of hers. It was a diaphanous
affair which revealed more than it concealed. She went
scarlet. 'Please do,' she said curtly. 'Where is. . .'

'He's gone, ma'am. He left quite early. He left you
the note, though.' She giggled again. Serena snatched
up the note.

My love,
You know I have to go, much as I hate to leave
you. I'll arrange another meeting as soon as I can get
away. Last night was even better than on St Just. All
my love — A.

Serena had had enough. She told the chambermaid to
leave her and got out of bed. There was a bowl and a
pitcher of hot water on the washstand. She scrubbed
herself till she felt sore and hastily dried and dressed
herself. The effort exhausted her, and she sat down for
a moment to rest and think. What was she to do? She
must find out what had happened the night before; she
must speak to the landlord. She went in search of him.
He looked at her stolidly as she approached.

'Landlord, did you see me arrive last night?' Serena asked.

'No, ma'am, I think I must have been busy in the bar. Your room was booked a week or two ago, so I didn't bother too much.'

'Who carried the bags up?'

'I don't rightly know. I think you had your own people with you——'

'They were not my people! You must know! You're the landlord!'

'I'm sorry, ma'am. Last night was a busy one. We had a lot o' guests here. I can't remember seeing you arrive.' Serena turned away impatiently. Then she had another thought.

'Where are the ostlers? I'd like to see them, if you please.'

'Certainly, ma'am. Jem'll fetch 'em. Jem!'

But when the ostlers came they could tell her nothing. The coach had arrived, deposited three passengers, and then driven away. The maid had carried two small bags up. The gentleman had carried the lady, who had appeared to be asleep.

'The gentleman told us you were tired after the journey. Very thoughtful, 'e was. Very fond, like.'

'Be silent! He was not fond! I was drugged!'

'Yes, ma'am. As you say, ma'am.'

Their faces looked stupid and wooden. She would get nothing more out of them. Serena felt she would go mad. She returned to her room and sat down to think. There was a wall of silence in the inn concerning her captors of the night before. She was sure someone must know more, but who? And why had someone drugged her and brought her here to this inn, apparently only to put her in a large bedchamber for the night and then leave her? The sound of wheels caused her to run to the window and she saw a post-chaise turning into the yard. Serena watched as its passengers got out and stretched. The temptation to ask them for help was very strong. They were strangers, but surely they would understand? She had to get back to London. But as one of the travellers looked up at her window Serena hastily drew back. Perhaps it might be wise to consider her position. In view of the attitude of the innkeeper and his servants this was equivocal to say the least, and it might be prudent to avoid exposure, at least until she knew more.

There was a knock on the door. The landlord was there.

'Excuse me, ma'am. Were you thinking of travelling today, or do you wish to keep the room for another night? I need to know because of the chaise.'

'The chaise?' asked Serena blankly.

'Yes, ma'am. There's one booked in your name for today — Calvert, that's right, isn't it? For London. At least that's what's paid for.'

'Are you sure?'

The landlord looked as if he thought her weak in the head. Indeed, she almost felt it. He said patiently, 'A well-sprung chaise and four, together with coachman and boys, hired for twenty miles, two guineas. I can show you the bill, if you wish.'

'Yes, I'd like to see that, if you please. Immediately.'

But the bill was unrevealing. It had been paid on the spot by the tall gentleman.

Further questioning of the landlord about the chaise produced nothing more than the conviction that this, at least, was above board. She would be safe to take it.

But she was conscious of a touch of knowingness in the landlord's manner which went ill with his apparent stolidity. She became convinced that he knew more than he was acknowledging, and that he had probably been bribed.

'What is your name, landlord?'

'Samuel, ma'am. Samuel Cartwright.'

'Well, Mr Cartwright, I will take the chaise to London. It is clear I can do nothing more here. But, if you have taken part in this conspiracy, I warn you you may well lose more than you have gained by it.'

The landlord's expression did not change. 'I don't know what you mean, ma'am. I keep a respectable house here,' he said. 'In fact, begging your pardon, I'd rather your friend didn't book any more rooms at the Black Lion.'

Serena turned on her heel, and went out to the stable yard, where the chaise was waiting.

On any other occasion Serena could have enjoyed the journey back to London, for the countryside was pretty, and they passed through some places with famous names. But she pressed on, merely stopping once for a change of horses. The landlord of the Black Lion was a rogue, she was sure, but she dismissed him from her mind. The man behind him was more important. Her head still ached, and the drug had left an unpleasant taste in her mouth, but she ignored both of these and tried to concentrate on what her mysterious enemy was trying to achieve. Why Hoddesdon! Why the Black Lion, a coaching inn, and much in the public eye? If he had intended harm to her person he would have chosen a more out-of-the-way spot. So, if she was right, he had

not intended harm to her person, he had merely
intended her to be noticed. She vaguely remembered
the open door to the bedchamber that morning. There
had been faces in the doorway, she had tried to reach
them. He must have left that door open deliberately!
He had wanted her to be seen, not just in the inn, but in
the bedchamber! With a blush she remembered the
nightgown—there was no doubt about the sort of
rendez-vous that garment was intended for! Serena's
heart sank as she saw the scheme for what it was. It was
no more or less than an effort to discredit her. And
unless she could prove otherwise, that was exactly what
it would do!

She walked in through the door of the Dover Street
house as the clocks were striking five. Mrs Starkey was
waiting for her with a smile, but her expression changed
when she saw Serena's face.

'Mercy me! What has happened, Miss Calvert?
You're ill!'

'No, no. Just a little tired. But I am hungry. Could
you bring some tea and a little bread and butter to the
small parlour, Mrs Starkey. I shall rest there for a while.
And would you tell Sheba I have returned, please.'

She lay on the sofa in the small parlour and when
Sheba brought in the tea she asked her to close the
shutters. Sheba tried to persuade her mistress to go to
bed, but Serena's thoughts were too chaotic for sleep.
And they were leading her to one inevitable conclusion.
As far as she knew, there was only one person in
London who wished her ill. One person who had tried
to bribe her to leave England. One person who had told
her just the day before that he had changed his mind
and had other plans. One person who had taken her off

her guard by his pretended concern for her. She buried
her face in her hands and let the bitter tears flow
unchecked.

But Serena was too much of a fighter to give in to
tears for long. After a while she dried her eyes, and
considered what to do. It all depended on those people
in the door. If they had not recognised her then all
might not be lost, and a great deal was to be gained by
saying nothing. Perhaps her captor had made a mistake
in hiding her face against his chest so closely? She would
wait to see. Lucy was returning tomorrow and they
would be out most of the time. She would not alter her
plans for the moment.

Serena went upstairs and changed her dress. Lady
Pangbourne was giving a dinner party and had asked
Serena to come with an old friend of her husband's.
Serena must be ready for him. Sheba used her skills,
which were now considerable, to disguise the ravages of
the past two days, and when General Fanstock called,
Serena was waiting in the drawing-room as cool, as
composed and as beautiful as ever. They arrived at the
Pangbourne house in Grafton Street at exactly ten
o'clock. They were received graciously by Lady
Pangbourne, and soon found themselves among what
Lucy called 'The Pangbourne set', usually wrinkling her
nose at the same time. It was true that the average age
was high, and the average level of conversation worthy
rather than scintillating, but Serena nevertheless
enjoyed herself. She began to feel safer. Perhaps the
people at the inn had either not recognised her or they
did not belong to the very limited numbers which make
up London society.

Halfway through the meal she found herself the

subject of a penetrating stare from an elderly dowager some way up the table. She asked her partner who it was. 'Hrrmph! Let me have a look. I think. . . Yes it's Valeria Taplow, my dear. Charmin' woman. A bit of a stickler, you know, but none the worse for that, none the worse for that! John, her husband, is a very nice fellow, too. Hrrmph! Great friends of mine.'

Serena was uneasy. That stare had not been one of approval. But the evening passed without incident, unless you would call it an incident that neither of the Taplows had come over to speak to their old friend.

Lucy arrived back the next day, glowing with happiness. She had had a wonderful week, with wonderful weather. The Warnhams and Mrs Galveston were wonderfully kind! Serena smiled in spite of her own worries and waited. Eventually Lucy said hesitantly, 'Sasha?'

'Yes?'

'Sasha, you like Mr Warnham, don't you? Isabella's brother.'

'I think he's charming.'

'If he. . .if he came to see you—to ask you if you would let him pay me his addresses—you wouldn't say no, would you?'

'Well. . .let me see. . .'

'Sasha!'

'Of course I wouldn't, you goose! You mean to tell me that he hasn't already "paid his addresses"—or some of them, anyway?'

Lucy blushed. 'Not exactly. But he wanted to talk to you before we. . .before anything was made public.'

'He's a charming boy, Lucy. You are both fortunate.'

'He's not a boy, you know, Sasha,' said Lucy seriously. 'He's a man — the man for me.'

She was shortly to be proved right.

Lady Pangbourne's dinner party was followed the next evening by a rout party with dancing given by the Countess Carteret. Once again Serena was invited to go with a friend of the family who had been waiting for some time to escort the lovely Miss Calvert. Mr Yardley was a lively bachelor and an excellent dancer, and Serena was looking forward to her evening. She was a little disappointed therefore that Mr Yardley seemed to be somewhat subdued as he ushered Lucy, Serena and Mr Warnham into the large ballroom in Marchant House. Lucy was immediately taken off to dance by Mr Warnham, but Serena's partner seemed strangely reluctant. When Sir Harry Birtles came up Mr Yardley willingly performed the introduction he demanded, and then seemed to slide away.

'I hear you're a great sport, Miss Calvert,' said Sir Harry with an engaging smile.

'I beg your pardon?'

'You know — the inn at Hoddesdon. I was there, too. A great lark, what?'

Serena felt herself growing pale. 'I don't understand you, Sir Harry. What do you mean?'

'Oh, come! I won't tell, you know. Soul of discretion, give you my word.'

Serena walked away without looking at him. She went upstairs under the pretence of repairing her dress and stayed there for as long as she dared. She must not lose her head! After a while she was calmer and came down again. Lucy and Mr Warnham came over from the other side of the ballroom to join her. Lucy's face was stormy. Before they arrived, however, a man, a perfect stranger, came up behind Sasha and put his arm round her waist. She turned swiftly and took a step away from him. He smiled cynically and moved on, but his friend, who seemed to have drunk more than was good for him, lingered.

'Serena!' he whispered. 'What a lovely. . .lovely name. Beautiful Serena! I could adore you.'

'Sir!' said Serena. But she did not have to say more. Michael Warnham interposed himself in front of Serena and said coldly, 'I think your friends are waiting for you in the card room, Dauncy. Miss Calvert is just leaving.'

'Come, Sasha,' whispered Lucy. 'Come quickly!' Considerably shaken, Serena allowed herself to be taken away, Mr Warnham in close attendance on them both.

The short journey back to Dover Street was accomplished almost in silence. Lucy began to speak as soon as they left Marchant House, but Mr Warnham put his hand firmly over hers and said,

'Not yet, Lucy!'

'But —' She subsided when he shook his head at her.

Serena was shivering. The plot appeared to have succeeded all too well if the reaction of Mr Dauncy and his friend was anything to go by. Now she was forced to face the problem of what to do about it. They reached the sanctuary of Dover Street, where Mr Warnham suggested that they went into the small parlour. Here he said gently, 'Now Lucy. Now you may talk.'

'I know what you are going to say, Lucy,' said Serena wearily. 'Let me spare you what must seem an unpleasant task. London is buzzing with the story that Serena Calvert is having a secret affair. That she was seen in an inn outside London, having apparently spent the night with her lover.'

Mr Warnham made an involuntary movement towards Lucy, and Serena turned to him.

'Lucy and I have no secrets, and have never minced our words in speaking to each other, Mr Warnham. However, if I *were* guilty of the behaviour I have just described, you may be assured that I would protect my niece from any knowledge of it.'

Young Mr Warnham relaxed. 'I knew there must be something wrong with the story. It isn't true.'

'There, I'm afraid, you are taking too simple a view. It isn't true, and yet it is.' Lucy jumped up and ran over to kneel by Serena.

'Sasha! Oh, Sasha, don't speak in riddles like this, I can't bear it! I know you cannot have done anything wrong; why can't we just deny the story, threaten to go to the law. How can they say such things of you?' Serena gently drew Lucy to the seat beside her.

'Because people who don't know me as you do, Lucy, would find it difficult, if not impossible, to believe that I am the victim of a very carefully laid plot.'

'A plot!'

'Yes, Mr Warnham.' Serena went on to give the two young people most of the details of what had happened the day before and at Hoddesdon that morning. She finished up by saying, 'The conspirators were particularly clever in that they saw to it that the story would not only be spread—but believed, as well. I know now for certain that Sir Harry Birtles saw me there, and, unless

I am mistaken, we will find that Sir John and Lady
Taplow were also present at the inn, and also saw me.'

Lucy flung her arms round Serena as if to shut out the
dreadful picture her aunt had conjured up. But Mr
Warnham was silent. Serena said sadly, 'It is an extraordinary tale, Mr Warnham, I agree. Hardly credible,
indeed.'

At that he came over to sit on her other side.

'Miss Calvert, if I did not speak straight away, it was
not, believe me, not in the slightest degree because I did
not believe your account of what actually happened. I
have known you for some time now, and Lucy has told
me a great deal about you. To me, what you have told
us is completely credible. No, I was thinking rather how
one might best challenge the version going round
London. Because you must! Your own good name, and
Lucy's as well, are at stake.'

Serena turned swiftly to Lucy. 'Has anyone spoken to
you. . .?'

Mr Warnham said grimly, 'No gentleman has
approached Lucy, no. They would hardly dare while I
am there to protect her. But. . .' He seemed
embarrassed.

Lucy finished for him. 'The ladies are not always very
kind, Sasha. I do not mean Lady Warnham—she is
upset, of course, but she has been very sympathetic.
She has suggested, however, that we—Michael and I—
do not for the moment publish our engagement.' She
looked defiantly at Mr Warnham. 'And I agreed with
her.'

Serena looked towards the young man.

'I would publish it tomorrow, Miss Calvert, and so I
told my mother,' said Michael Warnham. 'But Lucy is

adamant. And perhaps she is right. It is better to postpone our own celebration until you are cleared, then we shall all rejoice together.' He got up, went to Lucy's side, and took her hands in his. 'You must not think that putting off the announcement of our engagement alters my determination to marry Lucy.' The two smiled at each other. Then he turned back to Serena. 'But, more immediately, I should like to help you in any way I can. Do you wish me to challenge Dauncy?'

'For heaven's sake, no!' cried Serena. 'You would soon find yourself challenging half the men in London! No, we must look for evidence to convince London society that it is wrong!'

'What about Sir Harry Birtles!' cried Lucy. 'Was he alone at the inn?'

'Most unlikely, I'd say.' Mr Warnham seemed to recollect himself. He turned to Lucy and suggested that she might like to leave her aunt and himself to discuss the matter. 'I dare say you will accuse me of being stuffy, Lucy, but you really shouldn't be involved in discussing Lord Harry's behaviour and similar matters. You can support your aunt in other ways.' Lucy looked mutinous, but he said firmly, 'I am not discussing this unsavoury business in your presence, Lucy.'

'Well, I shall go, but do not imagine I shall stop thinking about it. I wonder who Sir Harry was with?' With that she went, after hugging her aunt and giving Mr Warnham a slightly cool curtsy. Serena smiled.

'I see I have no need to worry about Lucy's future happiness, Mr Warnham. You will manage her very well. I cannot say how happy I am that you wish to marry.'

'Lucy is a darling,' he said simply. 'I think I am very

fortunate. But this is not solving your problem. You know, Lucy's question was an acute one. Your conspirators had to ensure that the necessary witnesses were there at the right place, and at the right time. The Taplows frequently travel to Huntingdon. It would be easy to find out when they would next be staying at the Black Lion. But Sir Harry. . . Who was Sir Harry's companion? You didn't see her, I suppose?' Serena shook her head. 'Would you like me to try to find out?'

'Can you do so?'

'Easily, I should imagine. Sir Harry is not noted for his discretion.'

'I would certainly like to know. And I think I will see Mr Rambridge—my lawyer. He is dealing with another matter for me, and may have some suggestions to make about this one. But now, Michael—you see, I regard you as one of the family—I would like to ask you to do something more for me.'

'Anything!'

'I wish you to make sure that Lucy and yourself are not seen in public with me for the moment.'

'Miss Calvert!'

'Lucy calls me Sasha. Could you? In private, of course.'

'I am honoured. Thank you. . .Sasha. But Lucy would never agree to desert you—nor would I.'

'I know that you wish to show society your regard and support, and I am touched. But it is better for Lucy's sake that she should be kept away from this scandal as much as possible—at least for the next day or two until I find out what I have to do. Will you do this? From what I have seen you are the person to persuade her.'

'Very well. But you must let me know if there is anything else I can do.'

'I will.' In spite of her weariness Serena smiled. 'I feel we have a man in the family again, Michael. It is very comforting.'

Mr Warnham left, wishing he had a white charger or an army or two to defend Miss Calvert. Keeping Lucy safe seemed a small thing compared with all Sasha's other problems.

What he did not realise was that Serena was at least as anxious to keep Michael himself out of danger. In his eagerness to defend her honour he might well find himself picking quarrels with gentlemen more experienced than he in the art of the duel. And it was for this same reason that she had not mentioned her suspicions of Lord Wintersett.

But she had not forgotten them either. Thus it was that the next morning found her demanding to see Lord Wintersett at his residence in Upper Brook Street. Percy was alone in the entrance hall at the time, and found it difficult to deal with this totally unorthodox occurrence. He was only saved by Lord Wintersett himself, who came out of the library and invited Miss Calvert to enter.

'How can I help you, Miss Calvert?' he asked when the door shut behind Percy.

'You know how you can help me! Withdraw this rumour about me that you have set round London!'

'I have heard the rumour, of course. I have had no part in spreading it.'

'You are too clever, and too cowardly for that,' said Serena, her lip curling in scorn. 'You, Lord Wintersett,

stay in the background, merely pulling the strings for
your puppets to hang me!'

Lord Wintersett looked down at the snuff box he was
holding. His hand tightened, then relaxed. When he
looked up again his voice was arctic. 'If a man had said
that to me, Miss Calvert, I would have knocked his
teeth down his throat — as an alternative to killing him.'

'I have no one to defend me, Lord Wintersett. It is
easy for you to be brave with your threats.'

'What about your mysterious lover? Is he not a man?'

Serena looked at him with loathing. 'How can a
creature such as you live with himself?' she asked, her
voice quivering with feeling. 'You have ruined me,
Lord Wintersett, and yet you still taunt me with the
creatures of your own invention. You know I have no
lover!'

'Is there no foundation for this rumour, then? You
were not at. . .Hoddesdon, was it? You were not seen
by the Taplows?'

'Why are you fencing like this with me? There is no
one else here; why cannot you be open?'

'Tell me what you think I did.'

'I will not waste my breath on such an exercise. But I
warn you, I intend to expose you, if it kills me! You may
have bribed that landlord with all the wealth in
England, but one way or another I shall rip your
conspiracy wide open!' She went to the door.

'Serena!' He strode over to the door and put his hand
on her shoulder. She wrenched herself free.

'Don't touch me!'

'Serena, what are you going to do?'

'Expose you for the villain you are!'

'And meanwhile?'

'Meanwhile I shall outface the scandalmongers and the gossips. I shall carry on as if they did not exist. I will not give in to your blackmail!'

'Serena, society can be cruel; it isn't wise ——'

'You may save your efforts to dissuade me, Lord Wintersett. I will not let you win.'

'Serena, what if I tell you that I had no part in any plot against you?' he asked rapidly.

'Who else wants me out of London?' Serena asked contemptuously. 'Who withdrew the offer of Anse Chatelet and told me that he had "other plans"?'

'But I only meant that I was going to St Just myself! I am leaving in two days' time.'

Serena whirled round. 'To St Just? You have wasted little time in your anxiety to review your new possession! I am sorry for the snakes on the island, for no viper, no fer-de-lance could rival your poison. Take care you don't bite one!' With that she pulled open the door and ran out.

CHAPTER ELEVEN

IT TOOK Serena some time to calm down, but then she went to see Mr Rambridge. He was not sanguine about the outcome of any action on the Anse Chatelet case, but promised to continue. When he heard the story of her abduction he was horrified. 'Why, Miss Calvert, I have known only one other case like it. What do you wish me to do? As you say, it would be impossible to scotch the rumours without first finding the villian behind the plot. Who wishes you so much ill?'

When Serena tentatively voiced her suspicions concerning Lord Wintersett Mr Rambridge was dismissive. 'All things are possible, I suppose, and a lawyer hears more than most. But that Lord Wintersett should stoop to such dealings I find it impossible to believe!'

'But I know of no one else who bears me any kind of grudge!' cried Serena. 'Mr Rambridge, I should like to hire a trustworthy fellow to investigate the inn for me. I found it impossible to get any information at all from the landlord and his tribe. Perhaps a trained investigator, and a man, might be more successful. Do you know of such a person?'

Mr Rambridge said he did, and if Miss Calvert wished he could present Mr Barnet to her in a very few minutes. 'He is just writing up the details of another case in the office next door. Can you wait? May I offer you a glass of Madeira or some other refreshment?' Within a short time Serena had engaged Mr Barnet,

given the particulars of the inn and everything she could
remember which might be of use, rejected with scorn
his suggestion that the Ambournes might have had
anything whatsoever to do with it, and had taken her
leave of both men. Mr Rambridge's last words were, 'I
am glad you did not tell Barnet of your suspicions of
your noble friend, Miss Calvert! I do not acquit the
gentleman of ruining a lady's reputation. But that he
should resort to such villainy to do so is quite out of the
question.'

That evening Serena went to a concert in
Northumberland House. She had taken a long time
deciding what to wear. The temptation to put on a
poppy-coloured India muslin dress was strong. Equally
strong was the desire to wear stark white or discreet
black. Each would make a statement to the world — but
all had their obvious disadvantages. In the end she wore
her topaz silk dress. Sheba brushed Serena's hair until it
gleamed like silk, then twisted it into a knot high on her
head. Aunt Spurston's diamonds glittered at her ears,
throat and wrists, and the amber-coloured silk of the
dress reflected the tiger gleam of her eyes. Lucy was
spending the evening at Lady Warnham's, so she was
not there to give her verdict on Serena's appearance. It
was as well. She would not have recognised her loving,
impulsive aunt in this creature of shining gold and ice.

Serena entered the great doors of Northumberland
House five minutes before the concert began and
started to walk up the wide staircase. Groups of people
were standing on the stairs chatting and viewing each
new arrival. As Serena passed silence fell on each
group, and though the gentlemen eyed her, the ladies

studiously avoided meeting her eye. Serena appeared not to notice. Her head held high, one hand holding the hem of her dress up, she mounted the stairs without haste, and without pause. The man standing at the top of the stairs looked down and thought he had never seen anything so graceful or so courageous.

'Cool customer, ain't she, Wintersett? Magnificent creature, though,' said a young buck standing nearby, eyeing Serena through his glass. Lord Wintersett gave him such a glacial stare that he vanished, and avoided the noble peer's company for the rest of the evening. As he remarked to one of his cronies, there was no sense in looking for trouble.

Serena reached the music room at last and took a seat near the front. She was studying her programme, so did not apparently notice that several ladies sitting near her got up and moved to a different part of the room. But a faint flush appeared on her pale cheeks. The silence that followed was broken by the rustle of silk and the voice of Lady Ambourne floating through the door.

'Serena, how pleasant to see you again! May I?' With a charming smile the Dowager Countess of Ambourne sat down next to Serena and proceeded to make light conversation until the music began.

In the interval it was even worse. The two ladies made their way to the supper-room, but, though the room was crowded, a space appeared round them wherever they stopped. There were smiles and greetings for Lady Ambourne, but no one offered to join them or to fetch anything for them. Lord Wintersett, watching from the other side, muttered a curse, and pushed his way through the crowd. 'Your servant, Lady

Ambourne, Miss Calvert? May I get you some refreshment?' he asked with a low bow.

The Countess expressed her gratitude, adding, 'Is it not astonishing, Lord Wintersett, how very many underbred people come to these concerts nowadays? One might have thought that a love of music would encourage courtesy, but the opposite appears to be the case.' The Countess's voice was soft but penetrating. A number of faces round them grew slightly pink, and one or two people actually came up to join her. For a while Lady Ambourne and Serena were surrounded. When Lord Wintersett returned, carrying some glasses and a plate of delicacies, he had difficulty in reaching the Countess. Serena had somehow been edged to the outside of the group. But when Lord Wintersett presented her with a glass of champagne Serena looked at him expressionlessly, and emptied the glass into a potted palm next to her. Then she turned and left the room.

Lady Ambourne was drinking her chocolate in the garden room the next morning when Purkiss came in to ask if she would receive Lord Wintersett. The Countess was surprised. Only the most urgent business could excuse a call so early in the day. She told Purkiss to show Lord Wintersett in and to bring some more chocolate. Lord Wintersett, when he came, was dressed in riding clothes.

'Lady Ambourne, this is good of you. I apologise for disturbing you at this early hour.'

'Sit down, James, and share my chocolate.'

Since Lord Wintersett's good manners forbade him to say that he disliked chocolate intensely, it was as well that Purkiss brought him some ale — 'As it's so warm, today, my lord.'

'Now, James, what is so important that you have to see me at this hour? I should think it is something to do with Miss Calvert?'

'Yes. She needs help.'

'Why are you concerned, James? I thought that you disliked her. Why do you want to help her now?'

'I don't know! That's the devil of it. Forgive me, Lady Ambourne, I shouldn't have said that.' He got up and went to the window. His back was towards her and his voice muffled as he said, 'I seem to be doing everything wrong! The trouble is that I don't know what to think or what to believe.'

The Countess looked at him with surprise. What had happened to self-sufficient, self-possessed Frosty Jack? She said thoughtfully, 'But you wish to help Serena all the same. Why do you not speak to Serena herself?'

'I. . . I cannot. She would accept nothing from me — not even a glass of champagne! Certainly not any kind of advice.' He came back and sat down. 'I'm doing what I can. In a few minutes I shall set off for Hoddesdon, to do a little investigating. My time is limited, however. I leave for Falmouth and the West Indies tomorrow night.'

The Countess's eyes widened. 'You're going to St Just?' James nodded. 'Then we must not lose any time. How do you wish me to help Miss Calvert? I would have done so in any case, you know.'

James came to sit opposite her, leaning forward in his chair. 'She's so obstinate, so fixed in her determination to defy society, and she will be badly hurt if she continues. You saw what happened last night.' He paused and looked down at his hands. 'She would not listen to anything I might say. Could you use your influence to persuade her to live quietly until this business is cleared up one way or the other?'

'I have already resolved on that. Indeed, I have been laying plans this very morning. But James, am I to understand that you believe her to be innocent?'

'Yes, I do! That is ——'

'Is that your heart or your head speaking?'

'It certainly isn't my head. The evidence is almost overwhelming.'

'Good! Then it is your heart. Trust it. Are you in love with her?'

'At one time I thought I was,' James said sombrely.

'In Surrey?'

'She has told you about the time in Surrey?' The Countess nodded. 'I didn't know who she was, of course. Then when we came to London I found out she was a Calvert. Sasha Calvert. Since then my life has been in turmoil.'

'Why?'

'Tony died on St Just. What the world suspects, but does not know for certain, is that he killed himself. For years I. . .we have blamed Sasha Calvert for driving my brother into taking his own life.'

'What rubbish! She was only fourteen years old at the time!'

'I know that now. I had always believed her to be much older. But Alanna said. . . No, I will not repeat it.'

'Do you really believe that Serena was responsible for Tony's death, James? Knowing her, as you knew her in

Surrey? Having observed her behaviour since she has been in London? Is there no alternative?'

There was a silence. Then James got up and said, 'That is what I am going to the West Indies to find out. It's what I should have done years ago.' He gave a wry smile. 'Serena believes I am going there to gloat over my new acquisition.'

'Have you tried to explain?'

'She would not listen. She dislikes me too much. I think I must go, Lady Ambourne. I have much to do before tomorrow night.' He said with feeling, 'I wish I did not have to leave England at this moment! Serena needs someone to help her! But I must; my journey to St Just cannot be delayed. I will be easier in my mind if I know she has someone she can rely on. I thought of writing to Ned, but I know he is anxious about Perdita. Oh, forgive me again — I am so wrapped up in my own concerns that I forget my manners! How is Perdita?'

'We have been quite worried about her, but things are better now. I think I can call on Edward if I need him, James. Meanwhile I wish you *bonne chance* and *bon voyage*. I will watch Serena's interests, never fear.'

'You believe in her, don't you, Lady Ambourne?'

'I have never doubted her for a minute.'

At Hoddesdon James soon got the landlord's measure, and with a judicious mixture of threats and promises of remuneration even persuaded him to talk of the night in question. Mr Cartwright had, it appeared, been asked — against suitable payment, of course — to provide a particular room at the head of the first flight of stairs. 'Best room in the house, that is.' He had agreed to be blind when a certain chaise drove up, to allow the passengers to see themselves to the room, to keep his mouth shut if the lady asked any questions in the morning, and to provide a chaise for her return to London. Everything had been paid for with shining, golden guineas by a man called the Captain. In answer to further questions he said that Sir Harry Birtles had stayed at the Black Lion more than once, always with the same lady, but he didn't know the lady's name. He thought it might be Aurelia, or Amelia — something like that. The Taplows — ah, they were a different sort, they were. Real aristocrats. They stayed regular as clockwork every six weeks when they visited their daughter in Huntingdon. Everyone knew that.

'Who arranged the matter of the rooms and so on?'

'The Captain. He came once beforehand to book the room and have a chat, like.' To discuss terms, thought James.

'Did he ask about Sir Harry and the rest? Or any other guests? To find out when they would be staying here?'

'I don't remember that he did. Not then. And apart from the night he came with the lady that's the only time I've seen him, before or since.' The landlord hesitated. 'One o' the maids — she got the impression the Captain knew Sir Harry's lady. But that don't mean nothing. Sir Harry's lady is the sort who'd know a lot o' gentlemen, if you know what I mean, sir.'

He gave James a vague description of the Captain and Sir Harry's lady-friend, but more he would not, or could not, say. James rather thought it was the latter. He paid Mr Cartwright what he had promised and asked to see the girl. Apart from giggles all he could elicit from her was that Sir Harry had called the lady 'Amelia'

and that the 'Captain' had winked at Amelia in the
corridor, and then said something to her. She too gave
some sort of description of Amelia and the Captain.
James was about to leave when she sidled up to him and
whispered that she had something to sell him. She
showed him a much handled scrap of paper.

'It were in the bedroom, sir. The one at the top o' the
stairs. The lady left it behind. It were all she left, too,'
she added resentfully. 'That and a funny little glass with
nothin' in it. I threw it away.'

With growing distaste James read the note which
Serena had found by the bed when she had woken up
that morning.

> My love,
> You know I have to go, much as I hate to leave
> you. I'll arrange another meeting as soon as I can get
> away. Last night was even better than on St Just. All
> my love — A.

As he rode back to London James was debating
whether the note could be genuine. Who could tell? It
was all so uncertain! Some of what the landlord had told
him could support Serena's story. On the other hand,
much of it could be explained by the very natural desire
of a couple sharing an illicit bed to keep themselves
anonymous. But — this was perhaps the biggest point in
her favour — Serena hadn't been kept anonymous. The
presence of Harry Birtles at the inn had made it certain
that the whole of London now knew of her 'affair'.
Harry. . . Harry had been with Amelia Banagher, he
was sure. It might be worth finding out which of them
had set up that assignation. He would call on Amelia
when he got back to town. He went over the note again.

Who was 'A'? If it wasn't genuine it was quite cleverly phrased. Not too much — merely the suggestion that Serena had known the writer on St Just. Well, he would be there in a few short weeks and would learn a lot more about Sasha Calvert and her family.

Amelia Banagher was resting in her boudoir, a pretty little room of satin, lace and roses, when James came in. She received him with little cries of joy, and fussed over him for several minutes. But she had a fright when he said he had been to Hoddesdon that morning.

'I believe you spent the night there recently. With Harry Birtles.'

She started to be coy, but he cut through her protestations and said directly, 'Amelia, you and I have usually managed to be open with each other. I will pay your outstanding bills if you will tell me how it happened that you and Harry were at the Black Lion on that particular night.'

'I'm not sure why you wish to know, James. And at the moment I have no outstanding bills!'

His eyes narrowed. 'Now that I find most interesting. Indeed, it is quite extraordinary. No outstanding bills, eh? I think no further proof is needed, Amelia. Who bribed you?'

She was really frightened. Wintersett was not a man to play with. But nor was Fergus O'Keefe, and it wouldn't surprise her if what she and Fergus had done to Serena Calvert was criminal. Amelia decided to risk losing any influence she had ever had with Lord Wintersett in the interest of saving her skin.

'James, I have to confess I was angry with you for the way you and that woman treated me about the necklace,' she said, improvising rapidly. 'I wanted to pay you both back. I could see you were interested in her, and. . .and I wanted you to see how she was deceiving you.' Amelia got up and fetched a handkerchief. 'Would you like some wine, James? I'll send for some, shall I?'

'Thank you, but no, Amelia. Please continue with your story.'

'Well. . . I decided to arrange that Harry should witness her meeting with her gentleman friend at the Black Lion. Nothing more. I knew Harry would spread it round. He's from the West Indies, isn't he? Her friend, I mean.'

'You knew him?'

'Oh, no!'

'He appeared to know you. One of the maids saw you both.'

Amelia felt her cheeks grow pale again. Then she pulled herself together and murmured, 'A lot of gentlemen would like to know me, James. Many even exchange a word or two with me. It doesn't mean I know them.'

Amelia could see that James was not entirely convinced, but she was confident that her story would be difficult to disprove. Then he asked, 'What was he like — this gentleman from the West Indies?'

What should she say? If she described Fergus too well, James might track him down. 'I didn't notice him particularly. Fair, I think. Not too tall.'

After a while James left, and Amelia sank back with a sigh of relief.

* * *

The next day James returned to Rotherfield House. The Countess was surprised but pleased to see him again. Once more he found her in the garden room, with a letter in her hand.

'Come in, James. Come in and sit down. I've had some pleasing news of Perdita. Edward says she is much better. Quite her old self again.'

James expressed pleasure and the Countess sent for some wine. Then she sat back in her chair and said, 'But now you shall tell me what you are here for. I thought we had said our farewells? Have you been to Hoddesdon? What did you find?'

James related to the Countess the result of his visit to Hoddesdon, and his interview with Lady Banagher. She grew grave immediately.

'A devilish conspiracy — I am not using the word lightly, either.'

'I think Amelia Banagher was lying. Her description of the man does not match what the people at the inn told me in any respect — they said he was tall and very dark. I am sure she knows him. Before I leave London I must engage a reliable man to investigate further.'

'James, Rambridge was here today to enquire after Perdita. He said that Serena had already engaged someone — a very good man, he said. Would you like me to pass your information to him?'

This was quickly decided on, and James promised to let Lady Ambourne have what he had learned in writing. 'But that is not really why I came, Lady Ambourne. It occurred to me after I left you yesterday that the Warnhams might well be reconsidering their approval of the match between their son and Miss Lucy Calvert. That would be most unfortunate.'

The Countess looked at him pityingly. 'And you think I have not thought of that? James, let me set your mind at rest by telling you what I plan to do. I shall persuade Serena, if I can, that she should retire to the country for a while — until we have time to establish the truth. I shall also suggest that I move into the house in Dover Street — everyone knows that I detest this place when I am alone — and that I sponsor Miss Lucy myself. I think the standing of the Dowager Countess of Ambourne is enough to silence any possible criticism of Lucy Calvert, do you not agree?'

James smiled for the first time. 'Lady Ambourne, you are, as always, completely right!'

James had one last interview before he left. It was with Serena, and was not planned. But he was irresistibly drawn to Dover Street on his way to the Gloucester coffee house, where he would pick up the coach for Falmouth. She would not receive him at first, but he eventually persuaded John to admit him. She was alone except for a large negress.

'Shall I stay, Mis' Sasha?'

'No, it's all right, Sheba. Lord Wintersett will not be here long.' The woman left, giving him a baleful stare as she went.

'I'm leaving tonight, Serena. Have you. . .have you any messages for the Pendomers?'

She smiled bitterly. 'What could I possibly tell them? That I no longer own Anse Chatelet? That I am disgraced and shunned by most of London society? That Lucy's marriage is no longer so certain?'

'No. Though I think Miss Lucy's happiness is not in danger. But I understand. Then I will bid you goodbye.'

'You could not bid me anything more welcome! Goodbye, Lord Wintersett. Enjoy your stay at Anse Chatelet. I hope you are prepared to explain to our — I beg your pardon, *your* people, why the Calverts have finally abandoned them.'

'Serena, what will I find when I get there? Was Tony's death an accident, after all? Is there another explanation?'

There was silence while a variety of expressions passed over her mobile features. A flash of temper, a desire to speak, hesitation, doubt and finally sadness. 'I cannot tell you,' was all she said. 'You must judge for yourself.' But her voice was gentle.

He moved closer. 'Will you be here when I return?'

'I don't know. I hope to see Lucy married but I am not sure when that will be at the moment. After that. . . I don't know.'

He drew her to him. She looked at him with troubled eyes, but made no effort to resist when he kissed her, a long, sweet kiss. The kiss grew deeper, more passionate until they were closely twined in each other's arms, murmuring to each other and kissing again and again. Serena broke free, but he pulled her back to him, holding her tight, pressing her head to his chest. He said into her hair, 'This business at Hoddesdon — do you really think me so despicable? That I would go to such lengths to ruin you, Serena? After the time on the hill in Surrey — William, Trask and Douce, and all those hours when we seemed to share so much?'

'I don't know!' she cried, pulling away from him again. 'I'm so confused. I've been told you were there at the inn yesterday, giving money to the landlord. But when you hold me as you did I cannot remember that.

One minute I think you're a devil, a monster, and the next you hold me in your arms and I cannot imagine wishing to be anywhere else! If you think we shared so much why did you treat me so badly? Oh, go to St Just and leave me alone, Lord W. . . Wintersett!'

'I thought you had mastered that stammer, Serena.'

'It is a weakness I despise, I assure you! It appeared after that first night in London. When you turned into someone I no longer knew. . . For a while I couldn't even say your name at all.'

'Then don't say it! Say James, instead! After all, I call you Serena — in private.'

'Serena and James — no, Lord W. . .my lord.'

'Never?'

'Perhaps. After your visit to St Just you may not wish to see me ever again.'

His face clouded. 'Will I hear of the Captain there? The man whose name begins with "A"?'

She looked blank. 'What are you talking about?' In silence James handed her the note he had bought from the maid. She glanced at it, then with a look of revulsion she threw it from her. She said in a strangled voice, 'For a moment I thought I had misjudged you, Lord W. . . Wintersett. I was even dolt enough to feel sorrow on your behalf! How glad I am that you have reminded me before you go of your true nature.' Serena's voice grew clearer. She said contemptuously, 'Did you enjoy kissing me so tenderly, arousing feelings I thought I had forgotten, while you knew all the while that this. . .this piece of filth was in your pocket, waiting to be produced? I acquit you of plotting to ruin me, Lord W. . . W. . . The devil take it! I will say it! Lord Wintersett! You were purchasing this note from the landlord in order to accuse me, not paying your bribe. But you are despicable, all the same. I have had enough of your tricks and postures. I never, never wish to see you again! And I wish you joy of your discoveries on St Just!'

She stormed out of the room, calling to John to see to Lord Wintersett.

The next day Serena and Lucy were sitting in the drawing-room of the house in Dover Street. It was a large, airy room furnished in shades of pale yellow and white, and the two ladies in their delicate muslins completed a very pretty picture. But it was evident that all was not well with them, for they were both pale and heavy-eyed. Serena had not slept at all. She had found it impossible to dismiss from her mind the vision of James Stannard travelling south-west to Falmouth. There was a long, tedious voyage ahead of him, and though he would find Anse Chatelet a worthy prize there would be little joy in it for him.

She had been haunted, too, by the events of the previous evening and the curious effect James Stannard had on her. She had told him that she never wanted to see him again, and she still meant it, yet the thought filled her with passionate regret. With a wry smile she recalled her conversation with Lady Pendomer before she had set out for England all those months ago.

'I wouldn't give up control of Anse Chatelet,' she had said. 'Not after all these years, unless I could find a husband I could trust to manage it better than I can myself. . .'

In Surrey, she had thought she had found such a man in Lord Wintersett, and the prospect had filled her with

incredulous and humble delight. It was bitterly ironical
that he should now be the man who had taken Anse
Chatelet from her.

He would return, knowing how unjust he had been
all these years. But it was too late. For all the feeling he
had aroused in her the night before, it was too late. In
London Lord Wintersett had been the cold-hearted
manipulator everyone had talked of. The man on the
hill had gone forever.

With a sigh Serena dismissed Lord Wintersett from
her thoughts and turned them instead to Lucy. She was
worried about the girl. It was so rare for her niece to be
listless and silent — and these should be the happiest
days of Lucy's life! But the shadow of society's reaction
to her aunt was casting a shade over Lucy, too. Michael
had been a constant caller, and the house was filled with
his flowers, but even he had failed to lift Lucy's spirits.
It was a relief when Lady Ambourne was announced
and Serena got up to meet her, smiling in genuine
welcome.

'Serena! How do you go on, my dear? And Lucy,
too? I have come with all sorts of good news, a basket
of fruit and fresh vegetables from Ambourne, and a
suggestion.'

Serena sent for tea and they were soon comfortably
settled.

'First, the good news. You must have seen how
preoccupied I have been recently — so much that I fear I
have neglected you. But, after worrying us all for a
while, Perdita is now quite fit again. I had thought I
should go down to Ambourne to be with her, but
that is no longer necessary. I will remain in London a
little longer.'

The two Calvert ladies both expressed their pleasure at this. The Countess continued, 'The fruit and vegetables I have given to John to take to Mrs Starkey. . .'

'And the suggestion?' smiled Serena.

'Ah, if I may, I should like first to discuss the suggestion with you alone, Serena. Perhaps Lucy could leave us for a while?' As Lucy jumped up to go Lady Ambourne said, 'Don't go far away, child. This concerns you, too.'

When Lucy had gone the Countess explained her plan to Serena. 'What do you think, Serena? Perdita would be pleased to welcome you to Ambourne.'

Serena hesitated. 'Thank you, Lady Ambourne, but I do not wish to give society the impression that I concede defeat. I have done nothing to earn their censure. And I have hopes that Mr Barnet will come up with something soon. . .'

'And if he does not? Oh, I know that James gave him a great deal more to work with——'

'Lord W. . . Wintersett?'

'Did he not tell you?' asked the Countess, opening her eyes wide in the full knowledge that James would certainly not have told Serena anything. 'He learned quite a lot in Hoddesdon. He is almost certain that the woman with Sir Harry was that wretch Amelia Banagher. Mr Barnet now has her under surveillance. He is hoping that she will lead him to this Captain fellow.'

'I see. . .'

'Do you, Serena? Do you really see?'

'What do you mean?'

'Why should James go to all this trouble to help you?

Going to Hoddesdon, undertaking this long journey to
St Just——'

'Oh, no! He's going to St Just to look at his property.'

'Did he say so? I think you are wrong. I think he is
going to find out what really happened on the island
thirteen years ago. It will be a sad day for him when he
does. Incidentally, why have you never told him about
Richard and Alanna?'

'I wanted to last night when he came to see me, but it
was for all the wrong reasons, Lady Ambourne. I was
so angry with him that I wanted to hurt him, to tell him
that his brother had died because of Alanna and
Richard, not me. He might have refused to believe me,
of course. He has refused to trust me so often before.
But then I realised I couldn't. However heartlessly he
has behaved towards me, I could not tell him this in
anger, hoping to hurt him. Perhaps if things had been
different. . .if we had still trusted one another, if I could
have told him. . .in confidence and. . .love, I might
have. But, feeling as I did about Anse Chatelet and his
efforts to discredit me, how could I just blurt out to him
that his brother had been betrayed by his wife, that his
nephew, his heir, the only link with Tony left to him was
perhaps not a Stannard at all, but part of the hated
Calvert clan?'

'Many would have. As you said, to hurt him.'

'I could not.'

'And I will tell you why, Serena. I think you love him.
As he loves you.'

'Lord Wintersett is not capable of the sort of love I
am seeking, Lady Ambourne. And if he did once love
me, in his fashion, then he will be cured of it by the time

he gets back. I told him I never wanted to see him again.'

The Countess smiled and said briskly, 'I think you are mistaken on both counts, Serena. But it is useless to talk about James for the moment. He must speak for himself when he returns. Now, about my plan. . .'

In the end Serena capitulated. 'But you would be doing so much for us, Lady Ambourne. I hardly know. . .'

The Countess leaned forward. 'The favour is not at all one-sided, believe me. Now that Edward and Perdita are settled I sometimes feel a little lonely — certainly in Rotherfield House! And I myself want to remain in London for the moment. Tell me, is Lucy in love with Michael Warnham? Does she wish to marry him?'

'Oh, yes! But —'

'But the Warnhams are worried, are they not? They are good, kindly people, but they have always been a touch over-conventional. You must let me help. Lucy deserves to be happy. She is a very pretty, well-behaved girl, and I guarantee that the Warnhams will accept her again once the world sees that she is sponsored by the Dowager Countess of Ambourne! Society will soon forget the scandal about Miss Calvert if Miss Calvert is not there to remind them of it. You may trust me, Serena. I know my world. And then, when the mystery is cleared up and your enemies are unmasked — as they certainly will be — you may return in triumph.'

After very little further persuasion Serena agreed to call Lucy in to see what she thought. She was afraid that Lucy might reject the offer out of hand, but she had underestimated the Countess. Within minutes all was settled, the only change in the plan being that Serena

would not go to Ambourne, but back to Lady Spurston.
She told the Countess and Lucy that she would not
think of imposing on Perdita at this time, and there
was enough sense in what she said for them to accept
this. What she did not tell them was that, once with
Lady Spurston, she fully intended to find her way
to Wintersett Court. She had to see young Tony
Stannard for herself! Almost the last thing Serena did in
London was to arm herself with a map of Surrey from
Hatchard's bookshop in Piccadilly.

The parting with Lucy was not easy, but both the
Countess and Sheba assured Serena that her niece
would be well cared for. Michael was also there to
support Lucy, and Serena had every hope that their
story would have a happy end. The Countess embraced
her warmly and extracted from her a promise that she
would visit Ambourne before long. Otherwise Serena
left London without regret. Her hopes had been so
high, the reality so painful. Lord Wintersett was now on
the high seas, and she might never see him again.
Perhaps it was as well.

CHAPTER TWELVE

SERENA gave Lady Spurston a limited account of her disastrous adventure, but it was enough to rouse all that lady's sympathy, especially when she heard that the Ambournes were championing her. She agreed that Serena's decision to retire to Surrey for a while had been a wise one.

'For you know, Serena, the season is three-quarters over. The world will soon have forgotten your story. And if you have retained the friendship of the Ambournes you will be able to return to London in time for next season.'

'Not,' said Serena with determination, 'not unless I am vindicated, Aunt Spurston. And perhaps not even then. Tell me, where can I find a new side-saddle?'

After some argument Lady Spurston had agreed that Serena could ride out as much as she liked as long as Tom, the stable lad, went with her. So Serena shook out her riding habit, learned, not without difficulty, to master the side-saddle again, and about a week after her arrival set off to find Wintersett Court.

Alanna had been burdened with a sense of doom ever since Lord Wintersett's lawyer had come down to Surrey and had announced that his client was off on urgent business in the West Indies. In three months — perhaps less if the winds were favourable — she would be unmasked. What was she to do? She was unable to

221

sleep at night or rest during the day. She was irritable
with the servants, and lost her temper more than once
with her son. Day after day she walked the gardens,
worrying over the problem. Should she go away — to
her home in Ireland, perhaps? The thought was not a
happy one. She did not relish living with her sister,
looking after an elderly father.

But soon another worry was added to her burden.
Fergus O'Keefe called, ostensibly to claim the last two
instalments of his money, but making it clear that this
was not to be his final visit.

'It's a fine house you live in, Alanna, my darlin'. I like
callin' on you here, I do. I'll come again next week,
shall I?'

She stammered, apologised, but gave in weakly
when he said with a laugh, 'Now, don't be puttin' me off
and me an old friend from Ireland. I'll leave you alone
when I have me gaming house in Dublin, I promise you.
But that costs a mint o'money, Alanna my love, a. . .
mint. . .of. . .money. You wouldn't have a bit more
put by now, would you? To help out an old friend. You
might call it a security. A security! Now there's a
thought!' He roared with laughter, but Alanna shivered
and promised him another hundred pounds.

She did not delude herself that this visit would be the
end of the story. In an effort to escape from the
treadmill of her thoughts she walked the gardens till she
was exhausted, but the fact was inescapable. In engaging Fergus O'Keefe she had put herself completely in
his power.

Serena rode up the drive to Wintersett Court, and when
she caught sight of a figure sitting on a bench under

some trees she stopped, dismounted and gave the reins
to her groom, who took the horse off to the stable yard.
She walked over the grass towards the bench.

'Mrs Stannard?'

Alanna stood up. 'I'm afraid I don't. . .'

'You possibly do not recognise me. I was only
fourteen when you last saw me.'

Alanna's eyes widened in horror. She jumped to her
feet shrieking, 'Oh, no! You must go away from here!
Get out, get out!'

'Please spare me the histrionics, Alanna!' Serena
made no attempt to disguise her scorn. 'You must know
by now that your brother-in-law is on his way to St Just,
and that he will learn enough there to expose your lies
for what they are.'

'Yes, but there may be a storm, or a shipwreck. . .'
Alanna's voice died away. 'Why are you here?' she
whispered at last.

'I have come to see the boy. And to ask you why you
did it.'

'Did what?' asked Alanna warily.

'Why did you tell the Stannards that it was I who
seduced Tony, not that it was Richard who seduced
you?'

'What else could I have done?' cried Alanna passionately. 'The Stannards would never have given me
shelter if they had known. . . Where else could I have
gone? I thought it was safe enough — St Just was the
other side of the Atlantic and I knew the Calverts would
hush up Richard's part in the affair. The Stannards were
desperate to have Tony's son with them. What else
could I do?'

'Tell the truth.'

'Tell the truth? And what was that? That your precious brother had rejected me, had laughed in my face when I told him I wanted him to marry me. Can you imagine what I felt when he told me he despised me? That he had no intention of marrying a damned tame bedmate, that he could have more thrills with the native girls in the village? That one bastard more or less made no difference to him, he had plenty.' Alanna was now hysterical. The successive shocks and lack of rest had been too much for her nerve. Serena tried to persuade her to sit down but she ignored her.

'He said that to me! Alanna Cashel! Not one of his native girls, but a Cashel of Kildone.' Alanna was striding up and down in front of the bench like a caged tiger. She had a handkerchief in her hand and was tearing it in shreds. 'He'd told a different tale when he'd been trying to get me into his bed. Oh, yes! I was mad for him, but I didn't let him see it. I held off till he swore he'd marry me if Tony were not in the way. So I let him love me. . . And then I found that the baby was coming. . .' Alanna sank down on to the grass. She was hardly conscious of an audience, but stared into space, reliving the past. She whispered, 'I went to Tony and told him I was going to leave him. He thought I didn't mean it. He refused to even discuss it. So I. . .so I. . . shot him.' She hid her face in her hands. Her voice was muffled as she sobbed, 'I got rid of Tony, but Richard didn't want me after all. . .'

'*You* shot Tony?'

Alanna was suddenly quiet. 'Did I say that? Oh, what does it matter?' she said wearily. 'There's no one else to hear and, anyway, no one can prove it now. . . I'll be gone soon and you're as good a confessor as any. Yes, I killed Tony Stannard. Everyone was so anxious to hush the whole matter up that no one questioned that it was suicide. But I wish I hadn't killed him!' She put her head back in her hands and wept bitterly. Serena gazed at her in horror. This was much worse that she had suspected.

Alanna looked up. 'I'm going away,' she whispered brokenly. 'But I don't know what to do about Anthony. He cannot travel. But how can I leave him behind? What will happen to him?'

'He's Richard's son, you say?' Alanna nodded. 'Then he's my nephew and a Calvert, whatever his birth certificate may say. I'll take care of him if the Stannards won't. He'll be safe, Alanna.' Serena tried to feel pity for this woman, but it was impossible. So many lives wrecked through her wicked selfishness all those years ago! Alanna looked up and caught the expression of disgust on Serena's face.

'I've tried to atone. All these years I've stayed here, hardly living. I have never been to London, never travelled. All I have done for thirteen years is to act as companion to Lady Wintersett, and to look after my son——' She caught Serena's hands. 'You won't tell him, will you? Anthony, I mean. You won't tell him that I. . .that his mother. . .'

'No,' Serena disengaged herself. 'Alanna, you know I cannot agree to keep silent if you stay here, don't you?'

Alanna nodded. 'I shall be gone by next week, I promise you.' She started to say something, hesitated, then started again, 'There's something else I ought to tell you. I was afraid you'd talk to James. So I. . .I. . .' She stopped and looked at Serena uncertainly. Then she said, 'No, I cannot. You will not help me if I tell you.' She ran into the house as if she was being chased by the hounds of hell. Serena stared after her. What had Alanna been going to say?

The next time Fergus O'Keefe called, Alanna was ready for him.

'I have no more money,' she said. 'But there are jewels — quite a lot. You can have nearly all of them. I'll just keep a few for myself.'

Captain O'Keefe's eyes gleamed. 'Where are they, Alanna, my soul?'

'They're in a safe place. You'll get them if you take me to Ireland with you. I could help you in your gaming club.'

'Now that is a surprise! It's not often that Fergus O'Keefe is taken unawares, but you've done it, my pretty one.' His eyes grew hard. 'I wonder why you're suddenly so fond of me, Alanna?'

She forced herself to laugh. 'I'm tired of living here, and that's the truth, Fergus O'Keefe! It's a bold man you are, and I've taken a fancy to see more of the world before I die — in your company.'

He looked at her appraisingly. 'Well, you've worn quite well; you might be an asset at that. It must be the good living you've had, but it won't be as easy a life with me, I warn you. What am I saying? Your jewels should make all the difference. A lot, you say?'

'The Wintersetts are rich — and generous. I've quite a few.'

'Where did you say they were?'

'I didn't. And I won't.'

Fergus paused. Then he smiled and said, 'Well I

won't say I don't have a fancy for you, Alanna Stannard.'

'Alanna Cashel, Fergus. Alanna Cashel. Wait for me at the end of the drive. I'll come in a short while — we can hire a chaise at the next posting station. My box is already there.'

With tears in her eyes Alanna went to her son's room. He was asleep. She kissed him, and went to join Fergus O'Keefe without a thought for anyone else or a look back.

As for Fergus O'Keefe, he was happy to wait for a while. He wasn't worried about the jewels — he'd find them all sooner or later. He might even keep Alanna Cashel for a time. She wasn't bad-looking, for her age.

Impatient as she was to see Richard's son, Serena delayed her second visit to Wintersett Court until she could be certain that Alanna had gone. For young Tony's sake she was prepared to give Alanna a chance to get away, but she did not wish to see her again. The revelation that Tony's death had been murder, not suicide, had filled her with horror. Nor did she believe that the act had been the impulse of a moment such as Alanna had described, for there must have been a gun. Alanna must have kept a cool head afterwards, too, for no one had ever questioned the cause of death. Serena felt burdened with the knowledge. Though she saw no sense in making it public after all these years, the Stannards ought to know. But what about the boy? She must do her utmost to keep it from him. In the end she decided to wait. The facts of Tony Stannard's death had remained secret for so long that another month or two would not make any difference.

 Confirmation that Alanna had disappeared came in
the form of an advertisement in the *Gazette* for someone to act as companion to two invalids — a widow of
high birth, and a child confined to a wheelchair. The
address given was Wintersett Court, Surrey.

 Serena went straight to her aunt and showed her the
advertisement. 'You must help me, Aunt Spurston. I
want you to write me a reference for this post.'

 'A reference, Serena? Whatever for? There is absolutely no reason for you to seek a post of any kind. Have
you forgotten who you are?'

 'No, Aunt Spurston, but if Anse Chatelet isn't
returned to me then I am almost penniless, and shall
have to find something to support me. And I wish to go
to Wintersett Court.'

 Lady Spurston was astonished, annoyed and finally
angry, but she could not persuade Serena to change her
mind. After a while she reluctantly agreed to provide a
reference, but was outraged when she was asked to
write it for a person called Prudence Trask.

 'Now, that I will never do, for that would be deceit.
Why can't you go under your own name, Serena?'

 'Aunt Spurston, the Stannard family would never
allow a Calvert to darken their doors.'

 'All the more reason for not going there, I should
have thought. What are you up to?'

 Serena knelt down beside her great-aunt's chair.
'There is something I can do at Wintersett Court, I feel
it in my bones — I know I can do more for this child than
anyone else could. Don't ask me how I know, I just do.
But if I go as Serena Calvert I will never get near him.
Please help me! You have been more than kind to me

here, but I know you secretly long for your peace and quiet again!'

Lady Spurston took a day to think it over, then agreed to write Prudence Trask a suitable reference. 'This is all against my better judgement, Serena, but you are clearly set on it. And you have a way with you, there's no question about that. I only hope you can carry it off. But what will you do when Lord Wintersett gets back?'

'I intend to be gone before that, but I can do a lot in three months.'

Serena's interview with Lady Wintersett in the presence of a representative from the family lawyers was a curious affair. Lady Wintersett looked ill, and said nothing. The lawyer fussed and fiddled interminably. Finally he said, 'Well, Miss er. . . Miss Trask, you might have been suitable, but I am disappointed that you appear to have had so little experience. Though your reference is excellent, it is your only one. We have had other, more experienced applicants. So unfortunately. . .er. . .'

Lady Wintersett leaned forward and put her hand on the lawyer's arm. She slowly nodded her head.

'You wish me to appoint Miss — er — Trask, Lady Wintersett?'

Lady Wintersett nodded again.

'Very well. Miss Trask, I have decided that your pleasant appearance and personality outweigh the lack of experience. The position is an unusual one in that you will be expected to oversee the running of the house. Mrs Stannard dealt with all this until she was er. . .called away. There is a steward, of course, and a housekeeper. . .' He went into details of salary and conditions of work, but Serena hardly heard him. She was elated at having passed this hurdle, but she was also puzzled. Lady Wintersett had appeared to take no interest in the interview, so why had she interfered? It was clear that before her intercession the lawyer had been about to refuse Serena the post.

The need for someone to take Mrs Stannard's place was so urgent that Serena was asked to start as soon as she could, and the weekend saw her installed in her own room in Lord Wintersett's country seat. She was occasionally overwhelmed at her temerity, but whenever she had doubts she thought of her nephew—sick and lonely in his darkened room. It had been explained to her that Mrs Stannard had been devoted to her son, but that she might have to be away for some time. The boy was already missing his mother, and he would need careful handling. Serena could hardly wait to meet him.

On the day after her arrival she was taken to Tony's room. Her heart was beating strangely as she entered, looked towards the bed, and saw the boy lying there. She had eyes for nothing else as she went over to him, and had to bite her lips to keep them from trembling. He was pale and thin, and had none of Richard's earthy robustness, but for all that Richard's eyes looked out at her from Richard's face—he was unmistakably her brother's child. The boy was staring at her. She saw now that he had been crying, and was trying to disguise the fact.

'You've come to take the place of mama,' he said. 'I don't want you.'

'I couldn't do that, Tony! I've just come to keep you

company. It must be rather boring lying here on your own.'

His head turned, and Serena saw Lady Wintersett was sitting on the other side. She was regarding them closely. Serena got up in confusion and curtsied. 'Ma'am. . . Lady Wintersett, I'm sorry. I didn't see you there.' Lady Wintersett smiled and shook her head. She indicated that Serena should carry on.

'Tony, I knew your parents had been in the West Indies, so I've brought you some pictures and books about the islands. Would you like to see them?'

By exercising every ounce of self-control and patience during the following days, Serena began slowly, tediously slowly, to win the boy's confidence. He was not a child. He was now nearly thirteen, at a suspicious, temperamental age, but by concentrating on interests outside the boy himself she was gaining ground. Lady Wintersett's own physician, Dr Galbraith, soon replaced Tony's former doctor and Serena had a long talk with him about Tony's state — the first of many. What he said gave her the courage to throw open the huge windows in Tony's room and let in some sunshine and fresh air. When Tony complained that the draught from the open windows made him cold, Serena was unsympathetic. 'That's because you don't move! Come, let me help you into your wheelchair, and you can throw your arms about a little. No, harder than that!'

It was all uphill work, but Serena persevered. She had never in her life shirked a challenge, and this one was perhaps the most important of all. She made sure that Tony did the exercises Dr Galbraith recommended, rewarding the boy with treats when she saw he was really trying. Lady Wintersett came to see her grandson one day with a small puppy in her arms, and Pandora, so-called 'because she was into everything', quickly won his heart. He exerted himself more for the puppy's sake than for anyone else.

'Look at her, Miss Trask! Quick, she's falling into the chest — no, don't bother, I'll get her!' and he would swing his wheelchair over to rescue the inquisitive puppy from whatever predicament she found herself in. He grew stronger with every day that passed, and seemed to miss his mother less as time went on — perhaps because his life was suddenly filled with so much that was new.

Serena told him stories about 'my brother Richard', who was always getting into scrapes — falling from trees, getting trapped in caves, doing all the things boys loved to hear, and it became a kind of continuous saga, where truth and fiction were mingled. She wheeled Tony out into the garden and they sat together on a bench under the trees and watched the birds and small animals at their work, while Pandora chased everything in sight, always with more optimism than success. Serena got the servants to seek out the bats and balls from the Stannard boys' childhood, and she improvised games with them on the lawn, games which often ended in laughter when Serena collapsed breathless on to the bench while a triumphant Pandora ran off with the ball or stick. Slowly she and Pandora together roused in the boy a desire to do more. He would stretch out for a ball thrown slightly wide and exclaim in frustration when he missed it, or he would watch Serena wistfully when she played with Pandora or rode one of the horses up to where he sat on the lawn. And all the time Lady

Wintersett watched and occasionally, in fact quite often, smiled.

Serena was waiting for the moment when Tony would realise that he could do so much more if he could only walk. She had talked the matter over with Dr Galbraith, who had said that the child had started walking at the normal age, and had made good progress.

'Then the poor lad was ill—I forget what it was, measles or chicken pox or the like—and there were complications. After that Mrs Stannard treated him as such an invalid that he lost the will to use his limbs at all. I argued with her, of course, but she dismissed me and engaged another doctor. It is scandalous, Miss Trask, how much damage can be done by an overfond mother, all in the name of love!'

Tony's cheeks were getting quite sunburned. He grew daily more like his father, his tawny hair bleached by the sun, and his eyes, so like Serena's, sparkling with life. Then one day Serena threw the ball too high. Tony stretched up from the bench, realised he was not going to reach it, and stood up to catch it. He remained there looking down at the ball in his hands for a moment. 'Miss Trask?' he said uncertainly. Serena wanted to shout, to dance, to sing, but did none of these.

'Yes, Tony?' she said casually.

'I. . . I stood up!' As Tony said this he sat down suddenly on the bench behind him.

'So? What's so extraordinary about that? Some of us do it all the time.'

'But I don't!'

'You do! I've just seen you. Try again.' Serena's tone may have been casual, but all her being was concentrated on this boy. She watched his face as the desire to

stand battled with his fear of failure. She strolled away,
turned and threw the ball high a second time. 'Catch!'

Without thinking Tony stood again. He missed the
ball, for in her excitement Serena had pitched it wide,
but he grinned all over his face as he realised what he
had done.

'Do you wish to try a step? I'll keep close by you.'
Serena nodded encouragingly. Stiffly, awkwardly, Tony
Stannard moved towards her, one step, two, three, then
he almost fell. Swiftly she took his arm and helped him
back to the bench. 'No more today,' she said firmly.
'Let's go back to the house. You must rest for a bit, and
tomorrow there's something I want you to see.' As she
put him back in the wheelchair she caught sight of Lady
Wintersett in the large window overlooking the garden
and impulsively waved to her. She was delighted to see
Lady Wintersett lift a hand in response. That night a
bottle of champagne appeared on the dinner table,
quite without comment. The following morning she
wheeled Tony round to the huge yard at the side of the
house. Here she took him into a disused stable.

'What are we here for, Miss Trask? I want to go back
to the bench! I want to stand again!'

'We shall go on to the lawn afterwards, Tony. I want
you to meet someone here first. Parks has two inven-
tions to show you. He's been waiting for you to be
ready. Parks, this is Master Tony. Show him your
puzzles.'

On the floor of the stable were two curious contrap-
tions. One was a kind of wooden frame, a bit like a
clothes horse but sturdier, and the other was a clumsy-
looking saddle. Tony studied them carefully in silence.

'I think one might be to put on a horse,' he said

slowly. 'But what are the things at the side for, Mr Parks?'

'To hold you, Master Tony. It's a special saddle to put on a pony.' Parks went out again and led in a broad-backed piebald pony. 'Like this one.'

Tony's eyes were wide with excitement. 'For me? I can ride? Now? Oh, Miss Trask!'

Serena laughed. 'Try the saddle,' she said. 'And then you can try the pony. If Parks is satisfied that you'll be safe you can ride round the yard. But first look at this.' She took the frame, held it in front of her and took some steps. Tony could now see that the frame took the weight of the body while allowing the legs to move. 'It's Parks's walking machine,' Serena said. 'I gave him the idea, and he made the design and constructed it. You must thank him for his trouble, Tony. He's spent a lot of time on it.'

Tony thanked Parks somewhat cursorily, for his eyes were on the pony. In a few minutes he was sitting on its back, well supported by the curious saddle. Parks examined it carefully and then led the pony out into the yard and they walked round it once in solemn procession. They did this several times, but when Parks gave Serena a significant look she said they must stop. Tony objected violently.

'I'm not tired, I'm not, I tell you!' But Serena was adamant.

'You'll have to go slowly, Tony. I want you to have some energy left for learning to use the frame. When you can walk properly on your own you'll be able to try riding on your own.'

That was the beginning of a time such as Tony had never known. Serena was hard put to it to restrain him from doing himself harm, so eager was he to be on the move all the time. The weeks passed and each day seemed to bring further improvement. The walking frame was used a lot at first but it gradually became unnecessary, and as Tony's muscles strengthened so the extra supports on the pony saddle were discarded. The boy fairly buzzed with happiness, and each evening as Lady Wintersett sat with him before he went to sleep he grew almost incoherent as he told her of his day.

It seemed to Serena that Lady Wintersett was less remote than she had been. She frequently joined them now out in the garden, and though she never said anything she was obviously taking an interest in their activities. Sometimes Serena was worried about the effect it might have on Lady Wintersett's recovery if she ever found out that Tony was not, in fact, her grand-child. She half hoped that it might never be necessary to tell her.

So high summer passed into early autumn. But though the mornings might be chilly the days remained warm and dry, and the gardens of Wintersett Court rang with the sound of boyish shouts and boyish laughter. Tony's tutor returned after the summer break, and it was decided that he should instruct Tony in the morning and late afternoon leaving the boy free to be outside during the main part of the day. Serena rode out with Tony regularly, always accompanied by a groom, but otherwise free to go where she wished. They rode far and wide, but Serena never took Tony up on the ridge. She felt no desire to see it again.

One afternoon in October they returned from their ride rather late. Tony was overdue for his lessons. They cantered into the stable yard, flushed and breathless, and were greeted by the sight of Douce waiting in the yard ready saddled, with a tall, bronzed gentleman standing next to her.

'I was just about to come in search of you,' he said.

'Uncle James!' shouted Tony, scrambling somewhat inelegantly off his horse. 'Look! I can ride!'

'So I see. My congratulations! Someone ought to teach you the finer points of the art — such as dismounting.'

Tony wasn't listening. He ran somewhat awkwardly to his uncle and said, 'I can walk, too!'

'It was worth coming four thousand miles just to hear that, Tony. How are you?' said James, smiling down at him. 'Though I think you have no need to tell me. Come inside, and tell me what you've been doing. Parks!'

'Yes, my lord?'

'See to the horses, would you. Come along, Tony! Miss Trask?'

Miss Trace...

CHAPTER THIRTEEN

ONCE inside the house Serena excused herself and started for the stairs.

'Miss Trask!' She stopped and slowly turned. Lord Wintersett smiled, presumably for the benefit of those around, for the smile did not reach his eyes. 'Where are you off to? I had hoped you would join us.'

'I. . . I have to change, Lord Wintersett. Lady Wintersett would not like me to appear as I am in the drawing-room.'

'Very well. I thought for a moment you might be attempting to avoid me. I shouldn't like that. . . Miss Trask.'

Serena put her chin up. 'I shall be down as soon as I can, my lord.' He nodded and followed his nephew. Serena continued on her way, but as she mounted the stairs her mind was on the scene in the stableyard. She was furious with herself for the sudden feeling of delight she had felt on seeing Lord Wintersett again. She had only just managed to stop herself from running to welcome him back with all her heart. What a fool she would have looked! His attitude towards her had been cool, almost unfriendly, and when she recalled her words to him before he had left for St Just she could hardly have expected otherwise. He looked well—the sea voyage had obviously suited him—but there were signs of stress and pain in the tanned face. It was no more than she had expected—not only had he been forced to relive the loss of his brother, but he had also discovered that he had been so wrong, so unjust all these years. For a man of his temperament that must have been painful. Serena pulled herself up short. Why was she feeling so sorry for him? He was nothing to her! She must go away as soon as she could, especially since his presence seemed to have such a devastating effect on her. He had appeared so unexpectedly that she had had no time to escape, not even any time to prepare for this meeting, to remind herself of all the things he had said and done. Then she frowned and stopped where she was. She suddenly realised that though Lord Wintersett had looked coldly on her in the stableyard he had not looked in the slightest degree surprised. But how could he possibly have known she was living at Wintersett Court under the name of Prudence Trask? She shrugged her shoulders and continued on her way.

Upstairs she had time to reflect on her position. Whatever his feelings for Sasha Calvert were now that he had discovered the truth, he must be furious to find her installed in his home under a false name. And what would Lady Wintersett think when 'Miss Trask' was unmasked? Serena could not regret her subterfuge, for the time spent with Tony had been such a joy to her and such an obvious benefit to Tony himself. But she had grown to like silent Lady Wintersett, and was sorry that her employer was about to find how her companion had deceived her. Perhaps her son was telling her 'Miss Trask's' real name at this very moment? Serena went downstairs again with reluctance, not knowing what she was about to face.

When she entered the drawing-room she found Lord Wintersett talking to Tony while his mother looked on.

A tray of tea and other refreshments was on the table by the sofa. It was a comfortable domestic scene, with no overtones of drama or untoward revelations.

'Ah! The worker of miracles herself. Come in, come in!' Lord Wintersett's tone was affable but patently false. Serena braced herself and walked forward, but as she sat down she was surprised to receive a warmly encouraging smile from Lady Wintersett.

'Tony has been describing your activities, Miss Trask,' Lord Wintersett began. 'I am astounded at his progress. Some of your machines sound most ingenious. Er. . .you perhaps have a gift for devices?'

Serena said calmly, 'You flatter me, my lord. Parks must have most of the credit for the machines.'

'But you designed them, Miss Trask!' cried Tony.

'Ah, a designer! That sounds more probable. But whatever you are, Miss Trask, you deserve our thanks.' Serena bowed her head. He went on, 'Though I could wish that you had taught young Tony here to dismount more gracefully. In the stableyard he reminded me of nothing so much as a sack of potatoes falling off a cart!'

Serena smiled at Tony's downcast face and said, 'But it isn't every day that his uncle returns from. . .where was it?'

'But, Miss Trask, you know! I told you Uncle James was in the West Indies. We've been studying the maps, Uncle James. I found St Just, and showed it to Miss Trask. It isn't very big, is it?'

With a sardonic look at Serena's pink cheeks Lord Wintersett said, 'Not big, but beautiful, Tony. And Anse Chatelet is a wonderful heritage. Now, it's time for you to be off. You have still to change, and I promised Mr Gimble that you wouldn't be too long. We shall have time tomorrow for more talk, but now you should go to your lessons.'

Tony objected, of course, but received little sympathy from his uncle. The boy gave Serena a resigned grin and left.

'Now, Miss. . . Trask. The improvement in your charge is incredible, and we owe you a debt of gratitude —— ' There was still the false note in Lord Wintersett's voice. Serena dared to interrupt.

'But now that you are back, Lord Wintersett, I dare swear you would prefer to choose a companion for your mother yourself. I was only engaged on a temporary basis. Much as I have enjoyed the work with Tony, I feel he hardly needs me any longer, and I shall understand if you wish me to go.' Her voice was matter-of-fact but her eyes pleaded with him not to expose her in front of his mother.

'The question is whether you yourself would rather go, Miss Trask — in the circumstances.'

'I would prefer Miss Trask to stay, James!'

The voice was Lady Wintersett's. Both Serena and James looked at her in astonishment, and James said, 'Wh. . .what was that, Mama?'

'I should like you to persuade Miss Trask to stay.' She smiled vaguely, got up, and before either of them had recovered enough to stop her she left the room, closing the door carefully behind her.

'Another miracle! Wintersett is full of them, it seems — since you have been with us!' Lord Wintersett turned back to Serena. 'But all the same,' he said grimly. 'All the same, Serena. . .'

'I know what you are going to say, and I agree with every word. It was deceitful, underhand, and a shame-

ful thing to have done. But I am not in the slightest
sorry! And now I shall go to pack my things.'

'You heard my mother. Those must be the first words
she has spoken for over ten years. She wants you to
stay.'

'It was very kind of Lady Wintersett to intercede for
me, but now you are back I would not be comfortable
here. I am glad to have done what I have done for your
nephew——'

'*My* nephew? I think not. Or at least, only in name.'

Serena grew pale. 'You know?'

James got up and walked about the room. 'I think I
know most of it now. The days I spent on St Just were
very enlightening, though they did little for my self-
esteem. For a man who has always prided himself on
being fair-minded, I had been singularly blind. I suppose I understand why you couldn't tell me the truth
about Alanna. But why didn't you make any attempt to
warn me?'

'Would you have listened to me if I had?'

'Perhaps not. Perhaps it was right that I had to find it
all out for myself. I should have gone to St Just years
ago, of course. But at the time there was so much else
to be done— my father's death, my mother's illness,
Alanna and the baby. Disaster on disaster.' He sat
down beside her, his head bowed, and though Serena
knew he neither wanted nor deserved her sympathy she
put out her hand and rested it on his arm. He took the
hand in his, holding it tightly. 'I thought so much about
this on the voyage home— how I would try to explain to
you. . . And now it seems so inadequate. . .' He got up
suddenly and walked away to look out of the window.

'It seems idiotic now, of course. but Alanna's story rang so true that we accepted it without question.'

'Parts of it *were* true, but the characters were changed.'

'She substituted you for Richard and Tony for herself.' He turned round and asked, 'Did your father tell Richard to leave the island?'

'Yes.'

'Alanna was ingenious in her half-truths.'

'And desperate,' said Serena quietly. 'She may have betrayed your brother, but she had been equally badly betrayed by mine.'

'It's a sordid story, Serena, and I am ashamed for my part in it. I think I have most of it now. The last piece fell into place when the boy came into the stable yard this afternoon. I could have sworn it was William with you.'

'William?'

'Yes! William the Turbulent, William Blake, William Serena Calvert — call him what you like. The boy is the image of you, except for his hair.'

'Richard's hair was tawny, not dark like mine. My father used to call him his lion.' Serena drew a deep breath and said, 'Lord Wintersett —'

'You called me James a short while ago.'

'It was a mistake. What do you propose to do about Tony?'

'What the devil *can* I do?'

'There's your family to consider — if you had no sons yourself Richard's son would inherit the Wintersett title! That would be wrong.'

'Oh, there's no risk of that! It may interest you to

know, Miss Trask, that I fully intend to have a wife and sons of my own in the near future!'

His arrogance irritated her and she said tartly, 'You can buy a wife, I suppose, with all that money you keep mentioning. But how can you be sure you'll have children, not to mention sons?'

He burst into unwilling laughter. 'You wretch, Serena! That's a possibility that had never occurred to me, I must admit!' He suddenly grew sober and said abruptly. 'I owe you an apology. . .much more than an apology. How can I possibly persuade you to forget the terrible things I have said and done to you? You swore the last time I saw you that you never wanted to see me again. I half thought you would run away when you saw me in the stable-yard, and I wouldn't have blamed you if you had.'

'You didn't appear very pleased to see me,' Serena said involuntarily. 'You didn't say anything except a haughty, '"Come, Tony. . . Miss Trask!"'

'I assure you I was not feeling haughty in the slightest — what a dreadful word, Serena! — I was never more nervous in my life!'

'Nervous! You?'

'Yes, nervous. I was afraid that if I said anything at all out of the way you would disappear. So I was being very careful — both in the stable-yard and afterwards.'

'Why weren't you surprised?'

'Come, Serena! Don't insult my intelligence! Who else could Prudence Trask be? You forget, I knew by then that Tony was probably Richard's son. I guessed you would be with him. I remembered Prudence from a conversation on the hill. And of course I remembered Trask!'

'I am surprised you remembered so much.'

'I don't think I have forgotten anything about you from the day we met.' Serena tried to turn away, but he took her hands again and added quickly, 'But this is beside the point. I was asking you if you could forgive me — and unless you thought me a graceless monster you must have expected me to do so. Have you thought about your answer?'

'I have thought about it all the time you have been away. I saw the heartbreak Richard's actions had caused in your family, and I weighed that against the heartbreak and tribulations in my own. I think the balance is about equal, don't you?'

'But you are the one who has suffered, Serena. And you have been completely innocent throughout.'

'I wasn't alone in that. What about your mother? And young Tony? And Tony's. . .your brother? No, I think it's time to draw a line under the past.'

'You are more generous than I deserve.' He put her hands to his lips and kissed them. Serena snatched them back and moved away from him. She was very agitated. He got to his feet, grimaced and then said abruptly, 'I have had papers drawn up for the return of Anse Chatelet.'

'No! I. . . I don't want it back!'

He looked astonished. 'But I cannot keep it, Serena!'

'Anse Chatelet must go to Tony. You should keep it for him.'

He frowned. 'Are you sure?'

She said, 'Quite sure. Richard would have inherited Anse Chatelet if he had lived, and it should go to his child. But it will have to come as a gift from you. His

name will always be Stannard, whatever his parentage.
You will make sure he uses his inheritance wisely.'

'You would trust me to do this?'

'Yes. Yes, I would. You have always been described
as a just man. You will do this. And now I must go.'

'No! Don't! You must stay! I have only just returned.'

'No, I must go, Lord Wintersett! I knew that you
would ask me to forgive you. And I do. But I always
intended to be gone from here before you returned.'

He saw she meant it. He spoke rapidly, jerkily.
'Serena, listen to me. I understand your feelings,
believe me.'

She shook her head, saying, 'You cannot possibly
understand what I feel! I don't even know myself.' She
started to walk to the door.

James strode after her and stopped her. 'Wait,
Serena! Please!' She looked at him coolly, clearly
unwilling to linger. James could see that her mind was
made up against him. He said rapidly, 'Let me try to
explain.' He led her back into the middle of the room,
where they stood facing one another. He took time to
find the right words, and at length he said, 'At one time,
on the hill, I think we were both very near to complete
understanding. More complete than I have ever known
with anyone else in my life. . . That friendship was very
precious to me, Serena.'

'You destroyed it,' she said stonily.

'I know, I know! In my blind prejudice against the
Calverts I destroyed it. But give me a chance to rebuild
it! I could, I think, given time. Say you'll stay!'

She shook her head. 'You are not the man I knew on
the hill. I could have loved him — no, I did love him.
But you forget, I have known you in London. I have

heard what they say about you ——' He made a gesture
of repudiation, but she raised her voice and went on,
'And I know it to be true! There is a hardness in you, a
lack of pity, which I hate. I could never love such a
man. I am. . .repelled.'

He grew white, and said almost angrily, 'There were
times when you did not seem to hate me, Serena. Or
will you accuse me of conceit for saying so?'

'I admit there's a strong attraction between us. And
given the right circumstances such feelings can lead to
love. But not with you. I do not trust you enough.'

'Serena!'

'Oh, I trust you to be fair with Anse Chatelet and
Tony, and all the rest. But not with my heart, not with
myself. You see, I too thought I had found my other self
on the hill. It seemed like a miracle, an enchantment.
More than I had ever dreamed of. . . And then. . .and
then. . .' She could not continue but walked about the
room in agitation. Finally she stopped and said decis-
ively, 'No, I will not allow it to happen again. And if I
stay here you will confuse me once more. I cannot stay.
I will not!'

He saw that she was not to be moved by appeals to
her feelings for him and switched his argument. 'What
about Tony and my mother?'

'Tony will manage now. He needs the companionship
of men, boys of his own age. . . Perhaps he ought to go
to school. If Tony is to live on St Just it is important that
he has the discipline that Richard never knew.'

'And my mother, Serena? She surely needs you as
much as Tony. I think with you she could in time
recover completely.' He saw that Serena was still
unconvinced and went to take her hands in his again.

When she stepped back he said desperately, 'Serena, I
cannot coerce you into doing my bidding as I did on the
hill. I know you too well to think of bribing you. I can
only appeal to your reason, if nothing else. Without
Anse Chatelet you have no real home. Stay here with
my mother. I shall remain in London as much as I can;
you will not have to see me very often.' He was pale
under his tan, and his hands were trembling. For the
first time Serena started to have doubts. Could she do
as he suggested? Could she keep her unruly heart under
control if she saw him only rarely? She was strongly
tempted to stay, for she had grown fond of Lady
Wintersett, and Tony would not be going to school
immediately. And though Lady Spurston would give
her a home, Serena knew that her great-aunt would
really be happier without her. James was speaking
again.

'I really will be in London, Serena. There is much to
do there. I was so impatient to see Prudence Trask that
I left it all.'

Serena looked at him without really seeing him. What
should she do? How was she to decide?

'Serena?'

'Oh, forgive me! What did you say?'

'I said that I have to return to London soon. I must at
least attempt to trace Alanna.'

'Is that wise?' Serena regretted this as soon as the
words were said, but James clearly understood her.

'What is it that you are not saying—is it about
Alanna? Do you believe, as I do, that she was behind
the plot against you? Isn't that a good reason for finding
her?'

Serena shook her head. 'Your sister-in-law couldn't

afford to leave me free to tell the truth about St Just. I had to be discredited.'

'As you indeed were! Have you heard anything from Barnet?'

'He has traced the coach and I believe he has spoken to its driver from whom he had a description of the conspirators. But he has so far failed to trace Lady Banagher. I think Barnet is in Ireland at the moment.'

'Perhaps Alanna is there, too.'

Serena said urgently, 'Surely it's better to let her disappear! You cannot wish for the Stannard name to be dragged into this business.'

'I shall do my best to keep our name out of it, Serena, but if disgracing Alanna publicly is the only way to clear you then I shall do that, too.'

Serena looked at him with troubled eyes. Should she tell him now that Alanna had more to hide than a plot against Serena Calvert? If she did it might make him more determined than ever to find the woman who had killed his brother. And what would happen to her nephew then? She decided to remain silent for the moment. Instead she said, somewhat formally, 'I should thank you for your efforts on my behalf. It will mean a great deal to Lucy, too.'

'Have you seen her since you have been in Surrey?'

'We. . .we thought it better not. She writes once or twice a week. After Lady Ambourne took Lucy under her wing the Warnhams were willing for the engage-ment to be announced, but Lucy refused to consider marrying Michael before I. . .until my reputation was cleared.' She tried to smile. 'So your efforts are very necessary!'

'Not for yourself?'

'London does not seem so important down here. But yes, I should like to be vindicated, certainly.'

'Then why not stay? I promise not to weary you with any more attempts to revive our. . .relationship, Serena — and I will be off to London quite soon.'

She took a deep breath. 'Very well, Lord Wintersett. I shall agree to stay here for the moment. We shall see how we go on.'

Once more she was amazed at the transformation of his whole personality as he smiled. He took her face in his hands and held it while he kissed her gently, saying as he did, 'To seal the bargain, Serena. That's all.'

She almost changed her mind there and then. This man was dangerous to her peace! This was a man who could win her heart again. It would be as well for her if this Lord Wintersett kept his distance!

James remained in Surrey for a little longer, but took care not to take up too much of Serena's time. Lady Wintersett began to speak more freely, and he spent hours walking, driving and sitting in the drawing-room with her. He gave Tony more of his attention than ever before, too. He took the boy out riding, and Serena found them one afternoon absorbed in the art of looping the whip. She was sometimes persuaded to go out with them, and the three of them roamed the countryside in perfect harmony.

James and Serena met at dinner each evening, but as it was always in the company of Lady Wintersett Serena was forced to play her role of Miss Trask. James watched with amusement 'Miss Trask's' efforts to stay in character — her struggles to subdue her natural liveliness and to disguise the air of authority which was as much part of her as her golden eyes. With each day that passed he grew more enchanted, and had difficulty in stopping himself from trying to spend every minute in her company. He constantly reminded himself that he still had a very long way to go before her confidence in him was restored, and that he must exercise caution.

Each day he put off his return to London, though affairs there were becoming increasingly urgent, including the one project which was of paramount importance to him — the clearing of Serena's name. He told himself that it was wiser to leave Wintersett before Serena realised how far their friendship had progressed. She might well run away from him if she saw how close they had become again, and he was eager to keep her at Wintersett Court where he could at least be sure of seeing her from time to time. But still he lingered, unwilling to tear himself away.

In the end the matter was decided for him, when Barnet sent a message that, after a long absence, Lady Banagher was back in London. She had suddenly left Dublin, where she had been staying with a certain Captain Fergus O'Keefe and his lady, and had taken the packet boat to Holyhead. Barnet was sure that her destination was Portland Place. James left Surrey that same day, promising Serena that he would soon have the truth out of Amelia Banagher.

Serena was astonished at the dismay she felt when James announced that he was returning to London. She had grown to depend on his company, and she suddenly became aware how much her opinion of him had changed. Without forgetting for one moment how hard he could be, here in his home she had seen another side to his nature, had marvelled at his patient gentleness in dealing with his mother and his apparently genuine interest in Tony. They had often sat long over the evening meals in the evenings, and Serena had found that she was enjoying herself more than she could have imagined. It had sometimes been hard to remember that she was ostensibly an employee in the house, and more than once she had caught Lady Wintersett eyeing her with amused speculation as she listened to the wit and laughter in the conversation between her son and her companion.

So after James had left for London Serena felt lost and uneasy. The weather had turned wet and she wandered about the house restlessly, unable to settle to anything. She was gazing unhappily out of the drawing-room window when Lady Wintersett said quietly, 'You are missing my son, Miss Calvert?'

Serena turned round to deny this. 'Oh, no, Lady Wintersett! It's just that the rain. . . *What* did you call me?'

Lady Wintersett smiled. 'I think it's time we had a talk. Come and sit down.' She patted the sofa next to her and Serena meekly sat down. 'James has told me a great deal since he came back from St Just. You have been made very unhappy because of Alanna's lies, and I wish you to know that I am sorry. I blame myself.'

'But why?'

'I should not have accepted what she said so blindly. Indeed, I sensed that there was something wrong with her story, for though I spent hours with the child, I could never see my son in him. Then you came, and of course as soon as I saw you and young Tony together I knew why.'

'I suppose you are angry with me for deceiving you for so long. I. . . I had no wish to distress you, but it was the only way I could be close to my nephew. Can you forgive me, Lady Wintersett?'

'Easily, my dear. In any case, you have never deceived me, for I knew from the first that you were Serena Calvert. You see, I was walking in the shrubbery the day you spoke to Alanna—before you ever came here. I overheard your conversation.'

'You. . .heard? All of it?' Serena was suddenly afraid. 'Even. . .'

'Even that Alanna Cashel shot my son?' said Lady Wintersett with a note of bitterness in her voice. 'Yes.'

'And you haven't told anyone?'

'I wanted Alanna out of our lives forever, and was afraid of saying or doing anything which might prevent that. It is better so, much better, and I only pray that James will fail in his present attempts to find her.'

Serena looked at her thoughtfully. 'You don't wish to make Alanna pay for her crime?'

'What good would that do? It would not bring back the dead, and it might hurt the living beyond redress. Over the years I have grown to love Alanna's child, and I love him still, even though I now know he was never my true grandson. Indeed, we have come a long way in the last three months, Tony and I. And that is thanks to you.'

'What do you mean, Lady Wintersett?'

'I mean that you taught Tony that he must have the courage and determination to live a proper life. Watching you both has made me look at my own life and I have seen how much I have wasted! When I heard Tony's laughter about this house I wondered at my own silence. Each night when he tells me of his day and I see how eagerly he seizes hold of every minute I am ashamed of my past cowardice. And you have done this—for him and for me. I owe it all to you.'

'Lady Wintersett, please! Don't thank me. Whatever I have done has been willingly done out of love for Tony. I do not deserve your thanks. I have tried to deceive you. And I have taken the last link with your dead son from you.'

Lady Wintersett smiled. 'Strangely, I see more of my dead son's spirit in Tony now—now that I know he is not my son's child—than I ever could before.' She fell silent, then after a minute she went on, 'And far from taking my Tony away, you have given him back to me. I see that that surprises you, yet it is easily explained. Until you came and uncovered the truth I could never understand Tony's death. That he would reject his wife, his child and all of us here enough to take his own life was beyond my understanding. I simply couldn't bear the thought that I had failed him so badly, and it seemed easier not to face it, to escape from it into a sort of dream world of my own. Now I know that he didn't take his own life, and for the first time in thirteen years I am at peace. And I owe that to you, too.' She paused and then continued, 'I suppose some time young Tony will have to learn the truth of his parentage. I hear that he is to have Anse Chatelet?'

Serena said, 'It is his more than mine.'

Lady Wintersett smiled. 'It is as well. You will not need Anse Chatelet, Serena.'

Serena was about to ask her what she meant, when a servant came in with a letter for Lord Wintersett from a Mr Barnet.

'I know his lordship has already left, my lady, but the letter is marked "Urgent". It is also addressed to Miss Trask, should Lord Wintersett be absent.'

Serena excused herself and opened the letter, which had obviously been written in haste. One paragraph leapt to her eye.

Since writing my last report I have learned more. First, Lady Banagher is no longer in Portland Place. She has accompanied Captain O'Keefe to Horton Wood House near Epsom Common. Second, further information from Ireland leads me to believe that O'Keefe is the man we have been seeking in connection with our case, but that he is also highly dangerous. I must warn you that it would be foolhardy to approach him with anything less than extreme caution. He left Dublin in order to escape being arrested for murder. I shall give more information when I return from Liverpool, where I have arranged to meet someone who knows more about Captain O'Keefe. Meanwhile be very careful, I beg you.

Serena sprang to her feet. 'Oh, no! Oh, my God!'

'What is it? What is the matter, Miss Calvert?' cried Lady Wintersett.

'James is in the gravest danger! I must go to him at once!'

'What are you saying? Why?'

'Read this note, Lady Wintersett! Barnet specifically warns us against O'Keefe, and James is almost certainly already on his way to meeting him! He will have failed to find the Banagher woman at Portland Place, and I have no doubt that he will follow her to Epsom. Lady Wintersett, you must forgive me. I must warn him!'

Serena ran upstairs and rummaged at the bottom of her clothes press. Somewhere, carefully wrapped up, were the boy's clothes she had worn so often before, and she secretly thanked the touch of sentiment which had preserved them so that she could use them again now. Without any hesitation she changed into them, sought and found her pistol, and hurried downstairs. Lady Wintersett was so agitated that she ignored Serena's unconventional dress and urged her to waste no time. As Serena reached the door she called, 'Do take care, Miss Calvert. From what I hear, you could be in danger, too!'

She gave a shriek as Serena waved her pistol and replied grimly, 'Not while I have this, I assure you!' Then Serena hurried to the stables and, after a short consultation with Parks, who knew the area round Epsom well, she set off on Douce with that gentleman in close attendance.

It was a wild night, and heavy showers alternated with periods of brilliant moonlight as the rainclouds swept across the sky. Parks had produced a greatcoat for Serena and she was glad of it, but as they galloped through the night she noticed very little of the wind or rain. Her one thought was to get to the house in Epsom before James.

CHAPTER FOURTEEN

JAMES had arrived in London to find the Portland Place house closed and the knocker off the door. Cursing Barnet for his inaccurate information, he set off on a search round the clubs of London for news of Amelia Banagher, and at White's he met with success. Harry Birtles, who was more than a little the worse for wear, was holding forth on the frailty of women.

'Take the fair Amelia,' he said aggrieved. 'Nothing too good for her—ribbons, furbelows, flowers—even the odd bit of jewer. . .jewellery. What does she do?' He stared owlishly round.

'What did she do, old fellow?' asked James sympathetically, leading Sir Harry to a nearby table. 'Have some more wine.'

Sir Harry drowned his sorrows a little more and turned to clutch James's arm. He looked vaguely surprised to see whose arm it was. 'Wintersett? It's kind of you to listen, 'pon my word it is! But you know what she's like.'

'What has she done now?'

'Gone off! Portland Place shut, no servants, not a word to me! Only got back two days ago, too.' He looked cunning. 'But I know where she's gone, Winsh. . . Wintersett. She can't fool me!'

'Where's that?'

'Tyrrell's place at Epsom. God knows why! He's away in France, know f'r a fact.' Here Sir Harry almost lost his balance in an effort to whisper in James's ear. 'It's my belief she's got someone down there. Why else go to a godforsaken place like Epsom? 'Cept for the Derby, and that's not run in the autumn, is it? She's with someone else, Wintre. . . Wintersett.' He looked melancholy, hiccuped and subsided quietly under the table. James left him there.

James returned to Upper Brook Street, deep in thought. Tyrrell was Amelia's cousin, and it was quite likely she would go to Horton Wood House if she wished to hide. But he had no means of knowing how long she would stay there — she might well decide to move on soon, tomorrow even. So, though it was late, he must attempt to see her that night. He quickly changed his clothes, wrote a note for Barnet, and set off on the old Brighton Road to Epsom.

He made good time in spite of the weather, for the road had a good surface, and he arrived at the door of Horton Wood House soon after seven. He had visited Tyrell with Amelia in the old days, and the manservant recognised him.

'I wish to see Lady Banagher on a matter of urgency, Parfitt. Please tell her I am here.' He was ushered into a small room off the hall and asked to wait. After a few minutes the manservant returned and showed James to a beautifully furnished salon on the upper floor. Lady Banagher was gracefully arranged on a sofa before the fire.

'James! How pleasant — and unexpected — to see you! I do believe you are looking handsomer than ever. Pray sit down. Have you dined?' Amelia looked relaxed, but her voice was pitched a little too high, and the hand holding the fan to shield her face from the fire was clenched.

'Thank you, but I haven't come to exchange civilised pleasantries, Amelia,' said James. 'I'm here to tell you that I now know all about Alanna's plot to discredit Serena Calvert. It was she who bribed you, was it not? You and Captain O'Keefe.'

The slender stick of the fan snapped, and Amelia turned white as she said with studied calm, 'I don't know what you're talking about, James. Why do you always think the worst of me?' With an effort she let her voice soften and she said with a pathetic look, 'It was not always so.'

'You may save your charms, Amelia. I know a great deal more than I did when I last saw you.' James paused. 'I know where the false Ambourne carriage came from, and the names of your hired accomplices. I even know what role you played — or should I say roles, *Betty*? And unless you do as I suggest all these details will soon be in the hands of the justices.'

'But that would ruin me!' she exclaimed, no longer able to hide her fear.

'As you attempted to ruin Miss Calvert. Yes. But I rather think in your case it might also mean prison.' Amelia burst into a shrill tirade, but James waited impassively till she paused for breath. 'Are you ready to listen to my suggestion?'

'What is it?' she asked sulkily.

'That you write a full confession, completely exonerating Miss Calvert, which will be sent to a number of prominent members of society, including Sir John and Lady Taplow, and Sir Harry Birtles. After they have read it, and you have confirmed it to them in person, I will help you to escape to Ireland or the Continent, whichever you prefer.'

'That sounds like a very fair offer, Amelia, me darlin'. But you'll keep my name out of it, if you please. It wouldn't be good for my health — or yours, either — if I was named in that document.' A tall, swarthy man came into the room. James regarded him coldly, ignoring Amelia's reply.

'Fergus O'Keefe?'

'So you know who I am already?' The Captain looked thoughtfully at Amelia. She shivered and said desperately,

'It wasn't me, Fergus! He knew before he arrived. I didn't tell him.'

O'Keefe turned his attention to James. 'I don't like anyone making free with my name, Lord Wintersett.'

'Why? Is it such an honourable one?' asked James, his lip curling in contempt. 'The name of a "gentleman" who accepts money to bring false disgrace to a lady? Of a brave soldier who makes war on women? Of a hero who goes to work on a defenceless gentlewoman, with no more than three or four accomplices? I assure you, I have no desire to make free with the name of a coward such as that. Once you have made amends to Miss Calvert I will willingly obliterate your name — and you — from my mind. They both disgust me.'

'James! Don't make him angry! Fergus!' said Amelia nervously. O'Keefe ignored her.

'You might regret those remarks, Wintersett,' he said softly.

'There isn't anyone here man enough to make me withdraw them, O'Keefe. Certainly not you!'

O'Keefe said slyly, 'I wouldn't get so positive about

that, my lord! Wasn't I man enough now to persuade
Miss Calvert to enjoy me company that night? Has she
not told you how she begged for me favours? Didn't Sir
John and his lady see her running to welcome me when
I came back to her? A fine story that would make in the
courts, would it not, now? And whether I was believed
or not, the lady's name would be blemished forever, I'm
thinking.'

James smiled grimly, and took a pistol out of his
pocket. 'You have just signed your own death warrant,
O'Keefe. I'll be damned if I let you tell that story in
public. And I'll be damned if I let a cur like you go
free!'

From his pocket he drew a second pistol, the twin of
the first. O'Keefe eyed them and laughed.

'A duel, is it? Begorrah, it's ironic! A fine gentleman
like you stooping to fight a duel with me. I'm honoured!'

'You shouldn't be, O'Keefe. It's the only way I can
kill you and keep roughly within the law. Here, catch!'

O'Keefe caught the pistol and examined it. Then he
walked a distance away, saying as he did so, 'But I
might kill you, Lord Wintersett!'

'By all means try, fellow! Or is it only against women
that you pit your strength?'

Just as O'Keefe turned with a snarl at James's last
remark a door to the side burst open and a sorry-
looking figure with wild hair and a torn gown ran into
the room towards James crying, 'James, oh, thank God!
James! Help me, please help me!'

But O'Keefe, beside himself with rage, had already
fired without waiting for the count. The figure, caught
right in the line of fire, staggered, tripped and fell.

'Alanna!' James ran to kneel down beside her, casting

his pistol aside. He ripped off a piece of her petticoat and made a rough pad, placing it on the growing stain of Alanna's gown. 'Help me, Amelia!' he cried impatiently.

These were the words Serena heard as she came softly up the stairs, closely followed by Parks. The desperation in James's voice was unmistakable, and, grasping her pistol more firmly in her hand, she hurried towards the salon. A dreadful tableau greeted her eyes. Alanna Stannard was lying on the floor covered in blood, and James was kneeling beside her making desperate efforts to stem the flow. Amelia Banagher was nowhere to be seen. A movement to Serena's right caught her eye. The man who had abducted her was moving furtively in the direction of a pistol which was lying on the ground near James. He picked it up and sprang away.

'Now, my fine hero!' he said. 'Now we'll see who it is who dies, Lord Wintersett!' He raised the gun. James looked up, his face a mask.

'Alanna is dying,' he said. 'And you have killed her.'

O'Keefe spared a glance for the woman on the ground. Then he said brutally, 'Amelia's worth two of her.' He grinned. 'And she'll soon have company.'

James's gaze had passed beyond O'Keefe to where Serena was standing in the door, pistol in hand. Without any change of expression he said, 'Any company is more welcome than yours, O'Keefe. Even that of a loathsome toad.'

O'Keefe's finger tightened, and Serena fired her pistol. A howl of pain filled the air as O'Keefe staggered away down the room, his arm hanging limply at his side and blood dripping down from his hand. The duelling pistol lay harmlessly on the ground.

'Take charge of him, Parks, if you please,' said Serena briskly, as she picked up the pistol and handed it to her companion. Then she hurried over to kneel down beside James. Alanna looked ghastly. Her breathing was very faint, her pulse almost non-existent.

'James,' she whispered. 'I have. . .to tell. . .you. Confess. . . I killed. . . Tony. Shot. . .him.'

'Don't talk, Alanna. We'll get a surgeon to you soon.'

'No. . .time.   Want   you. . .to. . .forgive. . .me. Please.'

James bent his head and kissed Alanna's cheek. 'Of course, Alanna.'

'A life. . .for. . .a life, James.' Her voice died away then grew stronger. 'Anthony?'

'Will be safe with us, I promise you.' Alanna's eyes closed, then she opened them again and looked pleadingly at Serena. She was beyond saying anything.

Serena took her hand. 'Anthony will have Anse Chatelet, Alanna. It is his right. You and I, we both love Richard's son. I shall remember that and forget the rest.' A little smile passed over Alanna's face, and then there was nothing.

James got up slowly and then helped Serena to her feet. His face was drawn and tired, and in spite of her own exhaustion Serena had a passionate wish to hold him in her arms and comfort him. Instead she stood looking on as he gazed down at Alanna. Finally he spoke.

'"A life for a life", she said. All the questions, all the anguish, answered in one sentence. Poor Alanna, to have lived with that all these years! And in the end she saved my life,' he said sombrely. Then his gaze turned to Serena. 'And so did you.'

Serena felt like weeping, but she rallied herself and said crossly, 'I very nearly decided to let him shoot you. Did you have to refer to me as a loathsome toad?'

His face lightened and he smiled slightly. 'I thought that would spur you on. O'Keefe had no idea what a defenceless gentlewoman was capable of!' But in reply to Serena's look of puzzlement he only smiled again and then said, 'You must leave here straight away. I take it Parfitt let you in? I can deal with him, but it would not do for you to be discovered here by the surgeon, or anyone else. Parks comes from somewhere round here and he will find you a place to stay.' She was about to protest but he stopped her. 'I cannot come with you now, much as I would wish — I must deal with poor Alanna and the rest. What happened to O'Keefe?'

'Parks took him downstairs. I don't think I wounded him seriously, but perhaps I should go to see?'

'On no account! You must stay in the background. I shall find out how he is and let you know. Meanwhile come with me.'

They went slowly downstairs, and James saw Serena safely hidden in the room off the hall. He came back a few minutes later to tell her that Parfitt had brought in some of the stable lads to guard O'Keefe, though he hardly appeared to need it. He had lost a fair quantity of blood, and was half sitting, half lying on a settle in the kitchen with his eyes closed. One of the lads had bound his arm enough to halt the bleeding, and O'Keefe was now waiting for the surgeon and the parish constable, muttering about a boy in the doorway. Everyone was so shocked at Alanna's death that little attention was being paid to him. Amelia had disappeared, and some of the men had gone in search of her.

'I have told Parks to come here in a few minutes. He already knows where he will take you. You'll be safe with him, Serena.'

'What about you?'

'I shall do my best to clear up the mess here to my own satisfaction. With a slight blurring of detail I think I ca atisfy the authorities, too. Thank God you're dressed in your boy's garb! Outside Parks and ourselves no one has the slightest idea who you are, so even if O'Keefe's mutterings do receive any attention the boy will never be found. Parks will take you back to Wintersett tomorrow, and I'll join you as soon as I can. You'll wait for me there?' He looked so anxious and so worn that once again she felt an urge to comfort him, and this time she did not resist it. She reached up and drew his head down to hers.

'I promise,' she said softly, and kissed him. He pulled her into his arms and returned the kiss, passionately and deeply, greedily even, as if he was trying to obliterate the memory of that scene in the salon. She made no attempt to resist, though he was holding her so tightly that it hurt. He was the first to pull away.

'I'm sorry,' he said. 'I'm sorry, Serena. Please, please forgive me. I don't know what came over me. Oh, God, I've said that before, haven't I? But it wasn't the same, I swear. Did I hurt you?'

'No,' she lied. 'And I do understand, James.' She smiled and caressed his cheek, and with a groan he drew her back into his arms, this time simply holding her and drawing comfort from the contact. Parks found them

like this and cleared his throat. Reluctantly they moved
apart.

'Sorry, my lord. But if anyone saw you they might get
a bit of a shock — seeing as how Miss Calvert is still in
her boy's clothes. Er. . .the surgeon is coming up the
drive, my lord. He'll be here any minute.'

Recalled to his duties, James kissed Serena's hand
and adjured Parks to take good care of her. Then he
went out, and after a few minutes of waiting while the
surgeon arrived and was taken upstairs Serena and
Parks slipped away.

It was nearly a month before James managed to return
to Wintersett for more than a night, though he sent
daily messages to his mother and to Serena. The
formalities of Alanna's death had to be completed, and
after that James decided that she should be buried near
her family home in Ireland. Her husband's grave was in
the West Indies, and no one felt that there was a place
for her in the Wintersett vault. James came down to
collect Tony, and they made the melancholy journey to
Ireland together. Serena visited Lucy and the Countess
quite often during this period of waiting, but always
returned to Wintersett after a few days. She heard from
Lucy that Amelia Banagher had been caught and,
though Amelia steadfastly denied having been present
at Alanna Stannard's death, she had publicly confessed
to helping in the plot against Miss Calvert. Perhaps to
save her own skin, she swore that Fergus O'Keefe had
in fact spent the night with her, only appearing in the
early morning to play his role before Sir John and the
others. Sir Harry rather shamefacedly agreed that he
had fallen asleep early the night before, and had known

nothing till the next morning. The news of Fergus O'Keefe's villainy had spread throughout a shocked London, and Serena's reputation was completely saved. Indeed, society eagerly welcomed her back, and the Warnhams were anxious to discuss plans for Lucy's wedding. But Serena had promised to be at Wintersett when James returned, and she would keep that promise — they must all be patient just a little longer. What kept her awake at night was the question of what she would do after that. James Stannard was gradually becoming too important to her once again. She had decided some time ago that she could not live with him. But could she live without him? She took the coward's way out and told herself that such questions would have to be shelved until Lucy's future was finally settled.

Eventually James and Tony came back to Wintersett on a brilliantly cold day in Nove...ber when an early fall of snow covered the ground. Serena had been for a walk, and they all arrived at the house together. There was much exclaiming and embracing, during which it seemed quite natural that James should kiss Serena. Confused and laughing, Serena broke away and said, 'Look at the view, all of you! To you it may be commonplace, but to me it is incredible — I have never, ever seen anything more beautiful!'

'Have you not?' asked James, studying her flushed face and glowing eyes. 'I believe I have, Serena.'

Lady Wintersett smiled and took Tony's arm. 'And I believe Tony has grown as tall as I. Come, Tony! I have so much to tell you, and I dare swear that Pandora would like to indicate how much she has missed you, too.' Her voice died away and Serena was left alone with James.

'You are recovered from your experience at Epsom? Unnecessary to ask — I can see you have.' James's voice was studiously light as he led Serena into the drawing-room. Here they walked to the window and gazed out at the dazzling scene. 'Serena ——'

'James ——'

They spoke together and apologised together, and both laughed. Serena said in a more natural tone, 'What were you about to say?'

'That I believe it is now truly over, Serena. The whole sad, ugly story. Alanna and my brother are both at rest ——'

'And Richard.'

'And Richard, too. Young Tony Stannard will have his Calvert inheritance — perhaps if and when he learns the truth he might even wish to change his name, and Anse Chatelet would then have Calverts in charge again.'

'The name is not very important, James. I don't believe the Calverts deserve any special consideration.'

'There's one Calvert at least who deserves mine, Serena.'

Serena flushed again and said hurriedly, 'What else were you going to say? You hadn't finished, I think.'

James had been smiling at her confusion, but his face grew sober as he said, 'Fergus O'Keefe has been taken to Ireland, too. He's to be hanged for a murder he committed there.'

Serena shuddered, and James put an arm round her shoulders. 'It's no more than he deserves. I would have killed him if I had had the chance, you know that. Don't think of him, Serena. He's a villain. He would have tried to drag you down with him if he had come to trial in this country. As it is, Amelia has made a full confession and you have been completely vindicated. Did you know?'

'Yes, Lucy told me.' Serena moved away. 'And that brings me to what I want to say to you.'

'I can imagine what the substance of it is. But say it.'

'The Warnhams wish Michael's marriage to Lucy to take place quite soon now, and I must go back to Dover Street, James. There are so many things to discuss, so many arrangements to be made. I must go.' Serena's voice held a challenge, and James smiled.

'Pax! Pax, Serena! I have too much respect for my skin to fight you!' He grew serious again. 'I have had time to think recently. There is nothing like a funeral for concentrating the mind on what is important. I know now what I want, indeed I am not sure that I can live without it. But it will take time, and keeping you here against your better judgement will not help me to achieve it. It is no part of my plan to attempt to persuade you to neglect your other loyalties — they are more important than any I can claim at the moment, and you must feel able to go whenever you wish.'

Serena studied him. She hesitated, and then her cheeks grew slightly pink as she said, 'Not more important, James. More urgent.' He drew in his breath, but listened patiently as she went on, 'I cannot decide anything before Lucy is married. That is what I came to England to do, and I must do it.'

James smiled suddenly, that wonderfully warm, all-encompassing smile. 'Then you shall do it with my good will, and any help I can render. Come, Serena! We have work to do!'

* * *

Within a week Serena was re-installed in Dover Street.
London was less full than it had been during the season,
but there were enough members of that small world
known as London society in town to show Miss Calvert
their delight at her return. Invitations were showered
on her, and no concert or reception seemed to be
complete without Miss Calvert's presence. Serena
smiled, talked, listened, and inwardly laughed at the
difference. Lucy and Michael had their own celebrations but were also carried along in Serena's wake
and the Countess stayed a little longer in London too.
The whole world suddenly seemed to be gloriously
amusing to all of them. Though James took care to be
discreet in public, he was often to be found at Dover
Street, visiting the Countess it was said. Serena found
herself relying heavily on his advice on matters connected with marriage settlements and the like. In fact
she found herself relying on him for more than just
advice — he was becoming far too necessary to her
altogether.

On the night of the reception held by the Warnhams
two days before the wedding the discerning would have
seen that Lord Wintersett was not himself. Because the
Countess had been called to Ambourne and had been
away for nearly a week, the frequency of James's visits
to Dover Street had been severely curtailed. He had not
seen Serena in private for several days, and he found
that he missed her company unbearably. Up till now he
had managed to maintain in public an air of cool
indifference towards her, limiting himself to the two
dances permitted by convention and never arousing
comment from the curious by paying her any undue
attention. This had been far from easy for, to his

annoyance, he suffered quite unreasonable pangs of jealousy. If the perfectly harmless gentlemen who gathered round Serena whenever she appeared — Mr Yardley, General Fanstock and the like — could have read James's mind, they would have retired to their country estates immediately, glad to escape unscathed. But though James counted every dance they dared to dance with Serena, though he knew to a hair how many seconds they spent in her company, he had remained calm.

But tonight was different. He suddenly found he could no longer tolerate their monopoly of Serena's time, and just as she was on the point of accepting Mr Yardley as her partner for the waltz, James cut in ruthlessly and whirled her away towards the other end of the room before Mr Yardley had collected himself sufficiently to protest.

'That was quite shamelessly rude, Lord Wintersett!' exclaimed Serena.

'Miss Calvert,' said James through his teeth, 'I have watched you charm the heads off enough sheep-shanked dolts and idiots in the last few weeks to last me a lifetime. I intend to suffer no more.' With a flourish and a neat turn he guided Serena into a small conservatory off the Warnhams' ballroom.

'Oh, no!' Serena said with determination. 'I have been in a winter garden with you once before, Lord Wintersett, and I do not intend to repeat the exercise. You will kindly lead me back to the ballroom immediately!'

'Just a few moments of your company, Serena! I promise to behave with the utmost circumspection.'

'You will call me "Miss Calvert" in public, if you

please. And forcing me into a private room, even to talk to me, is far from behaving with the "utmost circumspection"!' Serena was already moving back towards the ballroom, and James placed himself in front of her.

'A winter garden is not a private room, Ser — Miss Calvert.'

'Let me pass!' Serena was incensed, and tried to push him away. James laughed as he gathered her effortlessly into his arms, looked down at her flashing golden eyes and then kissed her. For a moment she resisted, then suddenly melted against him and for a moment he exulted in the feeling that once again flared up between them. But then she pulled away, exclaimed angrily, 'Utmost circumspection, indeed! I will not let you do this to me!' and slapped his face. The memory of what had happened once before on a similar occasion occurred to them both simultaneously. Serena's eyes widened and she stepped back. 'I didn't mean that, Lord W. . . Wintersett. Please — I didn't mean it!'

But the present situation was very different from the first, and James was amused rather than angry at the sudden change in Serena's manner. How could a man ever know what Serena Calvert would do next? Did she know herself? He started to laugh, and as she looked at him in amazement he laughed even more. Serena was offended and stalked out of the conservatory, head held high.

The Warnhams' guests were intrigued with the sight of Miss Calvert emerging flushed and angry from the winter garden closely followed by Lord Wintersett — whose appeals to her sense of humour were hampered by his inability to stop laughing. With real heroism, for

Lord Wintersett's skills were famous, Mr Yardley hastened to offer Serena his protection.

'Don't tangle with her, Yardley! She doesn't need your help. Pistols or fists, she'd outclass you every time I assure you!' said James.

Since Mr Yardley took great exception to Lord Wintersett's levity, it was as well that Serena regained her temper in time to intervene.

'Thank you, Mr Yardley. But it would be better to ignore Lord Wintersett's poor attempt at humour. I cannot imagine what he means by it!' She looked coldly at James, daring him to explain.

James, recalled to himself, apologised with all the solemnity he could muster—an apology which was graciously accepted. Later that evening, when a set of country dances brought them face to face, James said with a glint in his eyes, 'All the same. . .Miss Calvert. . . you have given me a challenge tonight which I will not forget.'

'Pooh!' said Serena, secure in the knowledge that James would hardly demand satisfaction in public, and that there would be little opportunity for them to be private for some time. It took a great deal of determination on her part to stop herself from wondering how that might be arranged.

The Countess arrived back in Dover Street the following day in time for the last-minute preparations for the wedding. It had been agreed that the ceremony should be held in London, and that the celebrations afterwards should take place in Mrs Galveston's Portman Square mansion. All the Ambournes had naturally been invited, but the recent birth of the youngest Ambourne of all made it impossible for her parents to be present, though they had sent the kindest of messages and gifts.

The Countess spent a busy day but made time towards the end of it for a quiet, and private, talk with Serena. After rhapsodising over the new baby and talking very affectionately of Lucy the Countess suddenly said, 'And when are you and James announcing your engagement?'

Serena almost dropped her cup of chocolate in astonishment. 'I. . . I beg your pardon, Lady Ambourne?'

'It should not long be delayed, Serena. From what I have heard all London is speculating on what happened in the Warnhams' winter garden. They are saying, not without satisfaction I may tell you, that James has met his match at last.'

'But James — Lord Wintersett — has never mentioned marriage to me! And if he did I should probably refuse him.'

The Countess, who had been looking mischievous, grew serious at this. 'You cannot mean it? You and James are made for each other.'

'I doubt it. Lord Wintersett can be charming enough when he chooses, and I will even admit that a surprisingly strong attraction exists between us. But there is a want of humanity in him which I could not live with. I have told him so.'

'So he has broached the subject!'

'Only indirectly,' said Serena flushing uncomfortably.

'Serena, I have heard about your exploits in Epsom. They seem to have gone far beyond what anyone would expect, even of a friend. I wish you to look at me and tell me that you do not love James.'

Serena lifted her head defiantly and started to speak, but found she could not finish. In the end she was silent.

'You see? For better or worse you do love this monster. Now I want you to forget his past crimes and listen to what I have to tell you of James Stannard.' The Countess spoke impressively, and Serena's attention was caught, almost against her will.

'James is not an easy man, I know. He has little patience with self-seekers, rogues or fools, and he doesn't bother to hide his contempt for them. This has made him unpopular in London, where there are many such people. I know what they say, and so do you.'

'I have experienced some of his contempt myself, Lady Ambourne. Am I to believe that I am such a person?'

'Serena, you are prevaricating. You know perfectly well that the circumstances of your acquaintance with James have been quite exceptional. And in fact James's violent reaction to you and your family arose from the deepest, most vulnerable part of his character — his love for his own family. For, in spite of the fact that James was a lonely, unloved little boy, in spite of the fact that his father treated him as a milksop and a coward if he showed a mite of affection or fear, in spite of being courted and flattered by half of London solely for his wealth, James has remained as true to those he loves as it is possible to be. It isn't easy to know him — he is very wary of others — but once he accepts you as a friend there is nothing he will not do for you. And if he ever allowed himself to fall in love — as I believe he finally has — then he would be as anxious to please, and as vulnerable to hurt, as anyone else. More so. Do not, I beg you, Serena, reject such a man lightly. You would be throwing away a chance of great happiness. Now that is enough,' Lady Ambourne added with a sudden change of tone. 'Tell me, where will Lucy live after she is married?'

They talked a little longer, but Serena was impatient to be gone. She knew she still had to see Lucy, and she wanted time to think.

Because of all the fuss of the wedding preparations, Serena had had little opportunity to have any real talk with her beloved niece. Though she knew it was unnecessary, she wanted a last reassurance that Lucy was happy with the thought of sharing her life with Michael Warnham and living in England. She need not have worried. Lucy had no doubts, was serenely certain that this was what she wanted.

'Everyone I love most will be here in England. How could I not be happy to live here?'

'Everyone?'

'Oh, Sasha, you need not pretend with me! I am young, but not stupid. Lord Wintersett may have returned Anse Chatelet to you, but you will never live there again.'

Serena wanted to say that Anse Chatelet was no longer hers, but for the moment that was Tony's secret, so she just asked, 'What makes you think so?'

'Sasha! You will be at Wintersett Court — everyone knows that! And, do you know, I like Lord Wintersett. He has been very kind to Michael and me.'

Serena tried in vain to disabuse Lucy's mind of the notion that Lord Wintersett meant anything to her.

'I know you, Sasha, and it has become clear to me during the past weeks that you are in love with Lord Wintersett. You cannot hide it from me, but don't worry, I won't say anything to anyone else — except perhaps Michael. It is plain for all the world to see that he is nutty about you.'

'Nutty!'

'Oh, forgive me — I meant to say that Lord Wintersett is more than a little enamoured of you. Oh, Sasha, I shall miss you! I shall be happy with Michael, I know, but I shall miss our fun together. Thank you, my dearest of aunts, for all the years we have had together. And I hope. . .no, I am sure that you will one day be as happy as I am. I cannot wait for tomorrow.'

They kissed each other and Serena left Lucy to her dreams. She herself had a more wakeful night. Everyone, it seemed, was conspiring to persuade her to look with favour on James Stannard. In the eyes of those closest to them they were apparently the perfect match. Serena wished she could believe they were right. Or that she could be sure they were wrong!

CHAPTER FIFTEEN

LUCY's wedding was the most joyous of occasions. The weather was cold but brilliantly sunny, the guests were cheerful, and the young couple radiant. The marriage of the Warnham heir would always have been an important event, but the Warnhams clearly loved Lucy for her own sake, and the pleasure they took in welcoming her into the family circle gave Serena every reassurance she might have needed. Long after the happy couple had left for a bridal tour to the Continent the celebrations in Portman Square continued. Lady Warnham, who was a great deal cleverer than her loving mama imagined, had suggested that Lady Spurston might be persuaded to come to London if Mrs Galveston invited her. As a result of Lady Warnham's forethought, the two old ladies spent a most pleasurable time before and after the ceremony indulging in an orgy of gossip and reminiscence and the rest of the party were left to enjoy the feast and the music of the military band provided by their hostesses.

Lady Ambourne was one of the first guests to leave. She had come to Lucy's wedding, but was anxious to return to Ambourne and her family. However, she took time to have a word with Serena before she left.

'Lucy looked a dream in her bridal clothes, Serena. She is destined to be happy, that one!' adding with a roguish look, 'I shall look forward to seeing you in yours! Oh, forgive me, my dear. I am an interfering busybody — Perdita could tell you more of that. But I find it impossible not to interfere when I see people turning aside from happiness. Be kind to James; you will not regret it. And come to Ambourne soon!'

Serena started to look for her aunt. They were leaving London the following day to return to Surrey and she wanted to be sure that the old lady was not too tired. But Lady Spurston was having a nap in Mrs Galveston's private parlour, and Serena had not the heart to disturb her. Instead she wandered down to the library, glad to escape from the revellers and find a quiet place to rest herself. Her head was aching — and her heart.

James finally found her here. He came in, closing the doors carefully behind him, then stood watching her where she sat on the sofa.

'You look tired, Serena. Or sad. Are you thinking of Lucy?'

'Why should that make me sad?'

'I'm not suggesting for one moment that you have any doubts for her — no one who has seen her with Michael Warnham possibly could. But you two have been so close — it would be natural for you to feel a sense of loss.'

Serena's eyes filled with tears. Through all the preparations and fuss no one else had thought of this, not even Lucy herself. She looked down to hide her distress. James came over, cursing himself for a tactless fool, and sat down beside her. He took her hands in his. 'Serena, don't!' He swore as a teardrop fell on his hand, and pulled out his handkerchief. 'You've no idea what it does to me to see you cry — I didn't think you could. Here, let me wipe your cheeks. We can't have the legend of the indomitable Miss Calvert ruined.'

She looked up and smiled through her tears at this, but the sight of his face looking down at her so anxiously entirely overset her, and the tears fell faster than ever. He took her into his arms and cradled her, uttering words of comfort, till the sobs gradually faded and Serena regained her composure. She smiled apologetically and gently removed herself from his arms.

'Thank you,' she murmured. 'Forgive me.'

'For what?' he asked with a wry smile. 'For sharing your unhappiness with me? I count it a privilege. And it gives me hope you might agree one day to share more, much more than that. Oh, God, Serena, if only you knew how I regret the past! You say you have forgiven me, but the past lies between us like a serpent. If it were not for that I could now make you forget the loss of Lucy, and every other unhappiness. I know I could persuade your body to love me — you tell me that every time we kiss, so how could I not know it? But I want much more than that! I want your mind, your spirit, call it what you will. I once knew the enchantment of that communion, and I shall never forget it, nor cease to desire it.' His voice dropped as he said this, and Serena had to strain to hear. She turned towards him.

'James. . .' she said tentatively. 'James, it isn't the past which divides us. I've told you before, it's your lack of. . .' She stared at the man before her, and could not continue.

His face dissolved, as numbers of images flashed through her mind — James giving an unknown boy a ride to console him on his birthday, James in the park with no reason to trust or like Sasha Calvert, yet sensing her loneliness and taking her for a drive, James comforting the woman who had killed his brother, looking on her with such sorrow as she lay dying, James taking trouble to get to know Alanna's son. The images increased — James teasing, James laughing, James with his mother, James looking so worried just minutes before — until finally all the images melted and refocused into one, beloved, familiar face. She gazed at him in wonder, then she smiled and her wonderful eyes glowed as she started to speak again. 'James ——'

The doors of the library opened and Mrs Galveston came in with a flourish. 'Ah, Lord Wintersett,' she began, 'There you are! Oh, forgive me, Serena, I didn't see you at first. We are just about to set up a whist table for the gentlemen. Would you like to play, Lord Wintersett? And if you'll forgive me for saying so, Serena, it isn't at all the thing for you to be in here alone with Wintersett. This may be a wedding party, but ——'

'I'd be delighted to join you, Mrs Galveston,' said James swiftly. 'Miss Calvert was saying she had the headache, so I am sure she will be glad to be left in peace. I will take my leave of you, Miss Calvert. Shall I see you again before you return to Surrey?'

Under Mrs Galveston's watchful eye what could Serena do but murmur regretfully that she was setting off the next day? But as he reached the door she asked idly, 'Are you intending to stay in London long, Lord Wintersett?'

'I think not. I have been away from home rather a lot recently and my mother will soon start complaining that she never sees me.'

Serena hesitated and said, 'My young friend William — I believe you know him? — has been asking after you. You might see him when you return to Surrey.'

* * *

The man standing by the graceful bay mare gazed over the countryside below. The brown and grey landscape was silvered with frost, but the afternoon sun was warm. He turned swiftly as he heard hoofbeats coming up the hill, and his heart leapt as he saw a woman with a laughing, glowing face riding to meet him. She came to a halt beside him and he held up his arms to help her dismount. But when she was on the ground his arms still encircled her.

'I half expected to see you dressed as a boy.'

'I was tempted, but I decided it was too dangerous. People might be shocked if they saw me as I am, but if I were dressed as William they would be infinitely more shocked. Besides, my groom is just below, at the bottom of the hill.'

'Very nearly respectability itself. But I thought it was William who wanted to speak to me?'

'No, James. I came as Serena, Sasha and William. All three of us have something to say to you, here on the hill where we first met.'

'What is it, my love, my torment and my very dearest friend?'

'We. . .' Serena hesitated, then she threw back her head proudly and said, 'I love you, James, and I trust you, completely, finally, for always.'

He gave a great shout of joy, and lifted her high in the air. The horses moved restlessly, and Serena said, laughing, 'Douce and Trask are shocked! Put me down, James, before they abandon such a disgraceful pair.'

James set her down and, still holding her hands in his, he said, 'Then I shall make us both honest again. Will you marry me, Serena? Will you give me, in William's words — the other William, of course, "Th'exchange of thy love's faithful vow for mine?"'

Serena smiled as she replied,

'"I gave thee mine before thou didst request it."'

James took her hands to his lips and kissing them he said slowly, 'I think Juliet had the best words after all.

My bounty is as boundless as the sea,
My love as deep; the more I give to thee,
The more I have, for both are infinite.

Serena's eyes filled with happy tears as he added, 'If you will marry me, Serena, I swear I will love you and cherish you for the rest of our lives.'

'Yes! Oh, yes, James, please!' He kissed her again and again, muttering incoherently as he did, and Serena laughed and eagerly responded. After a while he took her to the edge of the hill and they stood looking down on the patchwork of fields below.

Serena said dreamily, 'It seems an age since we first met here on the hill. The first words you spoke to me were a quotation. It is fitting that we are quoting again now, though Romeo and Juliet were a sad pair of lovers in the end.'

'Quite. I can think of a much more appropriate play.'

'Which is that?'

'*The Taming of the Shrew*, of course!'

'James!' Serena turned in his arms in mock anger.

He quickly imprisoned her again, and when she protested he said, 'I have to protect myself against those fists of yours, Serena! But now that you are here. . .' James bent his head to her again.

Finally she murmured, 'There's one other thing. . .'

'What is it, my love?'

'If I promise to be a model wife the rest of the time would you, just once a year, take me for a week or so to some remote spot where I might be William again? To dress and ride like William?'

'You may have a fortnight,' said James largely. 'As long as you promise to become Serena again at nightfall?'

'Done! Now I should go back to tell Aunt Spurston of our engagement. Will you come with me? She will be delighted, I think.'

'I thought she disapproved of me?'

'And you so *enormously* wealthy, James?' said Serena opening her eyes wide.

'Devil! But that reminds me, my enchanting, loathsome toad, — you gave me a challenge a short while ago in London. Are you prepared to answer it now?'

'What challenge was that, my darling viper?' asked Serena laughing.

'Just this.' And, taking her gently into his arms, James proceeded to demonstrate how calm, how breathlessly exciting, how comfortable, and how dangerous a kiss in reply to a challenge could be.

To the surprise of no one, but to the delight of all who were close to them, Miss Calvert and Lord Wintersett were married very soon after. When Lucy returned to London she was often heard to complain that she saw a lot less of them than she might have expected, for they spent much of their time at Wintersett Court, and took their nephew several times to St Just — until the arrival of young Edward Anthony Stannard made that difficult. And once a year they disappeared for a fortnight. No one ever found out where.

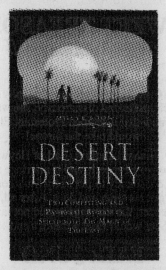
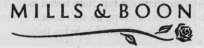

LEGACY *of* LOVE

Coming next month

SWEET TREASON
Marie-Louise Hall
London 1558

Seraphina Carey had made one politically expedient marriage, which had ended disastrously; she was *not* about to make another now that it seemed Protestant Elizabeth Tudor would take the throne!

Unfortunately, Richard Durrant, Earl of Heywood, had long been committed to Elizabeth, and if marriage to Sera would smoke out a conspiracy to put Mary Stuart on the throne, then he would grit his teeth and do it. After all, if Sera proved to be the ringleader, the marriage would not last for long, for Sera would meet a traitor's end...

FAIR JUNO
Stephanie Laurens
Regency 1818

Taking a short cut to gain the London road, the new Earl of Merton found himself—a gazetted rake!—playing the knight errant, rescuing a lady from kidnap. She refused to give her name, but Martin knew his fair Juno *was* a lady. Thus, on his launch back into society, he was bound to meet her again—he could bide his time.

But past scandals and present dangers were no mean obstacles to his pursuit of his mysterious lady...

LEGACY *of* LOVE

Coming next month

A CORNER OF HEAVEN
Theresa Michaels
Virginia 1862

When Colonel Colter Saxton found Elizabeth Waring hiding in
the chaotic Confederate city of Richmond, he vowed to learn
why she had betrayed his love and married another. Then he met
Nicole, Elizabeth's young daughter, and discovered what their
single night of passion had yielded. Although Elizabeth tried to
keep him at bay, Colter refused to leave her side. In spite of the
war, and in the face of constant danger, it seemed Colter was
determined to keep his new-found family safe—and to make up
for lost time with Elizabeth.

LAWLESS
Nora Roberts
Arizona 1875

The Arizona Territory was a dangerous place, but gunslinger
Jake Redman was half-Apache and all man—more than a match
for the wilderness. Sarah Conway was something else again. She
was every inch an Eastern lady, yet she was determined to make
Lone Bluff her home. Jake was annoyed to find himself playing
guardian angel to this tantalizing innocent—even more
disgusted to find he liked it. Little did he suspect that beneath
Sarah's ladylike demeanour beat the heart of a frontier woman
and that her body yearned for his hard embrace, her heart for his
words of love…

FOUR HISTORICAL ROMANCES

& TWO FREE GIFTS!

LEGACY OF LOVE

Witness the fight for love and honour, and experience the tradition and splendour of the past for FREE! We will send you FOUR Legacy of Love romances PLUS a cuddly teddy and a mystery gift. Then, if you choose, go on to enjoy FOUR exciting Legacy of Love romances for only £2.50 each! Return the coupon below today to:-

Mills & Boon Reader Service, FREEPOST, PO Box 236, Croydon, Surrey CR9 9EL

-------------------------- `NO STAMP REQUIRED` ---------- ✂ -----

Please rush me FOUR FREE *Legacy of Love* romances and TWO FREE gifts! Please also reserve me a Reader Service subscription, which means I can look forward to receiving FOUR brand new *Legacy of Love* romances for only £10.00 every month, postage and packing FREE. If I choose not to subscribe, I shall write to you within 10 days and still keep my FREE books and gifts. I may cancel or suspend my subscription at any time. I am over 18 years. Please write in BLOCK CAPITALS.

Ms/Mrs/Miss/Mr _____ EP61M

Address _____

_____

_____ Postcode _____

Signature _____

mps MAILING PREFERENCE SERVICE